MILKSHAKE

MILKSHAKE

A NOVEL

JOANNA WEISS

For Ava (inspiration), Jesse (field research) and
Dan (everything else)

CHAPTER 1

"BREASTFEEDING," the woman in the mumu said, "is every child's birthright and every mother's joy. So congratulations, ladies. You are the luckiest people in the world."

From where Lauren Bruce sat—in a folding chair in a windowless room on the St. Bart's-Pendergrass Hospital maternity floor—this seemed to be a massive overstatement. Lauren had only been at this breastfeeding business for 18 hours, but so far, the experience was not bringing her joy. *If I'm so lucky,* she thought to herself, *then why do I feel like my boob just got caught in a vise?*

She glanced around the room to try to catch somebody's eye, share a telepathic moment of sneering disbelief. But the other women in the room didn't seem to have the energy to sneer. Having given birth within the last day or so, they were perched uncomfortably in metal folding chairs, wearing sweaters over their hospital johnnies to ward off the air conditioning. A couple of them had dreamy expressions on their faces, but most of them stared ahead, glassy-eyed.

Lauren realized she would have to sort this out for herself. She raised her hand tentatively. "Is it supposed to hurt?" she asked.

The woman in the mumu, a certified lactation consultant, scrunched her forehead and looked confused, as if Lauren had just spoken in Swahili. "Sometimes," she declared, "there is discomfort."

On both sides? Like you just got bitten by a hyena, which is odd because you're pretty sure your baby has no teeth? Lauren wished she had the nerve to yell and beat her burning chest, but the woman in the mumu seemed eager to move on. Lauren regretted that she'd come here at all, leaving her day-old baby in the care of her terrified husband, but the morning-shift nurse had insisted she report to a breastfeeding lesson, no babies allowed. Now the woman in the mumu was droning on about "lobules" and "blockages," pointing to parts on an anatomically-correct stuffed breast. Lauren's mind kept wandering back to the small room down the hall, to baby Rory's fine and fuzzy hair, her tiny hands with perfect oval fingernails, her sweet pink lips that had been chomping with the fervor of someone who'd had nothing to eat for nine months.

"Can you repeat that?" The woman in the mumu sounded agitated: Someone had apparently asked another wrong question. Across the room, a pale brunette with sunken cheeks, wearing a pair of bunny slippers, leaned forward in her chair.

"I said, what kind of bottles do you recommend?" she asked.

"That's what I *thought* you said," the woman in the mumu growled. "Honestly, would you give your baby heroin?"

The new mothers looked at her blankly. The woman next to Lauren slowly shook her head.

"The bottle is just as addictive," the woman in the mumu said. "I can't tell you how many mothers I know who were pressured to give their babies bottles, and then found the child would not return to the breast."

"Even if it's pumped breastmilk?" said the bunny-slipper woman.

"Bottles are bottles," the woman in the mumu said dismissively.

"But for how long?" another woman piped up. "I got this free sample of formula—"

"FORMULA?" the woman in the mumu shouted. "WOULD YOU GIVE YOUR BABY CRACK?"

This required no response. The woman in the mumu put a hand over her chest and breathed deeply, trying to compose herself.

"I'd like to show you this movie," she finally said. "It's a Swedish instructional film from the 1960s, and it always brings tears to my eyes. Think about how magical it is to give our babies a part of ourselves. Breasts are just beautiful. Inside and out."

She slipped a videotape into an aging machine connected to an even older TV. Strains of gentle instrumental music came from the speakers. On one side of the screen was an infant, his mouth open wide like a bird's. On the other side was the biggest breast Lauren had ever seen. Perhaps it was the size of the lactation consultant's breasts, which swelled bountifully beneath her mumu. But it seemed bigger, not quite human—a beach ball, the planet Jupiter. The nipple was bigger than the baby's head.

Lauren stifled a giggle, then glanced around the room again, wondering again if anyone else felt like the bad kid in the back row of the junior-high sex education class. The other new mothers stayed expressionless. The infant in the video moved forward, entranced. The Swedish instrumental music twinkled on.

Lauren looked down at her own breasts, significantly smaller, and thought about what breastfeeding was going to entail. She was dreading the moments when she had to provide love in a liquid form, but her fear was no match for the power of guilt. She had read the pamphlets listing the vast health benefits of breastmilk. She had watched her friend Mia shake her head and murmur, "That poor child," when she saw mothers bottle-feeding on the banks of Jamaica Pond. She had seen the government-sponsored pro-breastfeeding ads: a dirty factory labeled "INFANT FORMULA INC."; a baby crying in a metal bassinet; the tagline, "Breastmilk. For mommies who care."

Lauren cared. She cared enough to have fretted for nine months over ancillary stroller features, to have outfitted her nursery with organic cotton sheets and an allergen-free rug, to have bought a set of flashcards with numbers, letters, and brightly-colored fruit. She'd do what the lactation consultant told her to do. And if it turned out that breastfeeding didn't nourish her own soul—well, that would be her small bad-mommy secret.

"ARE YOU SURE you don't want me to give her a bottle at night?"

Rob was adjusting his tie in the kitchen, guided by his half-visible reflection in the microwave. It was 7:15 a.m., and he was headed to work. If you wanted to make partner, it was best to show up at the law firm before 8.

"It must be nice to wear real clothes," Lauren murmured, glancing down at her polka-dotted pajama pants and her tank top, which was covered with splotches of spit-up and a long brown line of dripped coffee. Rory, wrapped in a soft pink blanket, was dozing on her shoulder. Lauren felt that she, too, would like an early-morning nap, possibly followed by a mid-morning nap, a late-morning nap, and an early-afternoon nap.

"You're ignoring my question," Rob said. "Seriously. If you'd just let me take one of the feedings, you could get more than two hours of sleep at a time. And I'd get to spend time with Rory. At this point, I don't think she even knows who I am."

"You have to work," Lauren replied. "You have to be sharp. I don't have to be awake for anything important. And the lactation consultants say—"

"I thought you said lactation consultants were evil Swedo-philes in house dresses," Rob said.

"I did," Lauren said. "They are. But that doesn't mean they aren't right."

Six weeks had passed since that breastfeeding lesson in the hospital, and Lauren had managed to maintain her promise to the woman in the mumu: No formula, no bottles, very little sleep, and a distinct sense that her conversation skills were slipping.

Rob poured himself another cup of coffee. "Well, you know what I think about them," he said. "Hey, how did your doctor's appointment go yesterday?"

"Um, fine, I guess," Lauren said. She barely remembered the obstetrician's check-up. Everything that happened these days felt vaguely unreal.

"You said at the six-week visit, you get the go-ahead, right?" Rob said.

"The go-ahead?" Lauren repeated.

Rob shot her a look. "For sex."

"Oh. Yeah," Lauren said. "You remembered. What a shock."

"I try to keep on top of these things," Rob said.

"Is that why you're so big on bottles? Trying to reserve some boob time for yourself?" Lauren couldn't help but feel annoyed. No matter what the doctor said about how "beautifully" she'd healed, it was hard to imagine anyone touching her still-delicate extremities.

"Trying to reclaim some of my territory," Rob said, taking a final gulp and putting his coffee cup on the counter. "What are you doing today?"

"Mia's coming over. I guess we'll probably take another walk."

"Her again?" Rob said. "With the baby T-shirts? And the natural-motherhood dogma?"

"It's not dogma," Lauren said. "It's information."

"Isn't she the one who convinced you to send away for $50 worth of herbal supplements? And that tea that smelled like rabbit shit?"

"To boost my milk supply," Lauren said. "And how do you know what rabbit shit smells like?"

"I know what bullshit smells like," Rob said.

"She's the only friend I have with a baby right now," Lauren said, defensively. "She's been my lifeline these past few weeks. I can talk to her about everything."

"That used to be my job," Rob said, kissing Rory's cheek before he headed out the door.

"You're still useful, don't worry," Lauren said, attempting a smile. "But sometimes, I need someone who has breasts."

WHEN THE DOORBELL rang at 10 a.m. precisely, Lauren was still in her pajamas, sitting on the couch, struggling to pull up a nursing bra with one arm and balance Rory on her shoulder with the other. Rory had just finished her mid-morning feeding. A half-eaten bowl of cereal sat on the coffee table. The newspaper was spread out on the cushions, open to the gossip page. With her free hand, Lauren started to flip it to world news, then decided the effort was pointless. It was impossible to keep up with Mia Hastings Hoberman, who managed to read the paper from cover to cover every day while taking care of a five-month-old and starting her own small business, a line of all-cotton onesies with slogans like "I need my beauty rest!" and "Get me a womb with a view!" Mia didn't struggle, like Lauren did, to get out of the house with every disparate piece of baby paraphernalia, always in danger of forgetting some critical item. Mia always arranged her designer diaper bag neatly the night before.

In short, Mia wasn't the sort of person Lauren would have naturally sought out for companionship. But they had sat beside each other for three years as account managers at Pinnacle Events, planning bloated corporate picnics on pumpkin farms and grand-opening parties at urban hair salons. And over the weeks and months, the late nights and commiseration, their battlefield camaraderie evolved into a tentative friendship.

Before long, they found themselves in sync, the way college roommates share mood swings and menstrual cycles. They got married in the same year, were promoted from junior to senior level the next, shared common enemies: incompetent bosses, sullen interns, the passage of time. When Mia announced her pregnancy one day, in faux-hushed tones that didn't mask her obvious pride, Lauren felt a jolt from her biological clock. She and Rob had already been trying in a haphazard way, but now Lauren started looking at the calendar. She visited online fertility sites, read reports of other women's vaginal secretions, encountered old-wives' tales involving sexual positions and phases of the moon. Before she got desperate enough to try any of them, Lauren was expecting, too.

But if she and Mia were equals at work, Mia quickly surpassed her on the pregnancy proving ground; she seemed to be a senior vice president of maternity, while Lauren was stuck as a junior trainee. When Lauren, racked with a ravenous midday hunger, was slinking to the vending machine for Ho-Hos, Mia was bringing in home-packed baggies of carrots and bottles of low-fat ranch dressing. When Lauren was discovering the trompe l'oeil powers of maternity jeans—How could her rear look like the back of a truck when her stomach barely registered a bump?—Mia was arriving at work each day in a flattering Lycra dress. Lyle was born precisely on his due date, and within days of giving birth, Mia was wearing couture sweatsuits and walking around her house in full makeup.

Mia left her job for good after Lyle was born, and her onesie line was more a vanity project than a moneymaking scheme. Her new job was motherhood, and she approached it in the highly-organized way she had handled her event-planning career. She attended weekly meetings of the Moo Coalition, a breastfeeding-support circle. She took Lyle to regular classes of The Smallest Spirits, which promoted a daily routine of infant yoga—baby limbs manipulated gently to the strains of Eastern music. She bought books and paraphernalia stamped with the label "Baby Mensa." She set her alarm for 5:25 every morning to pump milk at the time when her body had its greatest natural supply. Her freezer was filled with bottles of milk, neatly labeled and color-coded according to date.

She was also more than happy to serve as a motherhood resource, and Lauren found that she didn't need to read her pile of infant-development books when she could simply seek Mia's advice about sleep, swaddling, and the ever-changing colors and consistencies of infant poop. She let Mia get close—close enough, even, to peer at the sore, battered breasts that might have made Rob cringe—and it was Mia who helped her discover that if she adjusted Rory's chin the tiniest smidge, the sharp stabbing pain of nursing subsided, replaced by a bearable dull ache. For this, if nothing else, Lauren would be eternally grateful. Also, she was never sure what she was going to learn next.

This morning, in addition to Lyle, Mia was carrying a blue plastic bowl the size of a dog's water dish. When Lauren opened the door, Mia lifted the bowl and held it aloft in a victory pose. "Elimination communication," she announced, marching past Lauren to the living room, where she placed Lyle's car seat beside the couch and set the bowl down in the center of the floor.

"What's 'elimination communication'?" Lauren asked.

"I learned about it last week from the Moos," Mia said. "It's the best way to form an unbreakable bond with your baby."

"I thought breastfeeding was the best way to form an unbreakable bond with your baby," Lauren said.

"Breastfeeding is the foundation," Mia said. "EC helps you understand your baby's needs."

"I understand Rory's needs," Lauren said hopefully. "She needs to eat, sleep, and poop."

"You understand *that* she needs to poop," Mia said. "But do you understand *when* she needs to poop?"

Suddenly, Lauren realized what the bowl was for.

Mia lifted a blanket covered with blue and green dump trucks out of her diaper bag, laid it neatly on the floor, and gently extricated Lyle from his car seat. She laid him on the blanket, pulled off his shorts, and removed his diaper. Lyle cooed. Mia kissed his head, then turned him onto his tummy.

"Does Mommy's little sugar bear need to make a pee-pee?" she said.

Lyle gave his mother a broad, toothless smile. He was cute in a baby way, but Lauren secretly thought there was something odd about his face. His eyes were buggy, his cheeks misshapen. Rob said Lyle looked like a gnome.

"I don't think he's going to tell you," Lauren said, too tired to worry about sounding rude.

If Mia registered the sarcasm, she didn't let on. "A dog doesn't talk," she said, "but you know when a dog has to pee."

"Because he claws at the back door."

"Because he gives nonverbal clues," Mia said. "And so do babies. They grunt. They turn red. Sometimes they just glaze off, you know? Stare into the distance in just the right way."

Lauren looked down at Rory, who was lying on her back on a plush mat shaped like a fish. She seemed to be looking at the ceiling fan, but she could have been staring in the distance, too. Lauren wondered: Was she peeing, at that very moment?

"May I?" Mia said as she took a pair of throw pillows from Lauren's couch. She lifted Lyle from his prone position, propped him up with the pillows, and gave him a toy octopus whose legs made crinkling sounds. Lyle put one of the legs in his mouth. "Uhhh," he said.

"That's right!" Mia said. "Mollusk!" She kissed the top of his head again. "Don't you worry about the rug," she told Lauren. "We've been doing this at home, and he hasn't made an accident once. And he already had a poo-poo this morning, didn't you, bear?" She rubbed her hand over the top of his bald head. "He's been very regular lately. We've started a new yoga routine that's good for the bowels."

Lauren sighed. "How's Tom?" she said, changing the subject. Tom was Mia's husband, a financial planner who worked long hours, like Rob.

"I left him alone with Lyle for three hours last weekend when I got my hair highlighted," Mia said. "When I got home, they were watching HBO. I told him, 'You know, if you do this too much, your child's first word is going to be *fuck*.'" She uttered the swear word in muted tones, as if she hated to say it, but Lauren knew better. In moments of high stress, foul language coursed out of Mia like water breaking a dam.

"When *are* we supposed to stop swearing in front of the kids?" Lauren asked. So far, she and Rob hadn't censored their conversations a bit. Lauren was less concerned that Rory would start swearing than that she would enter full consciousness with the knowledge—direct from her parents' mouths—that her Uncle Tim was a deadbeat and her cousin Hank, at three, was already annoying.

"Oh, it's never too early," Mia said. "Babies recognize your voice in utero. Baby Mensa sells CDs for teaching Spanish in the womb." Her voice trailed off for a second, and Lauren wasn't sure which emotion she detected: sarcasm or regret.

"Education!" Mia said suddenly. "I almost forgot. I've decided we should be ambitious today. I think we should skip the park and go to the Stonewall Museum instead."

"The Stonewall?" Lauren said. "You've got to be kidding." The Stonewall was a mansion north of Boston that had been converted to an art museum, stocked with several Brahmin families' worth of magisterial collections.

"I'm a member," Mia continued. "I can get you in for free. We'll take the Bjorns. We'll walk through the galleries, we'll have lunch. We're mommies now. We get to spend our weekdays exposing our children to culture."

Lauren pictured a string of quiet rooms, a stern security guard, a wailing infant.

"I can barely make it to the supermarket," she said. "When I took Rory there last week, I left the car door open in the parking lot. When I got back, there was a bird in the front seat."

"I'll drive," Mia said.

"I don't know if I can handle art."

"You need art," Mia said, glancing at Lauren's newspaper. "Your brain is going to atrophy if all you think about is celebrities and poop."

"I read world news," Lauren said defensively. "And you think about poop a lot, too."

"I think about poop and art," Mia said.

"And what about when Rory needs to eat?"

"This is a cultured city," Mia said. "The Athens of America. People know what breastfeeding is. You stop on a bench, you feed her. You cover yourself with a blanket. If anybody minds, that's not your problem."

That's what the woman in the mumu would have said, too, but Lauren wasn't sure. "I don't know if Rory's ready for action yet," she said. "Lately, she's been having trouble latching. And I don't think anyone wants to see—"

Mia, who seemed to be listening at first, was suddenly in motion. She bolted off the couch, grabbed the plastic bowl and kneeled beside Lyle on the floor. "He's glazing! Lyle! Wait a minute, honey! Here comes Mama!"

Lauren hadn't noticed a change in Lyle's expression, but Mia seemed certain. She put her hand on Lyle's stomach and pulled him forward, slipping the bowl beneath his backside. Then she closed her eyes and waited. A few moments later, Lauren heard the sound of a robust stream of liquid on hard plastic.

"Great job, honey!" Mia said presently, picking up the bowl and holding it out for Lauren to observe. Inside, sure enough, was a sizable yellow puddle. And Mia was right. Not a drop had gotten on the rug.

• • •

TWO HOURS LATER, Mia's Volvo was parked in the Stonewall Museum lot, and Lauren was lugging her diaper bag onto the metal detectors. Rory was sound asleep in her Bjorn, her head resting against Lauren's chest, her legs dangling out limply like tiny pink sausages, capped with miniscule sneakers. The security guard looked suspiciously at one leg, then the other. "Hope she stays asleep," she said.

"Don't count on it," Lauren said with a weak smile.

The museum was hushed on a weekday morning. Mia and Lauren began on the top floor, in a gallery full of Impressionist work, where skylights left the room awash in soft October light. A few retirees moved slowly across the floor. An art student sat with her easel beside a small Monet, working intently on a passable copy. A Japanese couple walked silently in lockstep, each person holding an audio guide to one ear. A guard stood in one corner, looking blankly at the floor. From a distance, Lauren heard traces of a minor commotion: a sharp shout, a stifled laugh. She glanced down a corridor and saw a couple of teenage boys knocking elbows, pretending to fight. Someone made a loud *sssssssh*. Lauren could make out the faint sound of a docent, giving a lecture in monotone.

Mia moved at a faster pace than Lauren, five or six paintings ahead. Lyle was awake and facing forward in his Bjorn. Mia was holding his hand in hers and pointing at the walls. "Van Gogh. Van Gogh," she said, pronouncing the Dutch correctly, as if she were choking. Lauren stared back into the corridor and saw a group of high school students, the boys dressed in worn T-shirts and khakis, the girls in skinny jeans and tight-fitting sweaters. As they crossed the hallway from one gallery into the next, they parried and jostled, divided themselves by gender, then drew together again, attracted and repelled by the same hormonal forces.

Lauren stared at them, remembering a stage of life that felt impossibly distant. They were led by a heavyset docent with graying hair and trailed by a couple more adults. One was a tired-looking middle-aged woman, presumably their teacher. The other was a thin, sallow man with reddish hair, who wore black jeans and a rumpled plaid shirt and carried a slender notebook. The man's cellphone rang. He stepped away from the group and lingered in the hallway, a few steps from Lauren, whom he didn't seem to notice.

"McFeeney," he said into the phone. "Yeah. Yeah. I'm at the Stonewall Museum. Yes. Linda sent me on this idiot assignment…No. A feature. Suburban high school teaches kindness through the power of art, or some bullshit like that. Doesn't seem to be working. They're a bunch of fucking delinquents…What? No, I don't know when I'll be done. Just send a fucking intern to the press conference." He hung up the phone and headed back to the group, muttering to himself.

Lauren watched him go, then turned and followed Mia into another gallery. As she walked, Rory, nestled close to Lauren's chest, began to stir. Lauren knew that if the baby woke up, she'd want to eat. Sure enough, by the time Lauren caught up with Mia in a room full of Renaissance art, Rory was starting to whimper.

"Mia," Lauren stage-whispered.

Mia was standing in front of a painting of St. John the Baptist's head on a platter. She patted Lyle on the head and smiled at Lauren.

"Rory's hungry," Lauren whispered again, a little louder.

Mia cocked her head, indicating a bench at the far end of the gallery.

"In the middle of the room?" Lauren said out loud. Another woman in the gallery shot her a nasty look.

Mia gave an audible sigh and walked over to Lauren. "Drape this blanket over you," she said under her breath. "No one will notice." She reached into her bag and pulled out a small bundle. It was Lyle's dump truck blanket, rolled into a compact cylinder and tied together with a small blue ribbon.

Lauren hesitated. These days, feedings were unpredictable; sometimes Rory would refuse to eat, shaking her head with inexplicable fury. A voice inside Lauren's head urged her to bail, abandon the museum and head to the car, where she could breastfeed in peace to the strains of one of Mia's Baby Mensa CDs. But that, she told herself, would be demonstrating weakness, caving to social pressure. Mia and the woman in the mumu were right: Her breasts had a noble mission.

So Lauren walked over to the bench and gingerly lifted Rory out of her Baby Bjorn. "Be good for me, sweetheart," she whispered. Then she sat on the bench, unfurled the blanket, and draped it over her shoulder. She laid Rory's head on her lap and, beneath the blanket, unbuttoned her blouse and unhooked her nursing bra. She moved Rory's head into place so that she could nurse, hidden from view.

Beneath the blanket, Rory clamped, let go, and started to jerk and fidget. Through the corridors, Lauren could hear the high school tour group, the drone of the docent, stifled giggles drawing closer. She watched Mia round the corner into the next gallery. She reached under the blanket and tried to pat Rory's head. The baby whimpered, flailing her hands back and forth. Lauren tried to adjust her blindly, then gave up and pulled the blanket up so that it covered her head, too. As she did, she could hear the high school group enter the gallery. One boy shouted, "*Loser!*" A chorus of guffaws followed. Then came a sharp adult voice: "Gentlemen! You are supposed to be learning to be *nice!*"

Lauren wondered if the kids noticed her, a shifting, shrouded figure on a bench across the room. Beneath the blanket, she couldn't see anything but Rory's angry face, in shadows. "Come on, sweetie. Don't do this to me," she whispered to the baby through clenched teeth. She put her hands on Rory's cheeks and tried to pull her into place. Rory did not cooperate. Instead, she wriggled so violently that the blanket slipped and dropped to the floor. Lauren gasped. Her blouse was shifted to one side. The flap of her nursing bra had fallen to her belly. Her left breast was completely exposed.

And she was surrounded by teenagers.

"Whoa," one of them said, in a scratchy pubescent voice.

"Ho-lee crap," said another.

Several of the girls started to giggle uncontrollably.

Lauren knew she should cover up, grab the blanket and push her shirt back, but somehow, she was frozen in place. She felt as if someone had turned a cosmic knob, lowered the volume in the room, slowed down time. Even Rory seemed to melt into weightlessness. In her peripheral vision, Lauren spotted cellphones in the air, saw the reporter, McFeeney, scribbling furiously in his notebook. But all she really noticed was one of the boys. He had disheveled brown hair, pimply cheeks, a faint brush of stubble above his upper lip. He wore a T-shirt that said "Mountain Dew" and a pair of sagging jeans. His eyes were brown and opened wide, his gaze shifting between Lauren's eyes and her chest, the look on his face slowly changing from thrill to thoughtfulness. With a shudder, Lauren realized that she was going to play a starring role in some future sexual hang-up of his. This wasn't going to be the day his hormonal fantasies were fulfilled. This was going to be the day, for him, when breasts lost their magic completely.

Suddenly, Lauren felt a warm hand on her elbow, gently lifting her from her seat. She broke away from the boy's gaze and looked up to see a matronly woman with glasses and sandy brown hair. She had been leading the high school tour. Now, she spoke to Lauren in a gentle voice. "Let's get out of here, shall we?" she said. "There's a ladies' room this way."

Lauren rose, pulling Rory away from her breast and buttoning the first few buttons of her blouse. The woman moved her hand to Lauren's upper arm and grabbed the diaper bag and Baby Bjorn, which had fallen to the floor. Lauren leaned Rory against her shoulder and allowed herself to be steered.

Up ahead, indeed, was a ladies' room, its wide open doorway revealing an anteroom with a small sofa and two armchairs. One of the chairs, upholstered and blue, was directly in Lauren's line of sight. It seemed an attainable goal. But behind her, she could hear a new commotion.

"Hey!" Mia was shouting. "Hey! Stop! Where do you think you're going?"

The woman at Lauren's shoulder didn't respond.

"You're not going in there!" Mia yelled. "She is *not* going to feed her baby in a dirty place!"

The woman stopped and turned around. "It's not dirty," she said. "It's the ladies' lounge."

"It's not a lounge!" Mia spat back. "It's a bathroom!"

She had just run across several galleries, so her cheeks were flushed and her breath was short. Lyle was peering out from his Bjorn with wide, curious eyes. Mia pointed a finger in the air. "This is *not* appropriate," she said. "Who do you think you are?"

"I'm a volunteer," the woman said, and Lauren noticed, for the first time, that a pin on one side of her chest read, "JEAN." "I was leading a tour group from Woburn High. Believe me, you didn't want to rendezvous with those boys."

"Those boys are not her problem," Mia growled, indicating Lauren with her hand. "*You* are her problem. Her baby needs to eat in a sanitary place."

"Mia," Lauren piped up. "It's OK."

"It is not OK," Mia said, with a passion in her voice that Lauren hadn't heard since before Lyle was born. "It's bullshit. It's a fucking violation. It's a—"

"*Mia*," Lauren said. "We're in a museum."

"I understand your concerns. But this ladies' lounge is perfectly clean," Jean said, her voice steady and calm.

Rory, meanwhile, was still whimpering. Lauren gently broke free of Jean's grasp and headed toward the bathroom.

"Lauren Bruce!" Mia shouted. "Do not take another step further!"

Lauren ignored Mia and headed to her destination. She sat in the chair, unbuttoned her blouse, and lifted Rory to her chest again. She leaned back into the upholstery and placed the blanket across the baby's head. Now, miraculously, Rory latched, her tiny mouth working rapidly. Mia and Jean continued their argument as a few women hurried past them, out of the restroom and into the galleries.

"What about the fumes?" Mia was saying.

"I don't smell any fumes. Do you?" Jean replied.

"Excuse me? Ladies?" It was a male voice, and it belonged to McFeeney, the reporter Lauren had seen with the high school group. He was standing in the doorway, casting a shadow across the floor.

Jean and Mia stopped talking and stared at him.

"You are in the *ladies' room*," Mia said with a gasp. "You have to go away!"

"I'm in the doorway of the ladies' room," McFeeney corrected her. "I don't need to come inside. We can talk from here."

"Scott," Jean said. "What are you doing? You're supposed to be writing about my tour."

"I am," McFeeney said. "Your tour just got a lot more interesting." He turned to Lauren. "Scott McFeeney. Boston Herald. Do you spell 'Bruce' the regular way?"

Lauren looked up, alarmed. "Look, there's no news here," she said. "Just a bunch of boring ladies in a museum."

"That's not what those high school kids saw a few minutes ago," McFeeney said, smiling and raising his pen to his notebook. "This might just be the most exciting thing that ever happened in this godforsaken place."

CHAPTER 2

MAISY STREET DID NOT have children. Every once in awhile this caused her a slight pang, though she knew it was too late to do anything about it. Besides, she knew that a stable domestic routine, filled with soccer games and parent-teacher meetings, was incompatible with the itinerant life she had forged for herself in politics. At this stage in a campaign, she never had energy to spare.

It was 6 a.m., barely light out, dead quiet in the Calloway for Governor headquarters—early even for Maisy, but in the throes of campaign trouble she always found herself waking up early, mind spinning, ready to work. Problems often seemed to solve themselves in the early-morning hours, whether through some sudden caffeine-driven inspiration or as a byproduct of the brief and fleeting quiet. In the early-morning silence, she had to think quickly, focus sharply, before the interns came in, followed by the volunteers, followed by the candidate, and the place started buzzing with noise and confusion again.

In this case, the dilemma was especially confounding. State Senator Candace Calloway, sole female candidate for Massachusetts governor, holder of a perfect score on the Massachusetts Pro-Choice Coalition scorecard, had a woman problem. Her polls among men were passable. Her Republican opponent, a gregarious college professor, had a history of making impolitic comments about women in the military. But among suburban women, the voting bloc that mattered most this season, Professor Stuart Winkle was steadily rising while Calloway's polls were stuck. She was plagued with high negatives on trust and likability. And so far, the carefully choreographed biographical ads—in which Calloway looked directly at the camera and purred, "I'm a woman, just like you"—had only hurt her cause. The more Candace Calloway spoke for herself, the more women seemed to dislike her.

Maisy figured this had something to do with the fact that Candace Calloway was so impossibly feminine. She wore her hair long, favored expensive high heels, spoke in a husky near-whisper, carried herself with a WASP-y glamour that made her attractive to men but unapproachable to women. In truth, Maisy thought, Calloway *was* unapproachable: self-aggrandizing and haughty, uncomfortable with people outside her dinner-party set. At fried-chicken picnics and backyard barbecues, she tended to hang back by the tables of lightly-spiked fruit punch, waiting for people to come to her. A kind person could interpret this as shyness or reserve, but it was clear that some voters—mostly the suburban women the campaign needed so desperately—correctly sensed that Calloway wasn't rushing to shake hands because she didn't like the idea of touching these people. Maisy's challenge was to make Calloway seem nice, lovable, approachable. If not up close, then at least from a distance.

Anything was possible, Maisy knew; she had orchestrated too many come-from-behind victories to think otherwise. But house parties and TV commercials weren't going to do it. Changing the trajectory of a campaign had to do with capturing a moment, corralling the news cycle, making sure voters subconsciously connected the right person with the right idea. That was how her last candidate, a bumbling state representative running for governor of Maine, had managed to come across as a highly-competent leader. A near-miss on a Jet-Ski was spun deftly into a rescue attempt. And because it all happened so quickly and the press was eager for a storyline, the family he "rescued" didn't even realize they had nearly been killed. Like the public, they believed they had been saved by Byron Schnirdt—as they would be again, from the threat of global terror and the danger of politics-as-usual. Maisy was good at her job. Schnirdt had won.

So now, Maisy thought, brushing aside a strand of graying hair and chewing on the end of her ballpoint pen, she was waiting for Candace Calloway's moment to arrive—presumably now, a month before Election Day, when voters were just starting to pay attention. She needed a gift, and after 30 years of this, she knew they came, suddenly and usefully. It was part of the strange mystical power of campaigns, the magic mixed with adrenaline, that made Maisy love her life despite the indignities of corporate housing and the irritating qualities of candidates themselves. Maisy didn't want to latch onto a senator's office or a governor's administration. She had no hunger for policy work. After a campaign ended, she would spend a few months at her official home, a four-room cabin near Asheville, decompressing and painting watercolors. And soon, she would be ready for the next campaign, the next conundrum, the next unexpected gift.

Maisy took a chug of coffee, then winced; why did New Englanders insist on drinking this weak, watery stuff? She turned her attention to the papers she had brought from her furnished apartment in the corporate housing center. First, she picked up the Globe. There was nothing unexpected. A story about the latest fund-raising figures, which showed Calloway and Winkle in a virtual tie. A recap of the latest State House budget debate. A feature about an abandoned house in Brockton that had become home to a family of endangered loons.

Then she picked up the Herald and began to flip the pages. On page seven, she found her gift.

TIT-ILLATING!
At Museum, New Mom Lets It All Hang Out

By Scott McFeeney
Herald Staff

A group of high school students got an un-planned sex-ed lesson at the Stonewall Museum yesterday, when a woman went naked to breast-feed her baby in a room full of religious art.

Lauren Bruce, 35, of Jamaica Plain, was try-ing to expose her infant to culture, but wound up exposing her left breast, too.

"It was scary," said Shana Nichols, 17, a senior at Woburn High School, who said she could see Bruce's bare breast for "maybe five minutes. But it felt like ten."

Bruce said she was trying to feed her six-week-old daughter on a bench in a third-floor gallery when her blanket slipped. "The baby was hungry," Bruce said. "She wasn't trying to offend anybody."

To protect the high school students, museum volunteer Jean Thompson, 58, said she helped Bruce find a bathroom where she could nurse in private.

That caused another fracas, when Bruce's friend Mia Hastings Hoberman said it was wrong to feed a baby in a bathroom.

"This is about nutrition," said Hoberman, 36, of Brookline, who said breasts and art are a natu-ral fit. "It's a museum," she said. "There are nudes hanging on the walls."

But Thompson said breastfeeding mothers need to be modest. "Paintings of breasts aren't the same as real breasts," she said. "Just ask those teenagers."

Stonewall spokeswoman Myra Smith said the museum has no official policy on breastfeeding.

"We want everyone to feel comfortable here," she said.

But babies deserve to be the most comfortable of all, said Sheila McDonough, executive director of the Boston Organization for the Oversight of Breastfeeding.

"The world needs to treat breastfeeding mothers with more respect," McDonough said. "Breasts are just as beautiful as babies."

Go to BostonHerald.com for citizen video of the event. Images redacted. Safe for work.

Maisy fired up her computer. Then she scrawled the name "Lauren Bruce" on the notepad on her desk, leaned back in her chair, and waited for Candace to arrive.

CANDACE CALLOWAY APPEARED at campaign headquarters at 8:15—breezed in almost literally, brushing past desks so quickly that she left a trail of loose papers fluttering in her wake. Her high-heeled pumps clicked down the hall as she clutched a Starbucks coffee in one manicured hand. She made no eye contact with the scattered staff that had already arrived, or the three volunteers who were watching her with awe as they stuffed brochures into envelopes. Her driver, a youngish man hired by the limousine company, lingered by the front door and stared as well, presumably at the way her backside moved in her satiny peach-colored shift. Senator Calloway always dressed as if there were a decent chance that she'd be going to a cocktail party, perhaps in the mid-afternoon.

She click-click-clicked along the linoleum floor and into Maisy's office, swiped a few newspapers off of the tattered armchair, sat down, removed her pumps, and placed her feet on the coffee table. Maisy didn't particularly care for bare feet so close to her desk, but she had to admit that Candace's were exquisite.

"Honestly, I don't understand why we had to rent space in Downtown Crossing instead of Beacon Hill," Candace said. "Those extra ten minutes of traffic make me supremely irritated."

"Budget," Maisy said, pretending that she wasn't looking up from her newspapers. She had learned, over time, to treat her candidates the way she treated her nieces and nephews when they came to stay with her in Asheville for long weekends: Set strict rules, don't overpraise, and never let them think they can boss you around.

Candace took a sip of coffee. "This place is so austere."

"Budget," Maisy repeated.

Candace sank her head back in the armchair and had another sip. Maisy kept pretending she wasn't watching. She knew that this utilitarian space, above a dollar store, lacked the historic charm that was, for Candace, one of the attractions of political life. Calloway lived in a massive, pristine colonial with ocean views on Jerusalem Road in Cohasset, a town south of Boston whose toniest spots were known as the Gold Coast. It was there that her late husband, State Senator Bernard Calloway, had launched his 40-year political career. Candace had entered public life as a trophy wife, a University of Massachusetts-Dartmouth cheerleader who met the rich and handsome senator, twenty years her senior, at the staging area for a St. Patrick's Day parade. She learned the skills of backroom politics by his side, and when he died suddenly of a heart attack, she easily won election to his seat.

But where Bernard Calloway had been content to rule his corner of Massachusetts, his wife had different ambitions and skills. Her secret goal was an ambassadorship, but a real one, not a fund-raiser's sinecure in some quiet, unimportant African country, and so she needed a prime political perch. Being governor sounded glamorous, anyway, and this year, there was an open seat, since the current officeholder was leaving the state for a job with the malt liquor lobby. So Candace worked high-end parties with ease, won support from major political players, drew a stroke of luck when her chief Democratic foe grounded a campaign donor's yacht during a drunken late-night cruise. She won the primary, a low-turnout affair, with little effort. But the general election was bound to be tougher, so the party chairman—over Candace's limp objections—had brought in Maisy Street to seal the deal.

"What's my schedule today, Madame Slave Driver?" Candace asked, in a tone that was meant to sound joking, but wasn't entirely genial.

Maisy continued to keep her eyes on her desk, and rummaged around for the printout of the daily schedule. "Jodi arrives at 9," she said in her Southern drawl, referring to Candace's personal aide. "She'll bring you breakfast. At 9:30, we've got a fund-raising call. From 10 to 11:30, we prep for tonight's appearance on New England Cable News. At 11:30, you drive to a diner in Watertown. From 12 to 1, shake hands with the lunch crowd, say hello to the press, I think there might be a reporter there from the Cambridge News. Head back here, eat lunch in the car. When you get back, I'm hoping to have someone here for you to meet."

"Another donor?" said Candace. One thing she was quite good at, and rather enjoyed, was sweet-talking the moneyed set.

"A private citizen," Maisy said, leaving what she hoped was a dramatic pause. "I think I've found your issue."

"What issue?" Candace asked coldly.

"Your women's issue."

"I don't—"

Maisy interrupted quickly. "You've read the internals just like I have," she said, in the tone of an irritated schoolteacher. "But I

have an idea. So for the next half hour, I want you to start thinking about breastfeeding."

"What?"

"Breastfeeding," Maisy repeated. "You are going to come to
the defense of the latest victim of anti-breastfeeding discrimina-
tion in Massachusetts."

"Oh, Lord," Candace groaned. "I hate Earth mothers."

"I have a feeling this woman isn't an Earth mother," Maisy
said, finally looking up. "That's what I like about her."

At last, Jodi arrived with scones and Maisy sent the two of
them to Candace's small office, with strict orders that Candace
could not leave the room until she had read sixteen printed-
out clips about breastfeeding controversies. Then Maisy picked
up the phone and placed a call to her opposition research guy.
"Yo. Maisy Street in Massachusetts," she said. "I need an address,
ASAP. Lauren Bruce, Jamaica Plain." A few minutes later, she
hung up the phone, stood up and reached for her coat. This was
going to be delicate business, hard to entrust to anyone else, and
best performed in person.

AFTER A SHORT ride on the Orange Line and a ten-minute
walk, Maisy found herself in JP, in front of a renovated triple-
decker on a gentrified, tree-lined block. It was one of those perfect October days, crisp and only the slightest bit cool, and she
almost hated to go inside again. She stepped into the vestibule,
looked at the buzzers, found "BRUCE" on the first floor, and rang
the bell. Inside, she heard shuffling, the sounds of a baby crying,
a distant voice yelling, "Just a minute!"

When the door finally opened, Maisy couldn't help but smile.
If this was Lauren Bruce, she was exactly what Maisy had been
hoping for: brunette, average height, not mousy but not glam-

orous, perfect for projecting an everywoman image. She was wearing a T-shirt and sweatpants with a stain on the right thigh, holding a wailing baby in one arm.

"I'm sorry," she said, looking flustered. "Sometimes she wakes up mad."

"I hope the doorbell didn't wake her," Maisy said.

"No," Lauren said. "I think she was hungry. She's always hungry. Can I help you?"

"My name is Maisy Street," Maisy said. "I work for the Candace Calloway campaign."

"I haven't decided yet," Lauren said. "I'm sorry. Can you just leave a pamphlet?" She bounced Rory vigorously so that the baby's voice rose and fell, sounding vaguely like a lawn mower struggling to start up.

"Ms. Bruce," Maisy said, pulling a business card from her pocket and raising her voice to compete with the crying. "I'm Senator Calloway's campaign manager. And I'm here because I'd like to help *you*."

"Me? Help me with what?" Lauren said.

"Well, I read the Herald this morning, and—"

"Oh, no," Lauren said, as Rory bawled a little louder. "I didn't want to do the story. The guy was just there. It wasn't a big deal. I promise."

"It wasn't a big deal to you," Maisy said. "But it might be, to the people who read the story. Or see the video."

"Video?" Lauren said, her face turning white. "Like, YouTube video?"

"It's on the Herald website, at least," Maisy told her. "But you can't make out much. Seventeen-year-olds aren't so good at holding their phones steady. And you definitely can't tell it's you. They weren't looking at your face." She reached out her hand toward Rory, who continued to wail. "Can I help you with this, too? Really. I'm good with babies. I once had a very colicky niece."

"Come inside," Lauren said with a sigh, leading Maisy into

the living room and handing over Rory. Maisy pressed the baby up against her polo shirt and patted her quickly on the butt. "There, you go, dumpling," she said, holding her head close to Rory's ear and making a clicking sound with her tongue. "Settle down. Settle down," she repeated. Miraculously, Rory did.

"Wow," Lauren said. "You are good."

"My sister says I have some kind of smell that calms babies down," Maisy said. "But I think it's psychological. You have to be firm. With babies, and with cretins in museums who want to push you around. You must be just furious about what happened yesterday."

"I don't know," Lauren said. "It happened very fast. I'm mostly just overwhelmed. And a little mortified."

"Well, you *should* be furious," Maisy said. "And I can guarantee you that many women are outraged on your behalf. Candace Calloway, in particular."

"I didn't know she cared about breastfeeding," Lauren said.

Neither did she, Maisy thought. "Oh, yes," she told Lauren. "Candace believes that the way we treat new mothers is a symbol of the way we treat all women. And women juggling work and family life deserve the utmost respect."

"I'm not really working right now," Lauren said.

"Everything is a juggle," Maisy said quickly.

"Well, um, that's good to know," Lauren said. "But I still don't understand why you're here."

"I want to make sure what happened to you never happens to another mother," Maisy said. "And I think we've got a chance to use the power we have here—the power of our platform—to send the message: This must stop." She was talking quickly, making up her pitch as she went along, hoping Lauren didn't ask too many questions. Lauren looked tired, extremely tired. Maisy figured that would work to her advantage.

"I just want this thing to go away," Lauren said.

"Do you?" Maisy said. "Or do you want to help other mothers? Spare them from what you went through yesterday? Make it easier for them to feed their babies in peace?"

"Well," Lauren said tentatively. "Of course, I want to help people."

"Of course, you do," Maisy said. "So. Come with me to campaign headquarters. Meet Candace. Talk to her. It's a gorgeous day out there. You look like you could stand to get out of the house."

Together, Maisy and Lauren surveyed the apartment, where the furniture and blandly-tasteful home décor had been overtaken by the detritus of life with an infant. On the couch was a pile of baby toys, plush animals and alien-looking creatures of uncertain origin. On the coffee table were a stack of thank-you notes and an uncapped pen. On the floor lay a rumpled onesie covered with poop stains. In the hallway, a basket of laundry overflowed onto the rug. On the windowsill, a plant was wilting from lack of water. Over in the kitchen, a pile of dishes was toppling over the walls of the sink. In the dining room, an infant swing creaked emptily, as if filled by a ghost.

"Yes," Lauren said slowly. "Let's get out of here."

CHAPTER 3

ONE THING THAT STRUCK Lauren about Calloway Campaign headquarters was the way nobody fussed over the baby. In the circles Lauren traveled in these days, parks and supermarkets and baby clothing stores, there were endless amounts of cooing and affectionate tongue-clacking, along with volumes of unsolicited information and advice. The baby-shop salespeople were particularly eager to share their own birthing stories, even if their babies were adults by now; it was as if they felt the need to validate their presence among such tiny clothes.

Here at the campaign office, though, Rory was completely ignored, even when she roused and stretched into what Lauren thought was a fairly adorable yawn. Nobody stopped to look, though Lauren had been parked on a hallway couch in plain view of everyone, with Rory sleeping against her chest and a burrito by her side, provided by one of the interns at Maisy's instruction. Some other young interns across the room, wearing short skirts and boots, were stuffing envelopes and murmuring in low tones. A man in his mid-30s, in rumpled clothes, was writing on a giant chart. Some volunteers were arranged on the floor in one corner, painting signs. Lauren thought she could make out the words on one of them: "Don't Protest the Breast." She still wasn't quite sure why she had agreed to come here, but she had to admit this was a welcome change of scenery, a break from her living room TV set and the same long loops around Jamaica Pond, a reminder of the days when she felt part of the world instead of separate from it. She had never spent time in a campaign headquarters before. Now, she had no job, nowhere else to be, and a lunch she didn't have to prepare. Why not stick around and meet the candidate, at least?

Rory rustled again, extending her tiny arms and letting out a little mew. Lauren did a quick calculation in her head. Before they'd left for the campaign, she'd made Maisy wait until she'd fed the baby and changed into presentable clothes. But by now, Rory was surely hungry again. Lauren thought of going to the bathroom to nurse, but that didn't seem right, given the events of the past day. So she went to Maisy's office, tapped on the door, and—not realizing at first that Maisy was on the phone—asked if there was a private room anywhere.

"Candace is still out at an event. Why don't you use her office?" Maisy had said, without taking the phone from her ear.

A cheerful intern led Lauren into Candace Calloway's office and left, shutting the door behind her. It was a small, uncluttered room, unadorned with decorations, containing a desk and a brown leather couch. Lauren sank into the sofa, lifted her shirt, helped Rory latch, then closed her eyes involuntarily. She must have dozed off, since no time seemed to pass before she heard the creak of a door and looked up. There was Candace Calloway, looking the same as she did in the campaign ads, impeccably dressed, hair perfectly coiffed. For some reason, Lauren focused on her eyebrows, perfect arches, raised in what appeared to be alarm.

"Oh, for God's sake," the senator said, and shut the door.

A few minutes later, the door opened again. It was Candace, with Maisy beside her. Maisy was smiling, but her eyes were flashing like an angry kindergarten teacher's. "Lauren Bruce," she said, "This is Senator Candace Calloway. She really wants to meet you."

This time, the senator's demeanor was entirely different. She had a smile on her face that looked perfectly warm, a concerned look in her eyes. She held out a hand, then took it back and sat instead on the couch beside Lauren, keeping a safe distance from the still-feeding baby, extending one of her arms so that she could pat Lauren's shoulder. Lauren smelled perfume, some sort of exotic spice.

"I'm sorry," Candace said. "I was surprised to see you before. I didn't expect you so early. But I am so happy that you came and brought this adorable baby with you." She laid a manicured hand on Rory's butt and gave it a tentative pat. Rory's face remained hidden beneath Lauren's shirt.

"I cannot believe what you two have been through," Candace continued. "But don't worry, we're going to help you in every way we can."

"Thank you," Lauren said uncertainly. "I, um, appreciate your support."

"It's so important in times like this for women to stand together," Candace said.

"Right," Lauren said. "Of course."

"And don't you worry a bit about the press conference," Candace said. "Just be yourself. You'll be great."

"Press conference?" Lauren said, bolting upright.

"Just a small one," Maisy said, waving a hand dismissively. "To get the message out. It came together quickly. You don't even have to talk at all, if you don't want to. Just let Candace explain what mothers need."

"But I—"

"That's right," Candace said. "I'm going to say that mothers deserve to breastfeed wherever they want."

"And that babies deserve to be fed," Maisy said pointedly, "wherever and whenever they need to eat."

"Yes," Candace said. "This is a matter of doing what's right for babies." She and Maisy exchanged a meaningful look, and Lauren got the feeling that they had forgotten her altogether. But then Candace

gave Lauren's shoulder a firm squeeze. She stood up and bent down
to pat Rory's butt again, revealing her cleavage, perfect and tan.

"Don't you worry, Bruce girls," she said. "We're in this together." As she turned and left the room, Lauren noticed that
the senator's dress perfectly highlighted the sway of her rear end.

Maisy stood in place and smiled. "She has to make some
calls," she said. "Campaign business. Is there anything else we
can get you while you wait? Coffee? Water?"

"Um, no," Lauren said. "No, thanks. But I'm really not sure that—"

"Holler if you need me!" Maisy said, turning around. She
shut the door behind her and was gone.

ALONE AGAIN, Lauren settled back into the couch and tried
to decide whether to bolt or stay—the same calculation she had
made in the museum, a balance between self-preservation and a
sense of duty. She wanted to help other women, sure. She liked
having something to do. But she didn't know what to think about
Candace Calloway. She knew next to nothing about her, save the
images she'd seen in the inescapable campaign ads: soft-focus
shots of Candace talking to elderly people, reading a book to
schoolchildren, working a jackhammer at a construction site.
She remembered that the senator's hair stayed perfectly in place
when she took off her hard hat and said, "I approve this message."
But when it came to Candace's qualifications for office, her policies and principles, Lauren drew a blank.

"What do you know about Candace Calloway, Ror?" she
asked out loud. Mia had informed her that asking questions
of the baby, even rhetorical ones, was good for language development. Sometimes, Lauren just did it to fill the silence. But
when there was a pressing question to be answered, the baby
was little help. So Lauren stuck a hand into her diaper bag in

search of her cellphone. Her hand dipped into something soft and sticky, but she pressed on until she found the phone, covered with Vaseline. She wiped it clean with the inside of her shirt.

She thought of calling Rob, then hesitated. He was trying his best to impress the partners these days, and they frowned on personal calls in the middle of the day. He'd been busy, anyway, with an upcoming trial; he'd gotten home after she'd fallen asleep the night before, and left in the morning before she'd woken up. So she hit the speed dial for Mia's number, instead.

"You'll never guess where I am," she said when Mia answered.

"Pediatrician?" Mia said. "Drugstore?"

"Candace Calloway headquarters."

"What?"

"I know," Lauren said. "Her campaign manager came to my house this morning. She read the Herald."

"What did she want?" Mia said.

"To help. You know, help breastfeeding women. And babies. Using the attention they get from the press and all," Lauren said. "They're pretty excited about it. They're having a press conference this afternoon."

"A press conference?" Mia said. "A real press conference? About you?"

"Apparently," Lauren said.

"Don't worry," Mia said. "I'll be there right away. I can make it in half an hour. Where's the office? Never mind. I'll look it up."

"No, there's no need to come here," Lauren said. "Everything's under control. I just wanted to know if you knew anything about Candace Calloway. You know, whether she's trustworthy. Legit."

"Legit?" Mia said. "She's a powerful woman! You're the one I'm worried about."

"Because I'm not a powerful woman?" Lauren said.

"Because you've just been through a trauma," Mia said. "Stay calm! I'll see you soon." She let out a squeal of excitement, then hung up.

Lauren sighed and stroked Rory's head. It wouldn't be so bad to have someone there to talk to, someone who could actually respond. Maybe Mia could help her think of a pithy statement, so that she could sound truly political for once. The last time Lauren had embraced any grand cause was the day, in college, when she'd let some friends drag her to a "die-in" to protest nuclear proliferation. She had sprawled on the steps of the engineering building for ten minutes or so, sticking out her tongue and feeling profoundly stupid, before she'd finally gotten up wordlessly and headed to the library.

Just thinking of that day—the act of lying on her back, uninterrupted—made Lauren aware of her sleepiness again. She placed a firm hand around Rory, leaned her head back on the sofa, and let herself succumb to the weight of her tiredness. Her dream state was a jumble: teenage boys and security guards and interns holding antiwar signs. And then blackness, until she felt a tap on her shoulder. "Lauren," Maisy was saying. "It's 3:30. The press is starting to arrive. There's a hand mirror in the middle drawer of Candace's desk if you want it. But you look great. Be yourself. Candace will do most of the talking."

Just as quickly, Maisy was out of the room. Lauren stood, straightened her shirt, changed Rory's diaper as quickly as she could and brushed a spot of spittle off her romper. She pulled out Candace's mirror and laid it flat on the desk, looked at her image skeptically, then dug with one hand into her diaper bag again, tossing out a half-empty water bottle and the sticky remains of a cereal bar until she came across a tube of lipstick. She ran a finger through her hair, put Rory in her Bjorn, then walked out of Candace's offices and down the hallway, toward the open space in the middle of the campaign headquarters. Reporters and photographers had started to gather. TV cameramen were occupied with setting up their tripods. A few female TV reporters, wearing business suits and large quantities of makeup, stood together in a gaggle and chatted. Straining her ears, Lauren thought she could make out the words "Nordstrom" and "Ferragamo."

Across the room stood a few men with notebooks, not nearly as well-dressed or coiffed. These were newspaper reporters, clearly, and they were circled around Scott McFeeney of the Herald. He was looking triumphant, talking animatedly, and pointing toward one end of the room, where some interns were struggling to tape a hand-painted banner to the wall behind a podium. "BABIES NEED MILK," the banner said, in red and blue letters. The interns managed to wrestle it onto the wall, moved back, inspected it, adjusted it slightly, taped it down again, and then started to surround it with "Calloway for Governor" signs. A few older women headed toward the wall with signs of their own: "Don't Protest the Breast," "Breasts are Beautiful," "I Love Lactation."

Lauren edged away from the wall to read another poster and felt a jolt at her side. A woman with salt-and-pepper hair, wearing a peasant skirt and a billowing blouse, had broadsided her as she rushed through the room. "I'm looking for Maisy Street?" she said, not seeming to register the collision. Then she spied Rory, squinted her eyes, took a long look directly at Lauren's chest, and finally lifted her head and made eye contact.

"Are *you* Lauren Bruce?" she asked.

"I am," Lauren said.

"My hero!" The woman reached her arms out wide and wrapped them around Lauren and Rory, encircling them both in an awkward bear hug. Her breath smelled faintly of fennel. "I'm Sheila McDonough, from BOOB," she said. "Thank you for being so brave!"

"BOOB?" Lauren said.

"The Boston Organization for the Oversight of Breastfeeding," Sheila said, her cadence quick and clipped, as if she were a character in a 1940s movie. "Cute, huh? We had a pretty healthy debate, BOOB versus 'Breast Nazis,' but BOOB won out, and I'm glad. It looks a lot better on the signs."

"You brought more signs," Lauren said.

"I could only corral five other women today," Sheila said. "It was such short notice. But this is so important. This is awareness-raising."

Suddenly she glanced around the room, looking slightly panicked. "Sampson?" she yelled. "Sampson?"

"Mama!" A boy of about three, with light blond hair and tiny sneakers, was shouting from under a table.

"Sampson, come on over here," Sheila said. The boy didn't budge.

"Sampson," Sheila repeated. The boy let out a cackle.

"Sampson," Sheila said gently. "If you are not a good boy, you will get a time-out when we get home." She paused. "One…Two…"

Before she could say 'three,' the boy had zipped across the room and was clinging to his mother's leg. "Mama, I want nummers," he said.

"Sampson," Sheila said. "Mama's busy right now trying to find a nice lady. We'll have to wait for a few minutes to do nummers."

"But *people!*" the boy said plaintively.

"He gets nervous around crowds," Sheila told Lauren. "The breast helps to settle him down." To Sampson, she said, "Just hang in there, honey. Nummers soon. Yum."

Lauren looked behind Sheila and saw four other women with children. Two were wearing babies in brightly-colored slings. One held hands with twin toddler girls in braids. Another one was trailed by what appeared to be a five-year-old. Sheila motioned for them to come over.

"I want to introduce you to Lauren Bruce," she told them. "The reason we're here."

"Hello! Isn't this fantastic?" gushed the woman with the five-year-old, reaching out to shake Lauren's hand. "Bliss Mathers. I've been waiting so long for something like this to happen."

"How can you say that, after what she went through?" said the woman with twins. She shook her head and looked at Lauren sympathetically. "I am amazed at what people will do, even in this day and age."

"You're amazed?" another woman said, patting her baby in its sling. "I can believe it. I get dirty looks all the time when I'm nursing. I took a flight with Sam last month, and I thought the woman next to me was going to have a heart attack."

"Unconscionable," Bliss said. "But you will get used to it," she added, turning back to Lauren. "You learn to ignore what people around you think. Especially when your kids get older. And get support where you can. That's why we're here for you today. The BOOBs are all about support."

"Consider us your nursing bra!" Sheila said. The BOOBs started laughing raucously until Sam, in his sling, started to cry.

"Excuse me," said Sam's mother. "I'm going to go find a corner. Guess no one will look at me funny for breastfeeding here!"

Actually, as Sam's mother settled against a wall and lowered her son to her chest, Lauren noticed that two of the photographers pointed, smirked, and set up their cameras for a shot. She also saw, out of the corner of her eye, that Mia had arrived. She held Lyle in one arm and was dressed in one of the smart business suits she used to wear to major meetings at Pinnacle Events. Lyle was wearing one of Mia's custom onesies, which read, "Does it come in chocolate?"

Lauren felt a tap on her shoulder. Maisy was behind her. "Showtime," she said. "Come this way." She steered Lauren toward the podium. "Don't worry about the reporters," she said. "They'll be tough on Candace, but not on you. And they'll love the baby. Great image for the promos." She stepped up to the microphone.

"OK, folks, we're about to start," she announced. The reporters gathered around the podium, jostling slightly and looking up expectantly. It reminded Lauren of the crowds that always gathered to watch gorillas behind the glass at the Franklin Park Zoo. Except in this case, Lauren realized, she was the gorilla.

Candace Calloway strode to the podium, her hair bouncing gently with each step. She did not look like a gorilla, nor did she carry herself like a gorilla. More like a gazelle, graceful and serene. Lauren marveled at how she didn't wobble at all in her four-inch pumps.

"Thank you for coming," Calloway said. "I don't normally call you in on such short notice, as you know, but this is an important day. Yesterday, babies across Massachusetts were dealt a tremendous setback. A mother, trying to give her daughter the very essence of human sustenance—a food recommended by the American Association of Pediatrics—was told, in one of our state's cultural landmarks, that she had to feed her baby in a bathroom."

She paused, looking around the room seriously.

"Let me repeat that," she said. "In a *bathroom*. What self-respecting mother would stand by and let her baby eat in such an unsanitary place?"

Candace reached over to Lauren and grabbed her right hand. "Lauren Bruce could not abide," she said. "That is why we are so proud that she came to us. That is why we will not let her down. We will! Not! Let! Her! Down!"

Candace lifted Lauren's hand into the air with a triumphant flourish. A cheer went up among the volunteers and the BOOBs. Flashbulbs popped. Lauren tried to smile, but found herself replaying the morning's events in her head. As far as she remembered, Maisy had come to *her*.

Candace waited for the cheers to subside, then continued. "Every breastfeeding mother in Massachusetts has a friend in the Calloway campaign," she said. "That's why I'm proud to announce that, in my administration, any institution that gets state funding must allow breastfeeding, anywhere on its premises. When I'm governor, this state will be open for the babies' business!"

Another round of applause from the volunteers and the BOOBs. The toddler twins broke free from their mother's grasp and scurried across the room; their mother put down her "BOOBs for Babies" sign and ran after them.

"Anyone who would keep a woman from feeding her precious child," Candace said, "is striking a blow against women everywhere. But I can promise you: We will fight back. We will stand together, and make this state a haven for hungry babies!"

Another round of cheers, this one especially loud.

"Now, I'll be happy to answer questions," Calloway said.

"Senator!" shouted a TV reporter in a bright purple blazer. "What was your first reaction to the incident at the museum?"

"It was shock, Marissa. Outrage. Deep, deep sadness. And a sense of purpose," Calloway said.

"Do you think you can really understand this issue when you aren't a mother yourself?" shouted a man behind her, tall and thin, with a handlebar moustache.

Calloway shot him a steely look. "I am a woman, Fred," she said. "More importantly, I was a baby once."

"What about Professor Winkle?" asked another TV reporter, a middle-aged woman with bleached hair and dark roots. "Do you know his position on breastfeeding in public?"

"Frankly, Raquelle, I don't know my opponent's position on this affront to babies' health," Calloway said. "But as you can see, only one campaign has announced a plan to address this terrible scourge. Only one candidate is standing beside Lauren Bruce today." At this, she grabbed Lauren's hand again, pulled it into the air, and squeezed it so that everyone could see.

"Lauren!" said the reporter in purple. "Lauren! Can I ask? What were you thinking when this woman forced you to go to the bathroom?"

"Did you feel betrayed?" said the middle-aged blonde.

"Did you feel angry?" said a young reporter in high-heeled boots.

Lauren stood stock-still, aware that the room had hushed, that everyone was waiting for her to speak. She looked at the overdressed women from the TV stations. She looked at Scott McFeeney, his pen lifted in preparation. She looked down at Rory, who had somehow managed to fall asleep in her Bjorn. She looked at Mia, who was staring back with an expectant smile. She wanted to say something strident, something profound, something that spoke for womanhood at large. But all she could come up with was something dismayingly honest.

"I was thinking," she said tentatively, "that there's got to be a better way to feed a baby."

"Amen!" shouted Sheila McDonough, from somewhere in the middle of the crowd. The cameras turned toward her and she lifted her arms, eyes blazing. "There's got to be a better way to feed a baby!" she said. "A caring way! A natural way! That's what breastfeeding *is!* The rest of the world just needs to get with the program!" Then the BOOBs started chanting in unison: "Breast is Best! Breast is Best!"

That wasn't exactly what I meant, Lauren thought, as she watched the BOOBs wave their signs and mug for the cameras. Still, she had to admit, there was something nice about the way these women were cheering for her, treating her like somebody important. Lauren hadn't heard that kind of crowd support since she'd played field hockey in high school. And that was a long time ago. And she hadn't been a very good field hockey player.

After a few minutes of listening to the cheers, a wispy young man with mild acne stepped up to the podium. Maisy had introduced him earlier as Chip, the campaign press secretary.

"We're going to have to wrap it up now," he announced to the group. "Lauren's had a pretty exhausting couple of days, so I hope you'll give her some privacy. Thanks for coming."

Suddenly, Maisy was by Lauren's side, steering her toward the back hallway. As she rounded the corner, Lauren scanned the room. Scott McFeeney was scribbling furiously in his notebook. The TV reporters were huddled around Chip, except for one, who was pointing a microphone at Mia's face. Three of the BOOBs had already settled on the floor and started nursing their children. Candace Calloway was nowhere to be seen.

LAUREN HAD TURNED off her cellphone for the press conference, and didn't remember to turn it back on until she was already home, sitting with Rory on the living room couch, getting ready to unhook her nursing bra. Rob had called, it turned out. Five times. Once Rory was properly latched, Lauren dialed his number.

His secretary must have been gone for the day, because he picked up directly. "What's going on?" he said.

"Rory is eating, for the twelfth or fifteenth time," Lauren said. "I'm intimately involved. For dinner, for us, I think I'm going to take out those frozen burritos."

"No. I mean, what's going *on?* One of the partners' wives called in. She saw you on TV."

"Ah," Lauren said. "Yes. That. I guess I didn't have a chance to tell you, given that I was asleep and all. Something happened yesterday at the museum. I was feeding Rory, and some teenagers came by, and a woman told me to do it in the ladies' lounge, instead."

"So?"

"Well, that's what I thought at first. That it was no big deal," Lauren said. "But now, I don't know. I guess I'm kind of angry."

"How did you wind up holding hands with Candace Calloway?"

"Her campaign manager came by," Lauren said. "They had read the story in the Herald. And saw the video. And they were outraged. On Rory's behalf."

"The story in the Herald? The *video?*"

"Some kids took some footage with their iPhones," Lauren said. "But you can't really see anything. Or so I'm told. I didn't look. I thought it would blow over. But now I guess it's turned into a...thing."

"A thing," Rob said, sounding agitated. "Well, it's not such a great thing for me. A bunch of the partners have donated to the Winkle campaign."

Lauren sighed so deeply that her weight must have shifted; Rory popped off her breast and started to cry. "Arrgh," Lauren told Rob. "Hang on." She lifted the baby and switched her to the opposite breast. "This is what's nice about the Calloway campaign, as opposed to you," she said. "The women I met today want to *support* me."

"I support you by working all day so that you can be a mother!" Rob said.

"I'd be a mother whether you were working or not," Lauren shot back.

Rob was silent for a moment. Lauren briefly wondered if he had been stymied by her wit. Then she realized he was probably looking at his computer.

"I've got the Herald up now," Rob said, by way of confirmation. "Jesus, Lauren. Don't you think that volunteer was right?"

"What do you mean?" Lauren said.

"I don't want a bunch of teenage boys looking at you," he said. "And I don't really like it when your headlights are on in public."

"My *what* are *what?*"

"Your headlights," he said. "You know."

"My nipples," Lauren said. "Can you say that they're my nipples?"

"Come on, Lauren," Rob said.

"Repeat after me," Lauren said. "Rory latches to my nipples."

"Stop it," Rob said.

"Say it," Lauren said. "My *nip-ples* are sore."

"I'm in the office," Rob said. Lauren could tell that he was stifling a laugh. She considered: She could laugh herself and break the tension, or she could be like the BOOBs, full of righteous anger on her baby's behalf. She thought of the cheers, the chants, the hugs, the idea that she had unwittingly become a hero. If her husband couldn't handle these intimate anatomical details, she might as well side with the women.

"I think I'm becoming an activist," she told Rob, and hung up.

CHAPTER 4

THE NEXT MORNING, Maisy allowed herself to come to work later than usual, 7:45 a.m., a sleeping-in reward for a job well done. She whistled a little as she headed to the narrow doorway, wedged between the dollar store and a shop that sold specialty pens, that led to the campaign's upstairs offices. She gave a $5 bill, the full contents of her wallet, to the panhandler sitting by the door. Then she jogged up the stairs, clutching the Globe and Herald, which were filled with the fruits of yesterday's press conference.

The Globe had played the story on page one, and quoted a woman named Mia Hoberman, who called Candace a "guardian angel" for breastfeeding women. Stuart Winkle wasn't mentioned until after the jump—just a vague quote from his press secretary, saying the professor was "studying the issue with great seriousness." A Globe editorial demanded equal rights for nursing mothers and praised Calloway for taking a stand.

The Herald, meanwhile, had blown out its cover with a photo of Candace and Lauren Bruce, arms held aloft, and the headline, "ABREAST OF THE ISSUES." Inside, Dawn DeLuca, the feminist columnist, wrote that women had to "look out, above and below and at chest-level," for forces that were trying to oppress them. And Harvey Zane, the columnist known for sexist statements and ad hominem attacks, wrote that mothers had to "face the fact that nobody wants to see you old, shriveled, and naked." To Maisy, this was the best development of all. Angry readers were fund-raising targets.

And this was only one piece, Maisy thought with pride, of a multimedia frenzy. The night before, all five local TV stations had led their newscasts with the story, using the "open for the babies' business" line that Maisy had concocted. Newspapers across the state ran wire stories about the press conference. A website called ProudMamas.com named Candace Calloway its "natural woman of the day." And a message board on a site called MassMommies.com had 6,500 entries about the breastfeeding kerfuffle, which Maisy had skimmed while drinking coffee at home. These women weren't very good at spelling or grammar, Maisy thought, but they were engaged.

At 8:30 a.m., Maisy's phone rang. The front desk patched in Leroy Mason, the campaign treasurer.

"This is a gold mine," he said. "Online donations are soaring. We raised $12,000 in two hours yesterday, in $20 increments."

"I told you I'd come up with something, Leroy," Maisy said. "You doubted me."

"Oh, no, ma'am. I never doubted," Leroy said. He was a Brahmin investment banker with a 23-acre estate, where his wife bred Jack Russell terriers. But he had apparently once had a serious girlfriend from Georgia, so he fancied himself an aficionado of the South, and treated Maisy with un-Boston-like gentility.

"Now, you've got to find a way to keep this coming," he said.

"There are more trees to shake," Maisy replied, scanning her calendar and starting to think out loud. "We'll set up a string of women's house parties. We'll get her to make the rounds at some Moo Coalition meetings. She could go to some Mommy-and-Me-type classes…though Candace isn't great with toddlers, so maybe we should keep our distance. Of course, we could use Lauren Bruce as a surrogate. She's very female-friendly." She made a mental note to send Lauren along with Candace to a fund-raiser this weekend.

"I only have one worry," Leroy said. "You don't think there's going to be a backlash, do you? The young mothers all seem to breastfeed these days, but my wife bottle-fed our kids. Everyone did back then. The last thing we want to do is exclude any women."

"Do you have grandkids, Leroy?" Maisy asked.

"With the men my daughters have been dating? Thank God, no."

"When you do," Maisy said, "your wife will get on the breast-feeding bandwagon. Mark my words. Who can disagree with modern science?"

That seemed to satisfy Leroy, who agreed to draft a new fund-raising letter targeted at thirty-something mothers. Maisy promised to give it to her Motherhood Advisory Committee for review, then made a mental note to create a Motherhood Advisory Committee. When she hung up with Leroy, she dialed the receptionist. "Get Chip in here," she said.

Within 30 seconds, Chip Osterville had bounded into Maisy's office and was sitting on the couch, his legs splayed at about 140 degrees, as if he needed to air himself out. Three years out of college, he hadn't quite learned adult decorum, perhaps owing to the fact that he'd spent the previous two winters ski-bumming in Colorado. Chip's parents were active in Democratic politics, he had interned for a couple of previous campaigns, and Candace had insisted he be hired as press secretary. He was a pleasant enough kid to have around the office, but Maisy was still disappointed that she'd inherited him. He wasn't exactly a natural at courting the women's vote, and he wasn't quite cute enough to be a magnet for undersexed middle-aged women. Plus, Maisy wasn't sure that he wholly understood politics.

"Hey, Maisy," he said. "I was thinking today we could put out that press release about the Senator's environmental policy. I had it ready to go yesterday, but this whole breastfeeding thing came up."

Maisy looked at him and chewed on the back of her pen.

"Chip," she finally said, "I'm going to explain something to you about campaigns."

"Uh-huh," Chip said. He looked down at his iPhone.

"Some issues excite people," Maisy said, "and some issues do not. The environment does not excite people. Health care does not excite people. Economic development does not excite people. That doesn't mean people don't care about these things. It just means they won't pay a whit of attention when you talk about them. And you know who's going to be even less excited about an environmental policy press release than a voter? A reporter."

"Uh-huh," Chip said.

"Do you know what gets reporters excited, Chip?" Maisy said. "Sex. Puns. Women fighting women. Cats who learn how to flush a toilet. Anything that makes them forget how miserable they are when they have to write about issues they don't give a rat's ass about. This breastfeeding thing? It doesn't have cats flushing toilets, but it has sex and girlfights, and that's good enough for most reporters I know. And the best thing about it? A whole bunch of soccer moms are going to get excited, too. Because to them, breasts mean babies. They love babies. And starting today, we *own* babies."

She reached behind her desk and pulled out a dry-erase board. "It's brainstorming time, Chip," she said. "I need you to start thinking like a reporter. Either that or a lactating woman."

BY THE TIME Candace Calloway arrived at quarter to ten, the new agenda for the next two days was set. That afternoon, the campaign would issue a press release, saying Candace would make it a crime to stop a woman from breastfeeding in public. In the evening, at a fund-raiser, Candace would announce an overhaul of lactation rooms in state buildings, pledging that each one would have leather chairs and dimmable lights. The field staff would order yard signs that said, "Calloway: There's Got To Be A Better Way." They were discussing tax subsidies for nursing bras when Candace appeared in her doorway, with Scott McFeeney trailing close behind her.

"Are you still talking about breasts?" Candace asked.

"Are you still talking about breasts?" McFeeney repeated.

"What the hell is he doing here?" Maisy said.

"Oh—he's working on a profile of the senator," Chip said. "I told him he could shadow her for a couple of days."

"No," Maisy said. "No, no, no, no, no. He can shadow her at public events. Stand around in diners. But he can't just hang around the office."

"I'll be a fly on the wall," McFeeney said, leaning comfortably against the doorway.

"I've seen what you do as a fly," Maisy said. "Out. Out of my sight."

"Chip, I'll call you later," McFeeney said, and left.

"Chip, you will keep your distance," Maisy said after he left. "That guy is a weasel. I can tell."

"He's not that bad," Chip said. "He's old-school. And he's the one who got the museum story."

"I know. He's an old-school weasel with good instincts. That's why I don't want him anywhere near us," Maisy said.

"And I was just getting used to him," Candace sighed. She slipped off her shoes, sat down on the couch, and picked up a rough draft of the afternoon's press release. "I don't know," she said. "Should we really throw all of our energy into this breast-feeding thing?"

"Are you kidding?" Maisy said. "You were great at the press conference yesterday. You hit your stride. The women loved you."

"I know," Candace said. "They were very touchy-feely."

"And?" Maisy said.

"I'm just a little more accustomed to being touched by men."

Chip, sitting beside Candace on the couch, started choking

on his own saliva. "Excuse me," he gasped, rushing out of the room. Maisy looked at Candace accusatorily.

"You love doing that, don't you?" she said.

"Can't resist," Candace said with a smile.

"Well, speaking of being touched by men, the Pep Boys are coming for debate prep at noon," Maisy said. "I know they all want to get into your pants, too. Just try not to encourage them too much, OK? We've got to get down to business here."

"Pep Boys" was the name Maisy used for Bob Brooks, Mike LaDuke and Steve Albee, the three Washington consultants that Candace had insisted on hiring. The boys were Beltway insiders, a trio of divorced men whose resumes were filled with high-profile but losing presidential campaigns. Maisy knew their type, and didn't approve; they didn't know much about individual states and cared too much about unnecessary stagecraft. But Candace was so impressed by their pedigrees that she assumed their advice was sound. Before the last debate, they had presented a study that said that men prefer candidates who hold onto the podium, while women prefer gesticulation. Candace had spent the entire event trying to split the difference, holding her hands awkwardly in mid-air.

At five minutes past noon, the Pep Boys arrived, wheeling small black suitcases and wearing near-identical outfits: khaki pants and expensive oxford shirts with their initials monogrammed on the sleeves. They filed into the conference room, where an intern had set up Chinese take-out. They took turns kissing Candace on the cheek and nodding to Maisy. Then they quickly settled down to the business of eating. Brooks and LaDuke loaded up their plates with moo shi pork and beef lo mein. Steve Albee, a tall, wiry man with horn-rimmed glasses, spooned six of the eight dumplings Maisy had ordered onto his plate, then sat down and fired up his laptop. He loaded a PowerPoint presentation that was clearly recycled from other campaigns. The title was, "GENERAL ELECTION DEBATE."

"You look lovely today, Candace," he said as he tapped at the keys. "Did you see my new MacBook? Latest generation. Weighs less than two pounds. I just toss it in my knapsack when I'm biking."

"Nice that he can bring a knapsack along," said LaDuke, a heavyset man with a thick neck and a curly moustache, whose head reminded Maisy of a walrus. "I can't carry a computer around when I'm cross-training for a triathlon."

"I got him into those triathlons," Brooks said. He was a generation older than the other two, and nominally in charge. "Mike, you've been catching up nicely. But remind me to give you some pointers on the swimming."

"OK, we're very impressed with all of you," Maisy said. "You're manly and athletic. Can we get on with the presentation?"

Albee clicked to the first slide. "HOME STRETCH," it read. "AUDIENCE GROWS. MEDIA FOCUSES. TIME TO HONE MESSAGE." The second slide read, "CANDACE CALLOWAY MESSAGE: EXPERIENCE. ENERGY. COMPASSION." That was the tagline on their current crop of campaign ads. If they were going to be honest, Maisy thought, they would have added, "Legs."

Albee skipped to the next slide, "CANDACE CALLOWAY WEAKNESSES," it read.

"Campaigning is such an ego boost," Candace murmured, propping her chin on her hands. Maisy noticed that she hadn't taken a plate of food.

"It's just rhetorical," Brooks said. "You've got no weaknesses in my book."

"Moving on?" Maisy said.

"We threw a couple of questions about women into the last poll," LaDuke said. "Here's the thing. Women admire you. They want to be like you. But they can't relate to you. They think you're a little too perfect."

Albee clicked the next slide. "TOO PERFECT," it said. Albee smiled at Candace, who smiled back and reached for a Diet Coke.

The next slide had three bullet points: "EXHAUSTION. FRUSTRATION. VULNERABILITY."

"On Sunday, we think you need to show a little weakness up-front," Brooks said. "See if your hairstylist can leave a strand or two out of place—enough that you could push back from your face. You could start off the debate complaining about a bad hair day."

"Let's come up with some personal stories about insecurity," Albee said. "Did you ever get emotional when you were pushing through a bill? Can you get teared up on cue?"

"Also, the clothes," LaDuke said. "Women respond better to deep colors than pastels. So we're thinking a dark green suit. Maybe a little boxy. No cleavage. You'll be the only woman on-stage; no need to push it."

"She won't be the only woman on the stage," Maisy pointed out. "Lois Manson gets into this one." Lois Manson was the lowest-polling of the candidates, a member of the Green/Rainbow party.

"I don't think Lois Manson is a woman," LaDuke said. Albee let out a snort. Maisy had to admit, Manson did have a trucker's build.

"I've got to interrupt you here," Maisy said, "to remind you that we've had a shift in message. We're talking about babies now. And breastfeeding. Perhaps you missed today's news? That's all about yesterday's press conference?"

"The press conference you didn't call to consult us about?" Bob Brooks said, with his mouth full of lo mein.

"The very one," Maisy said.

"I wouldn't have recommended it," LaDuke said. "It was a little too…specific."

"We didn't have time to consult," Maisy said. "We had to capture the moment before Winkle had time to react. And if you happened to read the press, you would see that we caught him off-guard."

"I don't think we've ever polled this issue," Brooks said. "And you know what we say: You can't trust what you haven't polled." LaDuke and Albee joined in to recite their catchphrase in unison.

"I followed my instinct," Maisy replied. "Thirty years in politics and all. Raised us 12 grand overnight. Now, we need to come up with some good breastfeeding lines for Candace on Sunday night."

"Look," Brooks said. "Far be it from me to try to draw attention away from Candace's figure. But Sunday is an eternity away." He flashed her a smile, which she returned. Maisy rubbed her temples with her fingers.

"I think we need to run with this breastfeeding thing," she said. "Look at the papers and the blogs. Women across the state are going wild. Candace is their champion."

"What do you think, Candace?" LaDuke said. "Do you want to be the champion of breastfeeding women?"

Candace didn't respond. She was gazing, with deep concentration, into the depths of her Diet Coke. "What?" she finally said when she realized that everyone was staring at her. "I'm sorry. I didn't hear you. I was trying to summon up tears."

Suddenly, Chip Osterville barged into the office, looking flushed. Scott McFeeney was half a step behind him.

"What the hell is he still doing here?" Maisy said.

"He left and came back," Chip said. "Sorry to interrupt. But Scott came by to get some quotes for a follow-up story. About the Winkle campaign's official response to the press conference."

"Which is?" Maisy said.

"Mothers on Modesty," McFeeney said. "A new group they've started. Initials stand for 'MOM.'"

He handed Maisy a rumpled flier.

"*The MOM Manifesto,*" it read. "*Resolved: That modesty is a virtue. Resolved: That decorum is a sign of respect. Resolved: That cultural spaces should be safe for all ages. Resolved: That our children should be shielded from indecency.*

"*Mothers, grandmothers, and concerned women of all ages,*" it went on. "*Remember that babies grow up to be children, and children need protection. Pass this along to all of your friends. Tell them to support Stuart Winkle, the candidate with standards!*"

Maisy passed the paper to Candace, who passed it to LaDuke,

who handed it to Brooks, who gave it to Albee, who folded it into a paper airplane and shot it across the room.

"Apparently, that museum volunteer didn't like being the butt of your press conference," McFeeney said. "She called the Winkle campaign herself. I think this 'MOM' thing was her idea."

"The Winkle campaign is taking directions from a museum volunteer?" Maisy said.

"Well, yeah, but she's not just an art history buff," McFeeney said. "It turns out she was a founding member of the Moo Coalition back in the '70s. A classic bra-burner, coming out of retirement. Between you and me, I think she's kind of happy to get back in business."

"I see," Maisy said.

"So. You got a comment for me?" McFeeney said.

"On the record: Senator Calloway isn't concerned about the past. She's concerned about the future. And there will be no future if our babies aren't healthy or fed," Maisy said. "Off the record: Get out of my sight and let me think."

"Gladly," McFeeney said. "I've got a deadline."

After he left, Candace and the Pep Boys looked at Maisy expectantly. She wavered for a moment, wondering if she'd miscalculated, after all. Maybe the Winkle campaign was savvier than it seemed. Maybe there was an equally loud constituency for covering up.

On the other hand, she had finally found an issue with legs— legs that didn't belong to Candace and end in stiletto heels. The Calloway campaign would be the voice of young motherhood and modern science. The newfound mom-supporters would be doubly motivated. And the press would get to write as much as it wanted about girlfights and breasts.

"I don't think we have a choice now. We've got to be all in," Maisy said. Candace and the Pep Boys had to nod in glum agreement.

CHAPTER 5

"DOES MY HAIR look all right?" Lauren said uncertainly, trying to catch a glimpse of it in the windows of parked cars. She and Mia were walking along the cobblestone sidewalks of Beacon Hill, Lauren a few paces behind, stepping gingerly so that she wouldn't trip with her feet in kitten heels and Rory in the Bjorn. This was the first time she'd dressed up since Rory had been born, and on some level, it felt good—strangely human, after months of wearing elastic-waist pants. Except that she wasn't fully finished with all that; her pre-pregnancy clothes were still too tight, so after searching her closet frantically for the appropriate outfit for tea at a Beacon Hill townhouse, she had wound up doctoring a maternity skirt with safety pins.

That's what she had been doing when Mia had arrived at her house that Saturday morning, wearing another business suit and carrying a briefcase. She had left Lyle in his father's care, choosing to concentrate fully today on her new role as chairwoman of the Calloway campaign's Motherhood Advisory Committee. Maisy Street had called with the invitation a day earlier, praising the "inspiring" interviews Mia had given to the press. Mia had accepted immediately, then sped to an office supply store for folders, legal pads, and a small notebook for jotting down ideas.

She was already assembling an e-mail chain and a schedule of meetings, and contacting baby clothing stores and Mommy-and-Me franchises for lists of potential recruits. And right away, she had volunteered to accompany Candace and Lauren to a Beacon Hill fund-raising tea. Lauren, of course, was urged to bring Rory, who represented the Calloway campaign's official top priority.

"Come on," Mia was saying now, tugging Lauren down Charles Street. "We don't want to be late. These Beacon Hill ladies are sticklers for punctuality."

"What if they're sticklers for modesty, too?" Lauren asked. "What if they're MOMs?" When she had read about the new group, a small knot had formed in her stomach. She'd briefly wondered if Rob had been right, that it was better to nurse in some tucked-away place. Then she told herself that she was being weak. She was supposed to represent motherhood, open doors, set a strong example for Rory, who was currently asleep.

"Don't worry about the MOMs," Mia said. "They're a different generation. They don't understand modern life. Remember, these are the women who drank when they were pregnant. They put their babies to sleep on their *stomachs.*"

"But won't those be the women at the tea?"

"No, no, no," Mia said. "The women at the tea are older than the MOMs. I don't know if formula was even invented when they were having babies. Besides, they're super-liberal, so they'll definitely be on the side of progress."

She turned up a side street, past row after row of well-kept brick townhomes with impeccably-tended flower boxes. Finally, they reached the door of Tillie Lockerbie's house, around the corner from Louisburg Square. Tillie, as Maisy had explained, was a fabulously wealthy state Democratic Party stalwart, a personal friend of several presidents who had passed through her home for fund-raising events. She had served a brief term as ambassador to a small island in the Pacific before she returned home, claiming the hot air had been bad for her health. Now, at 83, she rarely left her townhouse, but she still hosted teas and fund-raisers for Boston's aging upper crust. Today's event was a women-only tea on Calloway's behalf, at a cost of $1,000 per head.

Mia climbed up the stone steps and rang the doorbell, a shiny black button beneath a polished brass eagle. A young black woman in a maid's uniform opened the door. Mia and Lauren stepped into a foyer with a grand chandelier. Above the wainscoting, the walls were lined with aging oil portraits of severe men and women, presumably Tillie's ancestors. A slender mahogany table, elaborately carved, held several small aboriginal sculptures, keepsakes from Tillie's ambassador days.

An archway led to a large drawing room with copious built-in bookshelves. About 15 women, all of them white, most with grey hair, were sitting in Chippendale chairs that had been placed in a large circle. The women wore skirts that fell just below their knees, in various shades of pastel or tweed, along with well-tailored matching jackets affixed with name-tag stickers. All of them wore nude pantyhose and orthopedic shoes. A few more black women in uniforms passed through the room with trays of finger sandwiches and delicate china teacups, which most of the ladies balanced expertly in their laps. Several other ethnic women congregated along one wall, beside a collection of folded walkers and oxygen tanks. Apparently, these were the health-care aides.

Lauren spotted Candace Calloway in one corner, holding a teacup and leaning down to talk to a woman in a hat adorned with feathers. Jodi, Candace's personal aide, was sitting in an upholstered chair in a corner, tapping into a BlackBerry.

"A lady with a baby. You must be Lauren Bruce!" a woman said loudly. Her voice was grainy, like a chain-smoker's, but still managed to have a melodious lilt. "I'm Tillie. So charmed to meet you."

Tillie Lockerbie stepped forward, dressed in the sort of outfit a little girl might wear: a bright red silk blouse with an enormous bow around the neck, a black pleated skirt, and a pair of flat black patent-leather shoes with bows on the toes. Her hair, bright white and wavy, flowed almost to her shoulders. Her face was wizened around the edges but still beautiful, high cheekbones giving frame to translucent skin. She wore blush on her cheeks, blue eye shadow, and lipstick in a muted shade of strawberry. Lauren shook Tillie's hand, which was also translucent, with bright blue veins. The socialite's skin was smooth. Her grip was strong.

"And this must be your baby," Tillie said, leaning into the side of Lauren's Bjorn to gaze at Rory's sleeping profile. "Isn't she just *darling?*" Her words were elongated in the Brahmin speaking style.

"Thank you," Lauren said. "Thank you for having us."

"Ms. Lockerbie," Mia said, tapping Tillie gently on the shoulder. "I'm Mia Hastings Hoberman, chair of the Motherhood Advisory Committee. It's such an honor to be here today."

Tillie turned to look Mia up and down. "Well, aren't you adorable," she said approvingly. "Welcome." Mia beamed.

"Let me introduce you to the girls," Tillie said, grabbing Lauren's hand in one of hers and Mia's in the other, and steering them both toward the drawing room. "Ladies," she announced. "Our guests of honor have arrived. Well, our other guests of honor, next to the candidate herself." She let out a low-pitched laugh. Across the room, Candace put on a practiced smile.

"This is Lauren, who was bold enough to feed her child in a museum," Tillie continued. "This is Mia, who is bringing other women into the fold. They are teaching the world a few lessons about women's resilience, I believe."

"Bravo!" one of the ladies said, setting her teacup on a dark wood table and starting to applaud. The other women who weren't holding teacups joined in.

"I think it's time for us to start our little group chat. We have a seat for one guest here," Tillie said, steering Lauren toward an empty Chippendale chair. "Can we get another chair here, please?"

She snapped her fingers, making a surprisingly loud sound, and one of the uniformed black women rushed out of the room. She reappeared a minute later with another fancy chair, which she wedged next to Lauren's for Mia. Lauren wondered if Tillie had a room filled completely with elegant spare furniture. Then she noticed that Rory was beginning to stir. She unhooked the Bjorn, gave Rory a kiss, and handed the baby to Mia so she could lift the Bjorn over her head.

"These contraptions you young girls have never cease to amaze me," said one of the grey-haired women, whose nametag read, "Effie." "When my children were young, we simply carried them around."

"And we didn't strap them into seats in a car," another woman piped up. "We held them on our laps. And most of them survived!"

"Every generation has its obsessions," a third woman said. "When I was a young mother, it was knowing which cigarette was the most fashionable."

Lauren noticed that Mia's smile was now as artificial as Candace's. She also noticed that Rory was starting to get hungry. She could see the baby's tiny head rooting around on Mia's chest, presumably smelling milk.

Once again, Lauren found herself hesitating: Should she duck into another room for a quiet feeding, or do her part for modernity and nurse in front of all of these women? With Candace and Mia here, she really had no choice. At least it was a women-only crowd; she could pretend she was in a bathroom lounge.

So as discreetly as she could, she reached into her diaper bag, pulled out the pink blanket she had packed for this purpose, and draped it around her shoulder. Then she reached into her shirt and unhooked her nursing bra.

"What are you doing?" one of the women asked loudly. "Are you taking off your bra?"

"Oh, my goodness, she is!" another woman gasped.

"Are you going to feed your baby? Right here?" said a third.

"Of course, she is," Tillie said sternly. "We are all enlightened here." She turned to Lauren. "Now, you go ahead, dear. We're so happy that you're giving us a demonstration, aren't we?"

Most of the ladies murmured in assent. Lauren looked up and noticed that all of them were staring at her chest in rapt fascination.

Across the room, Candace tapped a silver spoon against her teacup. She stood up, showing off a fitted tweed suit in the style of Jackie O. Lauren sent her a telepathic "thank you." Candace ran a hand through her hair, glanced around the room and started to speak.

"Thank you so much, Tillie, for hosting us today, and for lending your wisdom and support to my campaign," she said. "Ever since I heard about the horrible affair at the Stonewall, I knew I had a duty to act—as a woman, as a Democrat, as someone who cares about the future of the Commonwealth."

"Hear, hear," Tillie said, raising a teacup in the air triumphantly.

"In the coming days," Candace said, "you'll probably hear from a group that hopes to divert attention from the needs of our babies. They call themselves 'MOMs,' but they are, quite frankly, a front for my opponent's campaign. And I worry that with their sensationalism, they will distract the public from our very important work."

Lauren glanced around the room and saw that most of the women were now looking at Candace with expressions of concern. Only one, with the nametag "Geraldine," continued to stare directly at Lauren's chest.

"I'm worried about the misinformation they'll put out," Candace continued. "That's why I need your help. We'll need to blanket new mothers with mailings. We'll need to run response ads. I know how generous you've been in the past, and I would be honored if you would help me spread the word. State law, as you know, limits donations to $2,500 per person."

Several of the women reached into their purses and pulled out checkbooks. "Here's a bit more for you, dear," one of them said, in a voice that sounded eerily like Katharine Hepburn's.

Jodi passed through the room, collecting a dozen or so checks, as one of the maids made the rounds with more cups of tea and a tray of petits-fours. Lauren moved the blanket, as discreetly as she could, and shifted Rory from the left breast to the right. Finally, Mia tapped her spoon against her teacup, as Candace had done.

"I just want to take this opportunity to thank Senator Calloway," Mia said. "As a new mother myself, I can't tell you how much it means to have your support."

"You have a child, too, dear?" Tillie asked.

"Yes," Mia said. "A little boy. He's almost six months old."

"And do you feed him mother's milk as well?" asked a woman whose nametag read, "Martha."

"Of course," Mia said. "It's the best gift I can give to him."

"I felt sorry for my granddaughter when I heard that she was going to nurse her baby," the woman next to Martha said, in a raspy whisper loud enough for the entire room to hear. "When I was young," she continued, staring at Martha knowingly, "nursing was something that only the colored help did."

Two or three of the health aides turned and glared, but the woman didn't seem to notice. "I offered to give my Jessica some money for formula," she went on. "But she said it was something she *wanted* to do."

"Oh, there are many studies that prove the health benefits of breastfeeding," Mia said brightly, addressing the room at large. "It strengthens the autoimmune system and reduces the risk of allergies. Some studies show that breastfed babies have higher IQs than formula-fed babies."

"Well, that explains my son the schoolteacher," one woman piped up. Several other women erupted into throaty cackles.

"I have another question, Ms. Bruce," said Geraldine, whose gaze still hadn't shifted from Lauren's chest. "What does it feel like?"

"I'm sorry?" Lauren said.

"Does it hurt?" Geraldine said. "It seems as if it would be quite uncomfortable."

Lauren paused and thought about how—and whether—to answer honestly. "No," she said. "I mean, yes. At first, it hurt.

Pretty badly. But it gets better. I think babies get better at it after awhile. And you, um, get used to the feeling."

"But *what* feeling?" Geraldine demanded. "Is it a twisting feeling?"

Lauren felt herself blushing. "No," she said. "More like…a tugging, I guess. A light tugging. Honestly, you don't notice it after awhile."

"Really?" Geraldine said. "I'm quite sure I would notice *that*."

"All I know is, my granddaughter had a baby two months ago, and the child does not sleep," said another woman, whose nametag read, "Eunice." She sighed loudly. "He never seems filled up. It's impossible to tell how much he's eaten. And she refuses to hire a night nurse. Really, I think she's spoiling him."

A murmur of assent passed through the room.

"Oh, yes," said a woman whose nametag read, "Clea." "Today's babies are very privileged."

"Oh, come now," Martha said. "Perhaps you did the same thing with your children. I honestly don't remember it, myself. I can't recall giving birth to any of them."

"That's because you were drugged, dear," Clea said. "We all were."

"That's another thing about the girls today," said Geraldine. "They don't want drugs when they give birth. They want pain. My granddaughter calls it 'natural,' and she's quite proud of it. I told her, 'I'm a great believer in the synthetic.'"

The ladies murmured again.

"And the husbands in the room," Clea said. "Sometimes with a movie camera."

"*Mon dieu,*" Martha said. "If someone were to film such private parts of me, I'd expect to be getting paid."

Several of the women laughed loudly. One started to choke on her tea. One of the health aides rushed over quickly with a fresh handkerchief, and a maid disappeared and returned in an instant with a crystal wine goblet, filled with water.

"Oh, my," Tillie said loudly. "It appears we're having a bit too much fun. Motherhood today is just baffling!"

Lauren looked over at Mia, who had been a champion of natural childbirth, and realized she was looking defensive. Somehow, she felt compelled to give her friend a bit of support. "Modern motherhood is definitely different," she said. "But there's a lot that's good about it. Isn't there, Mia?"

Mia flashed Lauren a quick smile. "Yes! Modern motherhood is wonderful," she said. "There are so many innovations that bring us closer to our babies."

Lauren thought of some of the innovative modern items she'd bought for Rory in fits of pregnancy anxiety. A stuffed lamb designed to help the baby sleep by approximating the sound of an ocean, a jackhammer, or a yard full of crickets. A rubber duck with a sensor on the bottom that said "HOT" if the bathwater was warmer than 70 degrees. A plush Baby Mensa pig that said "Hello" in seven languages when you pressed its stomach.

"There is," Mia went on, "a growing sense that we've introduced too many synthetic things into our babies' lives. Like infant formula. Why create something in a factory when nature provides it right here?" She pointed to her chest. One of the ladies nodded.

"And how about diapers?" Mia went on. "They're filling up our landfills! In villages in the brush, babies don't wear diapers at all. The mothers just sense when their babies have to go, and hold them out over the dirt. And anthropologists who have studied those babies say they are *very* happy."

"My dear," Tillie said, "I have visited the brush. There are quite a few advantages to living here, instead. But do go on. I am always open-minded."

"Actually, it's easy to see the signs, if you know what to look for," Mia said. "I can show you right now, if you'd like. Lauren, I think we should demonstrate Elimination Communication."

Lauren looked at her, alarmed.

"Elimination Communication," Tillie repeated. "That sounds very complex. Does it require high-tech gadgets?"

"No," Mia said. "Just a bowl."

"A bowl?" Tillie said.

"To catch the baby's waste," Mia said. One of the ladies let out a gasp.

"It's a beautiful thing. Let me show you," Mia said, gesturing for Lauren to pass Rory back to her.

"Are you sure?" Lauren whispered. "I've never done this before. I'm not sure when she's glazing, or whatever."

"You're Rory's mother," Mia whispered back. "I'm sure you'll be able to sense her needs." Her tone was supportive, but Lauren suspected she was also issuing a challenge. She handed the baby to Mia, who held her in the air.

"Look at this adorable child," Mia said. Rory blinked appealingly and looked around the room. Several of the ladies cooed. Lauren felt a gush of pride.

"Now, imagine how uncomfortable she might feel if she were sitting in her own waste," Mia said. "Fortunately, there's another way."

"I suppose that's my cue!" Tillie said. She snapped loudly again, and one of her maids retreated into another room, returning quickly with a ceramic bowl that looked like a Chinese antique. She handed it to Mia, who placed it on the floor on top of the Persian rug.

"Lauren," Mia said. "Would you do the honors?"

For this occasion, Rory was wearing a onesie that Mia had rush-ordered from her silkscreen shop. "Candace Calloway," it read. "The Breast Governor Ever!" Lauren unsnapped the bottom and removed Rory's diaper, which she noticed was mostly dry. She rolled up the bottom of the onesie until it covered Rory's belly, revealing tiny private parts and a pair of chunky thighs. Rory cooed. Lauren kissed the top of her head.

"I'm new to this myself," she announced to the room. "But she's set. I think now we're just supposed to…wait."

"Wait and watch," Mia said. "We're looking for the natural signs that every baby gives when she wants relief."

The room fell quiet, all eyes now trained on Rory's small vagina. Lauren, feeling the need to fill the silence and the sense that she ought to be showing more campaign spirit, held Rory out and front of her and rocked her back and forth in a little dance. "Candace Calloway for governor!" she said in a high-pitched voice.

There was silence again. Finally, Candace Calloway spoke.

"While we're waiting," she said, with obvious irritation, "perhaps we can talk about some of our other initiatives. Our campaign isn't just about babies; it's about all of the citizens of the Commonwealth. I have a ten-point economic development plan…"

"Isn't the baby going to get cold?" the woman named Eunice piped up, as if Candace hadn't been speaking. "Her unmentionables are perfectly bare!"

"It's summer, dear. I'm sure she'll be fine," Clea said.

"Can you tell what she's thinking yet?" Martha called out. "I didn't know babies could think at this age."

Lauren noticed the flush on Candace's face and decided to speak up again. It felt unseemly, after all, to upstage her patron with her baby's private parts. "Senator Calloway," she said loudly, "I'd like to hear about your economic plan."

Across the room, Candace's eyelids fluttered.

"Or your environmental policy…" Lauren tried. But then she let out an involuntary yelp as she felt a drop of liquid on her thigh. A tiny trickle of urine was coming from Rory's bottom. The ladies, slow to detect it at first, now began to chatter.

"She's going!" one of them shouted.

"Did her face move?" another one asked.

"This was unusually fast," Mia said loudly. "She must have a small bladder."

As the volume in the room increased, Lauren stood and tried to position Rory's bottom above the Chinese bowl. But it was too late. The rug was dotted with several conspicuous wet spots. One of the maids rushed out of the room, then reappeared in seconds with a cloth and a bottle of carpet cleaner. As she knelt down to tend to the spots, she started cursing under her breath in a Creole dialect.

The other maids looked equally alarmed, but Tillie let out a laugh that was higher-pitched than usual, and sounded a bit like a tinkle, itself. "Don't fret for a moment about this old thing," she said, pointing to the rug as if it were something she had picked up at Home Depot.

Startled by the commotion, Rory started to cry, a whimper that soon rose into a full-fledged wail. As Lauren tried to comfort her, she heard one of the ladies say, in a clear voice, "Do you hear that, girls? Now *that* is communication."

CHAPTER 6

"I understand," Maisy said, "that it wasn't the way these fund-raisers usually go. But it's over. Now we have to get out of the car."

She was sitting beside Candace in the backseat of a Lincoln sedan, idling in the parking lot of Channel 6. Nearly a day and a half had passed since the event at Tillie Lockerbie's house, and Candace was still griping—about baby-obsessed old women, and also about the traffic, the weather, the man who sat beside her in the Senate, the tight straps on her newest pair of pumps. Maisy had never seen the senator in such a foul mood, but she had to snap Candace out of her funk. The televised debate was due to start in half an hour. And a Channel 6 producer had left Maisy five voice-mail messages and two urgent texts, wondering when the senator was going to arrive.

On the steps of the squat brick Channel 6 building, supporters of the candidates had gathered, waving signs. Stuart Winkle was busily working the crowd. Newspaper photographers snapped away.

"Let's get out there with him," Maisy said. "There's not much time."

"Not without Christopher," Candace said.

Christopher Bishop-Pryce was Candace's stylist and make-up artist, who accompanied her on shopping expeditions and primped her for TV appearances. He was supposed to meet them at the studio. So far, he had not arrived.

"I'm sure he's on his way," Maisy said. "He can meet us inside."

"I'm not going in front of those cameras with hair like this," Candace declared.

To Maisy, Candace's hair looked exactly the same as it did every day: highlighted and honeyed, slightly wavy, falling to her shoulders with a perfect bounce. But Candace insisted that it was frizzy. "When it rains in the morning, my hair is impossible all day," she growled, staring out the tinted window. "Where is he? He knows I need him."

"Your hair looks fine," Maisy said. "And it's supposed to look out of place, remember?"

"I need Christopher to take the right hairs out of place," Candace replied.

She was still under a directive to appear vulnerable and humanized, but given the campaign's newfound embrace of breasts, the Pep Boys had lifted their ban on décolletage. So she was wearing a fitted, cream-colored suit that showed off a hint of cleavage, along with a pair of peep-toe navy pumps whose straps she had yet to break in. *The cameras would love her,* Maisy thought, *if she'd ever get out of the car.*

"Well, I'm going," Maisy said, climbing carefully over Candace and exiting the Lincoln. As she headed for the station steps, Winkle gave a final wave and disappeared into the building. As usual, he had cultivated the look of an anti-politician, wearing a pair of khaki pants and a jacket of professorial tweed. Winkle was a government professor at Harvard, best known for teaching a popular course called "The Macroeconomics of the Seagull," which combined neoconservative economic policy with new-age philosophy: He preached such principles as "Never stray from your flock," "Don't be afraid to glide," and "Keep a keen eye out for Pirate's Booty." He had spun off his lectures into several self-help books, including a bestselling edition of "Seagull-Channeling for Dummies."

Winkle liked to talk about how the college students—"his kids"—had practically forced him to run for office, circulating petitions in the lecture halls, insisting that he was the only one who could save the ailing Commonwealth. Maisy didn't believe him for a second. The guy smelled like ambition.

But she had to admit that Winkle was good at rallying college-aged fans, who were here in force tonight, wearing torn jeans and peasant skirts, a few of them wielding cowbells. A couple of older women had joined them, holding hand-painted signs that said "MOM." Calloway's crowd stood on the opposite side of the steps: a small but passionate crowd of breastfeeding mothers, carrying signs that said "BOOB" and "Calloway for Governor," and handing out breastfeeding informational pamphlets. "Breast is best!" one of them chanted, as a few young Winkle fans flipped through their pamphlets with expressions of mild disgust.

"We *know*," yelled a grey-haired woman in Birkenstocks, the lone person holding a Lois Manson sign. "We've known that for *years*." Everyone else ignored her. The Winkle kids banged their cowbells to compete with the chanting.

At last, an orange Mini Cooper zoomed into the lot and pulled into the space beside Candace's sedan. Christopher stepped out of his car, unfolding himself to full height. He was tall and thin and carried an enormous black briefcase, which held his supply of makeup, hairbrushes, and travel-sized curling irons. Maisy rushed to greet him.

"What took you so long?" she said. "Candace is flipping out."

"I stopped for a latte," he replied with a sheepish grin. "There's a great coffee shop around the corner, a hidden gem, I never get out this far." He waved his hand toward the industrial highway outside the studio gates, pointing out that they were in the hinterlands beyond Boston's Back Bay. Then he opened the rear door of Candace's sedan, kissed the candidate on the hand, and helped her out of the car.

"Oh, my God, honey, that frizz is out of control," he said.

"Hang on. Let me get you something." He rushed back to his car and returned, moments later, with a wide-brimmed straw hat, which he placed carefully onto Candace's head.

"Do you just carry hats around in your backseat?" Maisy asked him.

"Always be prepared," Christopher said. "I was a Boy Scout once. Of course, today, they wouldn't have me."

Candace kissed him on the cheek, then bounded up the steps expertly in her too-tight heels and shook hands with the BOOBs, one by one. She posed for pictures beside a handmade sign that said, "MILK IT FOR CALLOWAY," gave a hearty wave to the Winkle and Manson supporters, then hurried through the door with Maisy and Christopher trailing behind her.

A production assistant met them in the lobby and led them to a small makeup room, explaining that space was tight and Calloway would have to share the room with Lois Manson. Lois and her campaign manager were already in the room, seated in a pair of folding chairs, reading identical dog-eared copies of Mother Earth Magazine. Lois was a tall, mannish woman with huge round eyeglasses and a haircut that looked like a balding man's comb-over. When she saw Candace, she nodded glumly.

"Hello, Lois," Candace said politely. "Would you like us to wait until you're done with your hair and makeup? The mirror here is awfully small."

"I'm already finished," Lois said.

Christopher gasped.

"Well, I guess we'll get started, then," Candace told him. Lois tapped on her campaign manager's arm. "Aerosol warning," she said under her breath. Both of them got up and left the room.

Christopher stared after them with narrowed eyes. "If I could just take a pair of tweezers to that woman…" he murmured.

"A boy can dream," Maisy told him. "Now, hurry. The producers are going to murder us, and then we'll never win the debate." She left and headed for the studio.

"Ten minutes!" a station employee in a headset was calling out as Maisy entered the studio, a small, black space that had been draped half to death in shiny red, white and blue bunting. A platform, with four podiums, had been set up on one side, in front of several rows of risers lined with folding chairs. Winkle was already standing at his spot, jotting down notes on a legal pad.

"Nice of you to show," said a voice behind Maisy. She turned to find

Asher Griffin, Winkle's campaign manager, a slender forty-something who looked perpetually young, like a kid dressed up in his father's suit. He was a campaign carpetbagger just like her, and they had faced off a few years earlier in a Florida Congressional race. Maisy had won; the chief issue had been alligator overpopulation, and her candidate had well-placed friends in animal control. But she had learned in the process that Griffin was cutthroat and prone to theatrics. For weeks, her candidate had been trailed, wherever he went, by an energetic intern in an alligator suit.

"Good to see you, Griff," Maisy lied. "And good luck with those MOMs. Nice acronym. Though maybe not quite as evocative as 'BOOBs.'"

"Mmm-hmmm," Griffin said. "This is finally turning into a campaign, huh?"

"One of the stranger ones I've seen," Maisy said.

"And one of the hardest to costume," Griffin said. "I've done dog suits, rat suits, dinosaur suits, Elvis suits, gator suits, as you might recall," he said. "But what do I do here? Dress someone up like a giant tit? Or maybe that's what you guys should be doing."

"Glad to know you're still classy as ever, Griff," Maisy said, wondering with a twinge of worry what Griffin had in store.

"Excuse me?" said the woman with the headset, jabbing Maisy on the shoulder with her finger. "We really need Senator Calloway here. We have to do her mike check."

"She's getting her makeup on now," Maisy said.

"Yeah, don't worry. Senator Calloway would never miss a chance to be on camera," Griffin said.

"All right, I guess we'll just do the Manson mike check first," the woman with the headset said. "Ms. Manson, can you say something for me, please?"

"Some people," Lois Manson said, staring coldly at Maisy, "do not have respect for this process."

"We're here!" Christopher's voice suddenly rang through the studio, so loud that it seemed to echo off the walls. Candace was behind him, her makeup flawless, her hair nearly identical to the way it looked before, save for a strand in the front that kept falling coquettishly onto her forehead. Christopher had a satisfied smile on his face.

"You look good," Maisy said, joining Candace at her podium. "How's your mood?"

"I look female, at least," Candace replied, glancing down at her cleavage. "And don't worry. I know how to smile for the cameras."

"I have no doubt," Maisy said. "So, remember. We're looking out for babies, but we're also looking out for women. We're all about female empowerment. Freedom from the prudes."

"Breasts are beautiful," Candace said, looking at her cleavage again.

Suddenly, a howl erupted from Lois Manson. "Get your hands off me!" she sputtered. "What do you think you're doing?!"

Christopher was standing beside her, both hands in the air in a "surrender" pose. In his right hand was a brush. In his left was a small jar of powder.

"Her forehead was so shiny," he said. "I couldn't help myself."

"Christopher!" Maisy scolded.

"What did you put on me?" Lois demanded. "Has this been tested on animals?"

"Of course!" Christopher said. "I like bunnies as much as you do. Maybe more."

"I'm very allergic," Lois said. "Parabens make me itch."

"It's hypoallergenic," Christopher told her. "Scout's honor. You can thank me later, when you see how you looked on TV."

"I think it's time to take our seats," Maisy said between clenched teeth, grabbing Christopher's arm. "You look lovely," she added to Lois. As they headed for the risers, she whispered in Christopher's ear, "Next time, do you think you can keep your hands off the competition?"

"It's a weakness. I want people to look their best," Christopher said, settling into his seat. "I could figure out a way to get to Stuart Winkle's hairpiece…"

"Don't you dare," Maisy said. Then she looked closely at Winkle's head. "Good call about the rug. I never would have guessed."

"When it comes to hair," Christopher said, "I can spot hypocrisy a mile away."

"Thirty seconds!" shouted the woman in the headset. At her podium, Candace ran a finger through her hair a final time. Winkle smoothed his jacket. Lois rubbed her forehead with her palm. Before long, pre-recorded music started, lights came up and the woman shouted, "We're live in five…four…three… two…one!"

A spotlight shone on Gil Zilman, the moderator, whose suit, beneath the lights, had a slight metallic sheen. He was the station's star political reporter, with a reputation for nailing politicians with unexpected questions. Once, he had made national headlines when a lesser presidential candidate, asked to name the capitals of six different states, had flubbed the answers to Vermont and South Dakota.

"Good evening," he said now, staring into the camera with a toothy smile. "And welcome to the gubernatorial candidates' debate on Channel 6. As you know, I'm Gil Zilman, and these are our candidates: Democratic Senator Candace Calloway; Republican professor Stuart Winkle; and businesswoman Lois Manson, the Green/Rainbow Party candidate."

"Businesswoman" was something of a stretch, Maisy knew.

Manson owned a share of a Cambridge co-op that sold goods handcrafted in Nepal and Tibet.

"As you might know from watching me in the past," Zilman went on, "I like to run an informal debate. So tonight, I want to start by letting the candidates ask questions of each other. Our first candidate, chosen by a draw of straws, is Lois Manson."

Lois rubbed her forehead one last time and turned menacingly toward Candace. "My question is for Senator Calloway," she said, with a tight smile. "Senator, I've heard you talking about breastfeeding a lot this week. But I don't recall you ever talking about this issue before, in all of the years I've been working for women's rights. So my question is: Where were you when I was protesting at St. Bart's-Pendergrass Hospital, to stop the formula companies from foisting free samples on unsuspecting mothers? Or when I was lobbying to get formula classified as a toxin? Were you thinking about breastfeeding at all?"

"Senator Calloway?" Zilman said.

Candace smiled at him, practiced and calm. "Thank you, Gil," she said. "And thank you to the viewers for watching this debate. And thank you to the women of the Commonwealth. I can assure you that I have always thought about breastfeeding. Even as a child. And as you may know, I took a stand on behalf of breastfeeding mothers this week, after one of Professor Winkle's supporters forced a mother to feed her helpless baby in a restroom. As governor, I know that—"

"I have a question for the senator!" Winkle shouted.

"Professor Winkle?" Zilman said. "How fortunate. It happens to be your turn."

"Ah, wonderful," Stuart Winkle said, "Gil, in addition to being an economist, I am a philosopher. I believe we always face a yin and a yang, a balance of duties. To get our babies to learn respect, we must teach them respect. A thought experiment, if you will: A train filled with people comes barreling toward a station, and the conductor sees a single person standing on the tracks.

If he swerves to avoid this person, he jeopardizes the safety of everyone on the train. If he stays course…"

"Is there a question coming?" Zilman said.

"And does it have anything to do with babies?" Candace said.

"Bear with me!" Winkle said. "My question is, what do you think is the right thing to do? Because it's not so different at all from what just happened at the Stonewall Museum! A woman tries to spare a large group of children from trauma. In doing so, she has to inconvenience a single person."

"Two people," Candace said. "A mother and a child. And it's not just inconvenience. It's health."

"Those impressionable minds!" Winkle continued. "That confusing situation!"

"It was a breast," Candace said. "They were high school students, and they saw a breast. I somehow doubt they've been traumatized for life. I'd imagine a lot of them have seen one before without getting permanently scarred."

"Wait!" Zilman interrupted, with a glint in his eye. "Are you saying that pornography isn't a problem for teenagers today?"

Candace looked at him and blinked. "Pornography?" she said.

"Or underage sex?" Zilman said. "Are you suggesting that parents shouldn't be concerned about underage sex?"

"It certainly sounds like it!" Winkle said enthusiastically. "And I know how many mothers across the state are concerned about underage sex."

Candace paused for a moment, as if to collect her thoughts. "Professor Winkle," she said, "I am not ashamed of breasts. I believe they are beautiful, functional parts of the female body. If we stop thinking of them as obscene, or objects of scorn, we will finally move this Commonwealth into the future."

Here, Candace stopped again and stared intently ahead. A few seconds went by, then a few more. Maisy shifted in her seat uncomfortably. Christopher made a small whimpering sound. And then Maisy saw why Candace had stopped: She was trying her best to cry. The senator blinked dramatically a couple of times, then lifted her hand to her face and wiped away a single tear.

"To love breasts is to love women," she said, her voice cracking. "To love women is to love breasts."

A burst of applause erupted from one of the top rows as Zilman announced a commercial break. Maisy turned around to see that several BOOBs were sitting together, nodding forcefully. One of the women was wiping her eyes. How could the Pep Boys have thought this would just go away?

Suddenly inspired, Maisy pulled her cellphone from her back pocket and dialed the number for one of her field directors. She could match Asher Griffin for theatricality, any day. Maybe not with a giant walking tit. But she had some ideas.

"Kevin," she said. "Maisy here. I need you to put in orders for ten dozen cream-filled doughnuts. No, make that fifteen dozen…No, not jelly. Cream. We're taking Candace to South Station tomorrow morning. And we're making some more headlines, mark my words."

CHAPTER 7

ONE UNEXPECTED consequence of having a baby, Lauren had discovered, was that she now watched more local TV news than ever. She turned on the news for company during early morning feedings, midday feedings, and sometimes late-night feedings. Now, she knew the names of several well-coiffed anchors and eager young reporters. One of them, Manuel Martinson, had slick black hair and an impossibly deep voice, and was doing a standup, this Monday morning, from the concourse at South Station. His report was about the Candace Calloway campaign, which was handing out cream-filled doughnuts to commuters.

"They're filled with white cream," Martinson was saying, "to evoke the breastmilk that the Calloway campaign says it cares about so deeply." He took an oversized bite of a doughnut to demonstrate, then wiped his mouth with an exaggerated sweep.

"According to breastfeeding mothers," he said, "their own milk is just as delicious as this."

"Manuel, you lucky duck," the anchor said. "This must bring you back to the good old days."

"If only I could remember them," Martinson said dreamily.

The next report came from Cohasset, where a correspondent named Frederika Lowe was standing at the foot of a long driveway, surrounded by a group of older women waving signs. They were at Calloway's house, accusing the senator of condoning pornography for teenagers. "Role Model or Porn Purveyor?" read one sign. "High School: Tests, Not Breasts," read another.

"These women say they fear for the country we've become," Lowe said intently into the camera. "A country where women will lift their shirts wherever they want, no matter who's around."

The screen cut to a woman with a sign and a "Winkle for Governor" T-shirt.

"Maybe Candace Calloway should run for governor of France," the woman said. "We don't do that kind of thing here in America."

The telephone rang, and Lauren sat up with a jolt. The receiver happened to be within arm's reach, and the caller ID read, "Private." Lauren wondered with dread if this was another one of the reporters whose calls she'd been avoiding all weekend, as she tried to think of pithy lines and Rob tried to convince her to stop talking altogether.

"My entire office knows about your breasts. I can't take it. *Moooooo!*" he had said the day before, as he lay on the living room rug beside Rory. He was performing his series of barnyard animal impressions, which he'd worked hard to perfect before Rory was born. The baby stared up at him intently, filled with either deep interest or gas.

"Next year, I'll wear something shapeless to the company picnic," Lauren had said from the couch, where she was writing thank-you notes.

Rob had tickled Rory's tummy, made a snorting noise that sounded exactly like a pig, then looked up at Lauren, exasperated. "Seriously," he said, "I don't get it. You aren't like these BOOB types. Why don't you leave the activism to Mia? You did your part. You went to that fund-raiser. Now tell them, 'Thanks, and good luck.'"

"I made a commitment," Lauren had said. "I can't back down now."

It was true. She was an inspiration to the BOOBs. She had

managed—she hoped—to convince a roomful of rich old ladies that breastfeeding was good. She was in too deep to quit. So she answered the phone in as bright a voice as she could muster. At first, all she heard in response was a sniffle, which slowly morphed into a full-fledged whimper. It took her nearly a minute to realize this was Mia.

"What's going on? Are you OK?"

"Yes," Mia said weakly. "I'm fine."

"Is it the campaign? Were you watching the news? Picketing in front of her house seems like a mean thing to do."

"No," Mia's voice shuddered, as if she had the chills. "The campaign is great. Senator Calloway is an inspiration. Did you watch the debate last night? She was so eloquent."

"I watched. She was fine. Now tell me what's wrong," Lauren said.

"It's Lyle," Mia said. "I think I've been doing something fucking terrible."

Of course. It had taken Lauren years to learn that Mia's put-togetherness was a kind of armor. Beneath it lurked some serious self-doubt, which bubbled up when she feared that she'd done something wrong. Mia did little in life, career, or motherhood without consulting the experts. She had read seven tomes on infant sleep before devising a careful plan to make Lyle "cry it out, with caring" in his crib at night. She obsessively checked several parenting websites that posted links to scientific studies, and often worried that she had unwittingly fed Lyle the wrong variety of wheat, or too many bananas, or food from jars lined with a potentially volatile chemical. Once, based on a longitudinal survey of children in Finland, she had panicked over whether she had started reading to Lyle too early. "He might have a lifelong aversion to books!" she had wailed when she realized that, at four months, he lacked the attention span for "Goodnight Moon."

"Mia," Lauren said. "Maybe you should stop looking at all of this baby stuff online."

"This is serious!" Mia wailed. "It's a study that was published in the journal 'High Intelligence.' It says that babies who didn't have mobiles in their cribs scored higher on intelligence tests and creativity. It's like the mobile saps a growing imagination. And we've been using Lyle's airplane mobile since day one. He loves it. He stares at it like he's really thinking."

"Maybe he'll be a pilot," Lauren said. "And really, how creative do you want those guys to be?"

"Go ahead and joke," Mia sniffled. "The worst part is, it was a Baby Mensa mobile. That's why the planes are all black and white and red. It was designed by a fucking pediatrician."

Lauren sighed as quietly as she could. She, too, was prone to baby-related paranoia. She had stopped eating peanut butter for fear of passing some dread allergy to Rory. She checked the baby's hairline obsessively for signs of growth. She worried about the shape of Rory's toes, feared that, later in life, her feet wouldn't look good in sandals. Still, she managed to maintain a cool demeanor, just as she'd always done at work. If Mia's career had been built on organizational skill, Lauren's had been built on composure. Event planning was all about recovering from last-minute disasters, and her clients—mostly mercurial types—needed someone close by who projected an air of control. A South End salon owner would be fussing over his grand-opening event, ranting about some minute detail involving the flower arrangements, and she would steer him steadily toward the alley behind his shop, grip his shoulders, stare him down, and hand him a cigarette. Though she didn't smoke herself, she carried a pack of cloves and a lighter at all times for this very purpose. Even now. Out of habit, she had stashed them at the bottom of her diaper bag.

Mia didn't smoke, either, but Lauren knew by now how to snap her out of a panic: Give her an opportunity to teach. "Can you come over?" she said. "I really need your help with something."

"When?" Mia sniffled.

"As soon as you can."

"I just have to get out of these fucking pajamas," Mia said.

"And calm down," Lauren said. "Stop swearing. Lyle can hear you."

WHEN MIA ARRIVED with Lyle an hour later, she betrayed no sign of frustration or worry, as if the previous phone conversation had never taken place. Her language had cleaned up, too. "I'm so sorry I'm late," she said, setting Lyle's car seat down in the entryway. She started to pull campaign paraphernalia out of her bag—a stack of brochures, a rolled up T-shirt, a pile of bumper stickers—and launched into a monologue as she laid it all out on Lauren's coffee table.

"I got a call from Maisy Street," she said excitedly. "She has all kinds of campaign plans that she wants me to help with. She feels we have a real chance to reach suburban women. And you're not going to believe this. They want Rory in an ad! A takeoff on the 'Got Milk' campaign. She's going to have a little moustache, and it's going to say, 'Got Calloway?' Isn't that adorable? Can you just picture it on the side of a bus? Your baby is going to be a model! And I'm coming with you. The shoot is at MicroStar Modeling, and they keep babies on file for other assignments."

Lauren contemplated bringing up the study and the mobile, but decided against it. Often, Mia's episodes passed quickly, especially when she got on one of her organizational highs.

"The ad sounds great," she said. "I think." Actually, she wondered whether it would damage Rory later in life to know that her face had been plastered across the state as campaign propaganda. But at this moment, she had a different focus, an ulterior motive for bringing Mia over.

"Come into the bedroom with me," she said.

"What for?" Mia said.

"To teach me how to use the breast pump."

For a baby shower gift, three of Lauren's aunts had pooled

together and given her a portable electric pump, explaining that their own daughters—faraway cousins, whom Lauren seldom spoke to—had considered it a godsend. Lauren wasn't quite ready to admit it to Rob, but she did want to have the option of using bottles, just in case. The trouble was, she was afraid of the machine. She had unpacked it once, taken one look at its intimidating array of parts, and stowed it away in the back of her bedroom closet.

"Are you sure you want to introduce the bottle so soon?" Mia asked Lauren. "I didn't start pumping for Lyle until he was three months old. That's when the Moos say babies are ready to tell their nipples apart. He's advanced, so I'm sure he knew the difference at two months, but I wanted to be safe."

"Well, if I'm going to do more of this campaign business, I'll probably need to pump," Lauren said.

"Hmm," Mia said. "You will have to learn eventually. But promise me you'll think long and hard before you give Rory a bottle."

Lauren promised, then led Mia into the bedroom, where they laid Rory and Lyle on Rory's fish-shaped exercise mat. Lyle quickly started batting at a plush purple seahorse that hung above his head. Rory gazed with wide eyes at a yellow seal. Lauren headed to the closet and got onto her knees, reaching into the nether-regions for the pump she'd stashed away. Her hands felt past a tennis racket, a yoga mat, a bag of worn clothes she had never gotten around to taking to the thrift store, and a squishy diaper that she hoped was filled with pee. Finally, she came upon the black faux-leather briefcase that contained the electric breast pump. She pulled it out, brushed off several large dust bunnies, and hauled it onto the bed.

"Here it is," she announced.

"It's a good brand," Mia said. The logo read, "Love & Suction," and featured a drawing of a stick-figure mother and an oval—a baby, presumably—off to one side, connected to her chest with a curlicue of wire.

Lauren unlatched the case and opened it up to survey the contents. It looked like a children's chemistry set: Two large, clear plastic funnels, a mess of plastic tubing, an orange box the size of a toaster, a yellow plastic cylinder, two six-ounce bottles with caps, and an electric cord.

"I've heard about these, but honestly, I've never seen one in action," Lauren said.

"Didn't you ever go inside the lactation room at Pinnacle?" Mia asked.

"I peeked in once, after it opened," Lauren said. "But not when anyone was in it."

After an earlier wave of pregnancies at Pinnacle Events, the company had converted a small utility closet into a designated room for breastfeeding. The commitment wasn't grand. The makeover consisted of pilfering a "Do Not Disturb" sign from a chain hotel, hanging some blue fabric over a shelf full of cleaning products—the janitors still had access to the closet after-hours—and setting a small end table beside a worn upholstered chair that the company's owner had found on the side of the road.

"A month before I had Lyle, Ginny Belliman invited me to watch her," Mia said. "She was a Moo leader once, and she wanted to show me the ropes."

"It looked depressing in there," Lauren said.

"It was, a little," Mia said. "But the key to pumping is that no matter where you are, you have to put yourself in a different mental place. Like a desert island. Where there's only you and your baby." She reached into the case and started pulling out the pieces, fitting them together with military precision. She screwed the bottles onto the funnels, used the tubes to connect the funnels to the box, snapped the cylinder onto the box's side, and plugged the cord into the wall. "Let's give her a try with air," she said.

She flipped a switch and the machine roared into action. The cylinder started moving rhythmically from right to left and back, making a wheezing sound, like an old man laboring to breathe.

"What's it doing?" Lauren asked.

"Creating a vacuum," Mia said, holding her hand up to the mouth of one of the funnels. "Feels like it's working. Let's wash these off and get going."

As Mia washed the tubes, bottles, and funnels in the bathroom sink, Lauren watched the babies lying peacefully. Lyle was wearing a diaper, which made Lauren wonder if his Elimination Communication experiment had gone permanently off-course. She thought about what it would be like to feed Rory from a bottle at last, to be able to see her tiny face while she was eating. Mia might disapprove, but at least Rob would be happy.

"OK," Mia finally said, returning to the room with the working parts wrapped in a bath towel. "Ready to go?"

"I guess so," Lauren said.

"All right," Mia said. "Take off your shirt."

For some reason, it hadn't occurred to Lauren that pumping milk would require an even greater level of exhibitionism than nursing. Though doctors and nurses had seen her breasts—and, of course, a few kids at the museum had, too—she was generally shy about undressing around friends. She wondered whether Mia would secretly think her small breasts were inadequate. She wondered if Rory, cooing on her mat, would see her bare chest and get excited. She wondered if Lyle, still batting at the seahorse, would record this sight into the recesses of his baby memory. When he was a teenager, would she be able to face him? On the other hand, she'd seen him diaperless enough by now that they weren't remotely even.

She lifted off her T-shirt and unhooked the flaps of her nursing bra. The babies looked indifferent. Mia also looked unfazed, too busy screwing the bottles onto the funnels to take note of Lauren's naked chest. Finally, she handed Lauren the funnels and ordered, "Put them on."

Lauren picked them up gingerly and cupped one over each breast. She tried to visualize a desert island, but her mind kept shifting to a less peaceful image of herself, standing onstage at a loud concert, wearing a conical bra. She noticed that her heart was beating a little bit faster than usual. "OK," she said. "Pull the switch."

Mia switched the machine to "on" and it sprang into action. The cylinder started to move again. The wheezing sound resumed, though, attached to her actual breasts, it sounded like a man's throaty voice, whispering, "*Will it help? Will it help?*" Lauren tried again to feel sand beneath her feet and convert the hissing noise to the sound of ocean waves. It only sounded more urgent: "*Will it help? Will it help?*" She felt the suction on her bare breasts and looked down, aghast, to see her nipples moving back and forth, as if invisible fingers were tugging at them and letting go. She let out a little yelp and dropped the funnels to the bed. A few drops of milk dripped onto the bedspread.

"What's the matter?" Mia said, perplexed.

"This is crazy!" Lauren said. "It looks insane!"

"What did you think it was going to look like?" Mia said.

"I don't know," Lauren said. "Not quite so…weird."

"Pumping isn't weird!" Mia said. "It's natural."

"Mia!" Lauren said. "This is *not* natural!"

"I'm starting it up again," Mia said. "You might as well pump something, to get the hang of it. You can freeze it and use it a month from now."

Lauren put the funnels over her breasts again. Mia flipped the switch. Lauren watched her nipples move, as if by magic. She envisioned herself sitting on a beach chair on a desert island, the pump sitting beside her in the sand, connected to an extension cord that ran toward the horizon.

Suddenly, the pump shifted into second-gear, tugging harder and a little more quickly. The voice changed, too, sounding more urgent, as if the whispering man inside the machine were now saying, "*Wake up! Wake up!*" Milk collected on the side of the funnels, then dripped into the bottles. The cry to "*Wake up!*" continued. Lauren started to giggle. Before long, she was full-on laughing, shaking so hard that she could barely hold the funnels against her chest. At first, Mia shot her an irritated look, but soon, she was giggling, too.

"I'm sorry. I'm not on a beach," Lauren said, gasping, still trying to hold the funnels in place. When they slipped, the "*Wake up!*" refrain slurred, and started to sound like "*Wank off. Wank off.*"

Lauren dropped the funnels onto the bed and put her hands over her eyes, wiping away tears. When she finally regained control of her breath, she covered her chest with her hands. "I feel like I'm in some kind of weird medieval science experiment," she said.

"In the dark house on a hill, where no one ever goes," Mia said helpfully.

"Deep in ze basement," Lauren said in her best bad German accent. "Professor Frankenboob lures women in to manipulate zeir breasts with his evil pumping machine."

"He says he's providing food for his caged monkeys," Mia said. "But really, he's just getting off."

Both of them collapsed into fits of laughter again. The babies looked confused. "Admit it," Lauren said, as the pump parts continued to move. "It's nowhere near this much fun to hang out with the Moos."

Mia looked up, suddenly alarmed. "Yes," she said, "but this is our inside joke, right? You won't tell anyone from the campaign?"

"Don't worry—the BOOBs and I aren't exactly best friends," Lauren said, still stifling giggles as the pump continued to groan, "*Wank off. Wank off.*" Then she saw that Mia was serious.

"Really?" she said. "You think they'd be mad? Over a breast-pump joke?"

"When you're fighting the Man," Mia said sadly, "you're not supposed to be having fun."

CHAPTER 8

FOR THE FIRST TIME in her long career in politics, Maisy Street was going undercover. Like most operatives she knew, she regularly sent interns armed with video cameras into the opposing camp's public events, hoping their wobbly footage would turn up a gaffe that could later be exploited in a TV ad. But while a fresh-faced young Calloway wannabe was here to do cinematography, Maisy also wanted to see this event for herself. It was a Mothers on Modesty rally, billed as a "Decorum Demonstration." And after spending time with so many breastfeeding activists and their small, fussy children, Maisy felt an urge to surround herself with women who were closer to menopause, like her.

So here she was, lingering near the back of a park in the exurban swing town of Walpole, far from the BOOBs and the pious, upscale liberalism that marked the towns closer to Boston. Twilight was approaching and a chill was setting in, a sign that winter wasn't far away. A couple of TV stations had set up satellite trucks on the street. A small bandstand near one end of a grassy, open field was festooned with two banners. One read, "MODESTY IS THE BEST POLICY." The other read, "KINDLY KEEP YOUR BREASTS TO YOURSELF."

The crowd trickled in, almost entirely women, wearing fleece sweatshirts, barn jackets and baggy jeans. Some carried "Winkle for Governor" signs. One held a handmade sign that said, "My Breasts Are Not Beautiful!" Most of them fit the brand of Massachusetts swing voters that Maisy liked to call New England Harshies. They were women over 40, with pear-shaped bodies and close-cropped hair that had been dyed to a neutral color, neither brown nor blonde. They dropped their "r's" in that Bostonian way and pronounced the word "can't" as if they were British. These were the women Maisy often saw scowling in the supermarket aisles, inexplicably angry at the presence of other customers. They turned down campaign leaflets handed out in the streets, or tossed them to the ground without looking at them. And the fact that they had come to a political event, on a Monday evening, spelled potential trouble for the Calloway campaign.

One Harshy was standing on the podium with a proprietary air, pointing decisively in various directions, giving orders to the women nearby. Maisy recognized a few mid-level Winkle staffers on the podium with her, along with Jean Thompson, the museum volunteer who had become the martyr of modesty.

Maisy milled about the rear of the crowd, trying to pick up snippets of conversation. "I'd never want someone to breastfeed in front of my 15-year-old," she heard one woman saying. "I know how his mind works."

A trio of women near her was making carpool arrangements for soccer practice. In her peripheral vision, Maisy spied two women dragging in their teenage daughters. The girls, both listening to iPods, looked sullen and bored. The group settled by an oak tree near Maisy, and the girls quickly slumped to the grass. The women, clutching Winkle campaign literature, continued their conversation. "There is something about that woman that I just don't like," one of them was saying. Maisy sidled closer to the tree trunk.

"Is it the hair?" the other woman said. "Because something really bothers me about her hair."

"It's way too long, that's for sure," the first woman said.

"If she had kids at home," the second one said, "she wouldn't have time to do her hair like that."

"She wouldn't wear heels like that, either," the first woman said. "Not if she had to cook dinner."

"Mary Kate had a teacher once who looked a little like her," said her friend. "I mean, younger. Much younger. But she walked into the junior-high school every day like she was trying out for a modeling job. At the parent-teacher conference, I wanted to tell her, 'Honey, this is Walpole, Massachusetts. Not *Vogue*.'"

"Was she a good teacher, at least?"

"It was French class. How should I know?"

They were interrupted by the chief New England Harshy at the podium, who tapped on her microphone viciously. "Welcome to Massachusetts' first Decorum Demonstration!" she said. "I am Alice Andrews, the founder of Mothers on Modesty. And I'm so glad you've come out here to help us send a message."

Several people toward the front of the crowd clapped dutifully.

"I think we can all agree that over the last few years, things have gone too far," Alice said. "People used to keep their bodies to themselves. They used to worry about what other people thought. Now, it seems, everything has to be up on the Internet or out in the open. Nobody has any shame anymore. And to blame it on a baby seems to me to be a very feeble excuse."

The crowd offered a bit more applause.

"You have read our MOM Manifesto," Alice said. "You have come here tonight to send a message: Enough is enough. We have to start teaching our children right from wrong. So to the women who take their shirts off with no regard for anyone around them, we say: *No, sir!*"

It came out "*No, suh.*" The crowd cheered, more loudly this time.

"To the people who let their daughters leave the house in tight clothes, we say: *No, suh!* To the people who make TV shows about teenagers having sex, we say: *No, suh!*"

The crowd started joining in the "*No, suh*" refrain as Alice continued with her litany of complaints: "To the people who sell high-heeled shoes for toddlers, *No suh!* To the people who sing songs about their booties, *No suh!*" Suddenly, Maisy felt something hit her left arm. She turned to find a large woman in an orange fleece, jabbing Maisy's bicep with her elbow.

"About time, huh?" the woman said. "It's great to see some ladies with common sense!" Her voice was thick and phlegmy, as if she hadn't cleared her throat since before breakfast.

You're undercover, Maisy reminded herself. "Common sense," she said agreeably. "Long overdue."

"Linda," the woman said. "From Peabody. Nice to meet you."

Maisy shook her hand. "I'm…Maureen. From Quincy," she said. "You came a long way for this."

"Hour's drive," Linda said. "But I'm telling you, I have had enough. You can't walk down the street without seeing some six-year-old dressed like a tramp."

She turned back to Alice Andrews, who was still shouting into the microphone. "Did you hear Candace Calloway at the candidates' debate?" Alice said. "Saying that breasts are beautiful? Well, maybe in a painting, but not in public!"

"Keep it in your shirt!" Linda yelled, cupping her hands around her mouth. Then she clapped. Maisy clapped, too.

"What does Candace Calloway say about pornography?" Alice went on. "That it's not a big deal. That our kids won't be scarred! Is this the woman you trust to be an example for your daughters? A vote for Candace Calloway is a vote for high-heeled shoes and tight-fitting skirts! A vote for Stuart Winkle is a vote for decency!"

Linda whistled with two fingers between her teeth. Some other women howled.

Maisy was surprised, even given what she knew about the Harshies, at the extent of the anger around her. The only people who didn't look mad were the two teenaged girls by the oak tree, who were still listening to their iPods, apparently unaware of the shouting. Maisy watched them intently for a few moments, then turned to her right. This time, she found herself face-to-face with a thin collegiate girl who was peering through a small video camera.

"What the—" Maisy sputtered. Then she noticed that the camera had a tiny "Calloway for Governor" sticker on one side. This was the intern assigned to spy at the rally. She had mistaken Maisy for a New England Harshy. Maisy glanced down at herself. Was she pear-shaped like these women? Did she look equally sour?

"*Pssst*," she whispered to the girl with the camera. "*Focus on the podium!*"

"What?" the girl said, looking confused.

"Don't look at *me*," Maisy whispered. "Look at them." She indicated Alice Andrews, who was now expounding on the virtues of abstinence.

"Why are you—" the girl was baffled.

"Honey," Maisy said. "I am your *boss*."

The girl's eyes widened in recognition, just as Linda noticed the minor commotion. "What's going on?" she said, putting an arm around Maisy protectively. "What's happening, Maureen? Who is this kid?"

"Oh, it's nothing," Maisy said. "No big deal. Just a misunderstanding."

"Hey, what's this?" Linda said, noticing the video camera. She reached out a thick arm and, with surprising speed, ripped the camera away from the intern, turning it over in her hands until she came across the Calloway sticker.

"Calloway for Governor?" Linda said. "The enemy! Hey, ladies! Take a look! We've got an enemy spy over here!"

A few women nearby stopped listening to Alice and turned toward Linda, who was waving the camera in the air. Within seconds, a group of Harshies had started to form a circle around the intern.

"Candace Calloway, huh?" one of them said. "So, you like boobs, do you?"

"Don't you dare take off that shirt," said another.

"Hey, guys," Maisy said, trying to divert their attention. "Listen to Alice! She's saying something great!"

But the women pressed forward, staring menacingly at the intern.

"Can I have my camera back?" the girl said in a meek voice.

"Why?" Linda growled. "So you can make a sex tape with it? Like your friend Candace Calloway? *With* your friend Candace Calloway?"

The intern gave Maisy a terrified glance, then ducked and bolted out of the park, leaving the camera in Linda's hands.

Shit, Maisy thought. *That thing cost $299.*

Linda examined the camera for a minute, a wild look in her eyes. Maisy worried that, in a MOM-driven frenzy, she might slam it on a concrete walkway or smash it against a tree. Instead, she placed into a roomy pocket of her jeans, then winked at Maisy. "Now I know what I'm giving my brother for Christmas," she said, turning her attention back to the podium.

"Now," Alice was saying, "I'd like to introduce one of the bravest women in Massachusetts, a woman who wasn't afraid to stand up and say 'no' to indecency. I am proud to introduce to you the patron saint of the MOMs, Miss Jean Thompson!"

Jean, who had been sitting on a folding chair, stepped up to the microphone and adjusted her glasses on the bridge of her nose. She wore a shift dress, generously sized. Her hair was slightly frizzy, her voice warm.

"Thank you for inviting me, Alice," she said, leaning into the microphone a little too closely, so that her words came out slightly garbled. She was reading, from a stack of note cards. "And thank you all for coming out here tonight. And thank you to the Winkle campaign for offering me so much support this week."

The women in the crowd clapped politely.

"I am not an opponent of breastfeeding," Jean said. "I nursed three children, and I loved it. I was a founding member of the

Moo Coalition. But I always considered nursing to be a sacred, private thing, a covenant between a mother and her baby."

Some women murmured quietly to each other. "What the hell is she talking about?" Linda said to Maisy.

"Who knows," Maisy said. This time, she was telling the truth.

"We had to fight a lot, in those early days, to make women understand just how important breastfeeding was," Jean said, reading from her cards. "Just as the birthing process was taken over by the patriarchal medical establishment, bottle feeding had become the norm. But nothing created in a lab could ever be as perfect as something created by the human body."

The crowd, buzzing with anger a minute ago, had now fallen nearly silent. "Enough with the bodily fluids," yelled one of the women near the oak tree.

"And yet," Jean went on, "I believe the breastfeeding experience does not need to be intruded upon. Certainly not by a group of boys who would not treat the act with the respect it deserves. And so, in the Stonewall Museum, I did what I thought would help both mother and baby. Now, I am glad the conversation has begun."

There was polite applause as Alice took the microphone again. Linda was staring at a hangnail. Maisy felt relieved. The momentum was gone. These MOMs could be mad for a minute or two, but they couldn't sustain the energy of the BOOBs.

"Thank you, Jean. You are a true heroine," Alice said, in a perfunctory way. "And now, I want to introduce another guest, who came to me after the founding of the MOMs and asked to share her story. She is a dynamic young woman and I think you will be interested in what she has to say. Please welcome Claire Langoon."

Maisy had never heard the name or set eyes on the woman who took the microphone. But she could see in an instant that this was no old-fashioned feminist. Claire looked to be about Lauren Bruce's age, but two or three times hipper; she wore trendy dark-rimmed glasses, a T-shirt with SpongeBob SquarePants on the front, and a pair of tight-fitting cropped jeans. She stood with one hip cocked to the right and one hand firmly gripped on the microphone, looked across the park with a slight smirk on her face, and started to speak.

"Hello, everyone," she said in a clear, confident voice. "I was so excited to hear about this group, because I saw the opportunity to talk about an issue I've been dying to address. I'm a mom. I have a four-year-old son. I live in East Cambridge. I vote. And with all due respect to Jean Thompson—because, really, you were brave to take a stand last week—I have a different perspective on this whole issue. Here's what I've been thinking, for about four years now: Do you know what's really oppressive to women? What really conspires to keep them down? Breastfeeding, that's what!"

A curious murmur went through the crowd. Maisy blinked, surprised, then scanned the podium, where Jean was frowning and Alice was smiling.

"I'm not sure how many of you have breastfed, but I have. And I am here to tell you that formula saved my life."

A lone person in the middle of the crowd clapped her hands.

"Do you know what breastfeeding is like? Well, I'll tell you. It hurts. I'm not sure I'm allowed to say this in front of TV cameras, but I'll say it anyway: When you start, it hurts like a *bitch*."

Shocked laughter bubbled up from a few places. Claire started to stray from the microphone stand, walking back and forth on the small gazebo, as far as the cord would allow her.

"There you are, lying in the hospital bed, and this tiny baby, as small as a doll, has the power to snap on you and make you bleed," she said. "This is what they call bonding! And every time he gets ready to eat, you start to cringe, maybe even cry a little, because you know how much it's going to hurt. You take him home, you're afraid to feed him, and you can't go anywhere. Not for weeks. Because you never know when the kid's going to wake up and want to eat again. You can't even get anybody to help you—like, make your husband do one of those feedings in the middle of the night—because the lactation consultants tell you that nooo, your milk will dry up! Your kid will get nipple confusion or some kind of dread disease because he won't get every possible drop of his mother's magic antibodies!"

The crowd had fallen into a mesmerized silence. Maisy noticed that the girls by the tree had taken off their earphones. Linda was watching with her mouth agape.

"And I'll tell you what," Claire continued. "For awhile, I listened to them. I did what I thought I was supposed to do. Even though I was raised on formula, like pretty much everyone in my entire generation, and I turned out perfectly healthy. And then one day, when my boobs were still killing me and I hadn't slept in weeks and my baby was crying in the middle of the night, I had a little moment of clarity. I told my husband to run out to the 24-hour grocery store and buy a can of formula. We didn't have one in the house, mind you, because some protesters had stopped the hospitals from giving them out."

A few women booed. Maisy shuddered.

"My husband is a very smart man, and he loves, me, so off he went. And he came home with the goods, and I gave my son a bottle of formula, and he chugged it down, and he slept beautifully, and he's been dining on Similac ever since. And ever since then, I've gotten wise. I realize what's going on. Our generation of women was taught that we could do anything. We could have careers. We could be doctors, lawyers, CEOs. We could be president or secretary of state. And at the same time that we're enjoying our freedom, along comes a movement that wants to put us right back in the house, barefoot and sexless and serving the needs of a child. These breastfeeding types are the same people who tell us that labor pain is a construct of the patriarchy, and that we have to give birth in a bathtub and wear our babies in slings 24 hours a day. Which is fine, if you want to be like one of those 'Feminine Mystique' types from the '50s. But I'll tell you what: You can't be a modern woman if you're attached at the tit to someone else!"

The assembled women gasped. Then someone started to clap, then a few other women joined in, and before long a wave of applause was washing over the crowd. Claire pumped her arms in the air and, as an afterthought, leaned into the mike and shouted, "Winkle for governor!" When she finally stepped down from the podium, Maisy spotted several people with TV cameras chasing after her.

Alice Andrews stepped back up to give some closing remarks, but by that point, the women weren't listening. They were talking among themselves as they headed out of the park. Maisy caught snippets of their chatter: "…amazing," "…refreshing," "…what a pistol."

"You know, I'd been feeling guilty for not breastfeeding my kids," she heard one Harshy tell another. "But maybe we were the right ones, all along."

She turned to gauge Linda's reaction, and found that her new friend had taken the Calloway campaign's video camera out of her pocket. Linda fiddled with the controls for a minute, figured out how to turn it on, and held it up, recording Maisy's face.

"Home movie time!" she said. "What do you say, Maureen? I think those BOOBs have a fight on their hands, huh?"

Maisy looked into the camera with deep seriousness. "Yes," she said. "There will definitely be a fight."

CHAPTER 9

"CAN YOU BELIEVE that woman?" Mia was saying. "The nerve of her. With no medical background, no real information, to just trash on breastfeeding that way."

She was driving her Volvo through Jamaica Plain, with Lauren beside her and the two babies strapped into car seats in the back. They were headed toward the suburban town of Canton, where the Calloway campaign photo shoot was set to take place in a warehouse that had been converted into a studio. Lauren had packed a bag filled with several changes of clothes for Rory, mostly gifts she'd gotten from older relatives: precious little outfits, covered with tiny pink flowers, hearts, and miniature teddy bears. To start, she had squeezed Rory into a fussy light pink dress with lace around the collar and sleeves, and a pair of white tights covered with pastel polka dots. Rory had fidgeted and whined until the car started moving. Now she was sleeping, and Mia was ranting about her new nemesis, Claire Langoon.

"And of course, the TV reporters lapped it up," Mia went on. "Did they even bother to talk to the other side? To the women who love to nurse?"

It was the day after the MOM rally, and the details of Langoon's anti-breastfeeding tirade had spread across newspapers,

TV reports, and blogs. Langoon had even started a blog of her own, at www.hurtslikeabitch.com.

"It's not affiliated with the Winkle campaign, which is why I'm allowed to swear," she had told one TV station. "But it's got a link to send a donation to him, and I hope everybody does."

This was clearly a setback for the Calloway campaign, and Mia was taking it personally—as an affront not just to her candidate, but to all breastfeeding women. "You have trouble, you get help!" she said, as she steered the car through a rotary. "You call a lactation consultant. You go to a Moo meeting. And if you do decide to quit, keep it to yourself. We won't get more women to breastfeed their babies if we go around telling people it hurts."

"But it does hurt," Lauren said.

"Not forever!" Mia said.

"No," Lauren conceded. "Just for awhile."

"That's part of the message we have to send," Mia said. "Fight through the pain. Be strong for your baby."

"Fight through the pain?" Lauren said. "That's your pro-breastfeeding slogan?"

"So come up with a better one," Mia said.

"'It's really not that bad'?" Lauren tried. "'Don't listen to that woman with the glasses'?"

"Listen to the women who want to help you," Mia said. "Not the ones who just want to tell you what to do."

"But the BOOBs are telling other women what to do," Lauren said.

"The BOOBs are telling other women to do what's *right*," Mia said. "It's different."

FIFTEEN MINUTES later, they had pulled into the parking lot of a nondescript warehouse, tucked into the back of an industrial park. The first few rows were lined with cars, many of them expensive SUVs, plus a few scattered compacts that city dwellers leased for outings into suburbs or vacation territories.

"It's an open call day," Mia explained. "MicroStar has gotten really popular."

MicroStar Modeling, the company hired to do the Calloway campaign photo shoot, had staked out a growing business as a baby modeling agency, finding local infants and toddlers to appear in ads for safety product packaging and clothes. Mothers from around the region—mothers with a certain amount of free time and disposable income—brought their babies to cattle call sessions, where, in exchange for a $500 "portfolio fee," they received a set of headshots and an assessment of their children's career prospects.

"Not everyone gets called for work," Mia had explained, "but at least this way you're in the system."

This afternoon, the lobby was filled with women and strollers, and hummed with the sounds of mothers chattering and babies whimpering. As Lauren and Mia rolled their own strollers through the crowd, Lauren scanned the room. Most of the babies were overdressed like Rory, squeezed into Burberry onesies and Lacoste sweaters. The mothers were equally well-dressed, if not better, in chic pencil skirts and kitten heels, designer jeans and tight-fitting sweaters or low-cut long-sleeved tees. Their hair, to a woman, was elegantly coiffed. Some of them clearly expected to be discovered, themselves.

A young woman in a miniskirt and platform boots was winding through the crowd, trying to impose some order. "Ladies," she yelled, sounding irritated, "there are different lines here! Initial assessment, in front of this red door! Children of the Soil All-Natural Clothing callback, over by the blue door!"

A new wave of fussiness echoed through the room as the women slowly started to sort themselves out, assembling into two jagged lines. The long one, by the red door, was filled with babies of varying ages and stages of fussiness, and mothers who chatted amiably as they pushed strollers back and forth or shifted their weight from side to side with infants in their arms. The line by the blue door was shorter and more rarefied. Some of the kids were toddlers, with remarkable features: a girl with fire-red hair, a pair of twin boys with afros and coffee-colored skin, an Asian boy with a shock of hair that stood up on end. The mothers looked intense, and didn't chitchat. A few older kids sullenly held onto their mothers' hands. Some were strikingly beautiful. Others were distinctive-looking, but odd.

"Is somebody going to take my picture again, Mommy?" one girl with dark freckles and flaxen braids asked her mother, a statuesque woman in tight-fitting jeans.

"Oh, no, honey," the mother said. "Don't worry. Just stand here by me and later we'll get that treat we talked about."

Mia bade Lauren farewell and joined the line of mothers by the red door. She immediately started chatting with the woman in front of her, and Lauren could see her reach into her diaper bag and pull out a Calloway campaign brochure. Lauren turned and hunted down the woman in the platform boots. She found her leaning against a wall, texting.

"Excuse me," Lauren said.

The woman looked Lauren up and down quickly. "Red door," she said, and turned back to her phone.

"No, I'm here for the Calloway campaign photo shoot," Lauren said. "The 'Got Milk' ad?"

"Oh, you," the woman said brusquely. "You're early. Follow me."

She walked so quickly that Lauren couldn't get closer than three long steps behind her, wheeling Rory around a corner and down a side hall to an unmarked grey door. The woman pushed it open with considerable effort. Inside was a small room, about ten feet square. In the center, a sheet of grey canvas was draped around a frame to create a backdrop. A three-legged stool stood on a patch of carpet beneath the sheet, a scattering of klieg lights around it. It looked like the setup for a school-picture shoot. In one corner, a man and a woman were sitting in folding chairs, eating takeout food from foam containers. Lauren could only see their backs.

"Salim," the woman said. "Your subject is here." She spoke in a tone she might have used to announce that he'd tracked dirt on a white rug.

"Give me a minute," the man said, in a thick Middle Eastern accent.

The woman left and shut the door behind her. Lauren waited for what felt like ten minutes. She looked down at Rory, sleeping peacefully in her car seat, and adjusted the lace on her collar. The food smelled seductively good, laden with curry and spices. She fumbled in her bag for a cereal bar.

At last, the photographer got up, turned around, and strode toward her. He was a handsome olive-skinned man in his late 20s, wearing an expensive-looking European-cut shirt. He didn't look at Lauren, but walked directly to Rory's stroller and looked down at the baby.

"So this is the girl who likes the milk," he said.

"This is Rory," Lauren said. "And yes, she seems to like breast-milk. Though she really hasn't had any other options."

"A nice, round face," Salim said. "Upper lip is small. What color are her eyes?"

"Blue," Lauren said. "They started out blue. Though I think they might be turning a little brownish."

"If the color is bad, we can fix it afterward," Salim said. "Mona! Come here, let us talk about the moustache."

His assistant stood up, and up. She was model-tall, probably over six feet, with long jet-black hair and dark brown eyes. Lauren felt shrunken beside her.

Mona gave Lauren a "hello" nod and quickly turned to Salim. "I brought a few things to try," she told him. "Cream of Wheat, marshmallow Fluff, Elmer's Glue…"

"Wait a minute," Lauren interrupted. "You want to put Elmer's Glue on my baby's face?"

"Well, we have to make the milk somehow," Mona said, sounding irritated.

"Can't you just use milk?" Lauren said.

"Milk is *translucent*," Mona replied.

"I'm sorry," Lauren said. "You're not using glue."

"Salim?!" Mona cried out.

Salim, who had been fiddling with a camera setting, looked up. "No worries, no worries," he told Lauren reassuringly. "We will make the milk without the glue. No glue. Mona, put the glue away. Let us get the lighting right. Come, bring the baby here."

Lauren lifted Rory carefully out of her car seat, trying not to wake her up. The frilly outfit had gotten creased during the ride, and Lauren tried to smooth it out with her fingers.

"Oh, no, no, no, no, no," Salim said, looking at the baby. "No lace, no, no. Do you have anything white?"

"Well, I mostly seem to have pink," Lauren said. "I can look in the bag…"

"Just one of those—what do you say, the onesies?" Salim said. "Like a T-shirt. Covering the belly. That is all we need."

"I can look…" Lauren said. "I'll have to go through my bag. Can, um, one of you hold her for a second?"

"I'll take her," Mona said, holding out her arms. Lauren looked at her suspiciously, worried that she'd secretly try to slather glue on Rory's face. But Salim looked a little impatient, so she complied. Mona hoisted Rory into the air, looking carefully at her face.

"Hello, cutie," she said to the still-sleeping baby. And then, to Salim, "Her skin tone is a little reddish."

Lauren decided to refrain from comment as she tore through the contents of her bag, looking for a plain white onesie. Everything was pastel, it seemed, and covered with some cute picture. "I'm sorry," Lauren finally said. "Is it possible she could wear pink?"

"Mona," said Salim, "go out into the crowd of women out there. Somebody must have a white onesie. Give them twenty dollars for it. Thirty. Go."

Mona handed Rory back to Lauren and quickly left the room.

"So," Lauren said, as Salim continued to adjust his equipment. "Do you do a lot of photo shoots of babies?"

"I do fashion," Salim said. "Children, grownups, everybody. But usually not babies so young. Or when you do, they are twins. How old is she?"

"Six weeks," Lauren said. "Almost seven."

"Mmm hmm," Salim said. "When does she wake up?"

"Oh! Um, I don't know," Lauren said. "Whenever she gets hungry, I suppose. She still sleeps for most of the day."

"We may have to poke her when we're ready," Salim said. "I need to see the eyes. This 'Got Milk,' it is not a sleeping thing. You must get milk when you are awake. And how do you make her smile?"

"Oh, she doesn't smile yet," Lauren said. "Six-week-olds don't smile. I mean, she looks like she's smiling sometimes, but I think it's just gas."

"Hmmm," Salim said.

"On 'America's Next Top Model,' they never smile," Lauren offered. Salim didn't acknowledge the joke.

Just then the door opened and Mona reappeared. "I found a woman with twin boys who gave us one of her onesies," Mona said. "It's size three-to-six months. Will that fit?"

"It might be a little big…" Lauren said.

"I have safety pins," Mona said.

"Maybe this is a bad idea," Lauren said.

"She will be a beautiful model," Salim said quickly. "Do not worry. The onesie will fit. We will not use the glue. Let's put her here, under the lights, and see what we see."

He grasped Lauren's elbow and led her to the stool. "The baby, she does not sit up?" he said.

"At six weeks? Oh, no," Lauren said.

"OK then. You will hold her. But hold her out away from you, yes? Like this?" He pantomimed holding a football in front of him, off slightly to one side.

"I'll try," Lauren said.

"Do it now," Salim said, positioning himself behind a camera. Lauren complied.

"OK," Salim said, peering through his viewfinder, shifting the tripod back and forth. "Mona, get me a 50 millimeter. And a 75. And the, what do you say, the Fluff?"

Mona handed Lauren the onesie, then went to the corner to grab the lenses.

"Should I change her now?" Lauren asked Salim. "I suppose I should change her diaper, too." She laid Rory gently on the carpet and took off her lace outfit and tights. She pulled off the diaper, noticed a trace amount of poop, wrapped it up quickly, and tossed it in her bag. She put on a new diaper, then the onesie. Rory had opened her eyes by now and was looking around, in a state that the parenting books called "active alert." Lauren brought her to the stool and held her upright, propping up her neck with one hand.

"Hello to the beautiful eyes!" Salim said, switching lenses. "And yes, they are blue. OK. We'll be ready soon. So tell me, because I live in New York, this Candace Calloway, what is her story? She is a beautiful candidate, no?"

"She's very pretty, yes," Lauren said.

"If she is so beautiful, then why are we taking a picture of a baby?" Salim said.

"Well," Lauren said slowly, "we want to tell people that she supports babies. Their right to be breastfed in public."

"And the men do not like it," Salim said. "To the American men, the breast is very sexual. Where I am from, the men prefer the other parts of the body. The buttocks. The legs. A woman with beautiful legs is very valued in my country. But here, with the breasts, the men get very happy. And perhaps when they see a baby with the breast, they get jealous. They get angry."

"Well, maybe," Lauren said. "But they shouldn't. That's what breasts are for, isn't it? To feed babies."

"But if the men get angry, nobody is happy," Salim said. "That is why it is good not to show them what is happening. What they don't know does not hurt them."

As he spoke, he raised the camera slightly in the tripod, peered intently through the lens, and snapped his fingers.

"Beautiful," he said. "This is it. The light is good. Now, the milk."

Mona approached with a jar of Fluff and what looked like a lip-liner brush. "Hold her still," she said, as she started to apply the thick, sticky marshmallow paste to the skin above Rory's upper lip. Rory's eyes widened, and Lauren wondered if she'd miraculously stay calm. But then she noticed a tiny quiver in Rory's lower lip, and knew what was coming next. The baby's eyes creased at the sides. Her lower lip pushed out into a pout. Her mouth opened, and she let forth the sort of howl that usually comes from a cat in heat.

"Oh, baby," Lauren said, pulling Rory close. "It's OK. It's OK." Rory only wailed more loudly.

"No crying!" Salim shouted. "No crying! Here. Give me the child. Quickly!"

Before Lauren realized what was happening, Salim had grabbed the baby and hoisted her into the air. "No crying!" he shouted, bouncing Rory vigorously up and down. "Happy! Happy! Happy baby!"

Lauren reached out instinctively and took a few steps toward Salim, but then she realized something: Rory had quieted down. As the photographer lifted her high into the air, her facial features relaxed. She didn't seem to notice the marshmallow Fluff on her face. And as she stared into Salim's brown eyes, her mouth opened wide into what Lauren believed was her very first bona fide smile.

ONCE RORY HAD settled down, the photo shoot seemed to last for only a few minutes. Salim took a series of shots while barking orders: "Hold her higher! More to the left! Jiggle the butt! Yes!" He let Lauren take a quick glimpse into his camera, at a picture of Rory with an ever-so-slight smile. Lauren was impressed. Rory actually looked kind of sly.

Then Salim and Mona quickly packed up their equipment and hustled out of the building, and Lauren ended up waiting for nearly an hour for Mia to be finished with the cattle call. She nursed Rory in a folding chair in one corner of the lobby, passing the time watching women leave the building. The red-door mothers seemed cheerful as they left, cooing to their babies or talking on their cellphones. The blue-door mothers seemed agitated. Some of their kids were in tears.

"Why?" the mother of the flaxen-headed girl said to her daughter, grasping her by the wrist as they hustled through the lobby. "Why did you insist on making that silly grin? The man was telling you to look serious!"

"On 'Mickey Mouse Clubhouse,' they tell you to smile when somebody takes your picture," the girl replied. Lauren was sure she detected a note of sarcasm.

Finally, Mia emerged from the room, pushing Lyle's stroller beside two other mothers.

"…and that's why we need a candidate like her," she was saying.

"Well, I am so thankful that I met you," said one of the women beside her, who wore a frilly shirt, short shorts and high-heeled sandals, and pushed a stroller upholstered in suede. "I have been arguing with my mother about this for days. This will give me new ammunition."

"Your mother is a doll, but I think older women simply don't understand," said the woman beside her, who held a toddler's hand. She and her daughter were wearing matching dresses.

"My mother is no doll," the first woman said. "You only say that because you never had to live with her. And she and her friends are up in arms over this. It's like they've found a new hobby to replace tennis."

"That's why we have to organize and fight," Mia said. "If they're banding together, that's what we have to do, too. Please. Come to one of our meetings. We need smart women like you."

She kissed each woman on the cheek and waved to them both as they left the building. Then she walked over to Lauren and sat down beside her.

"You would not believe the score I just made," she said. "The woman in the shorts? Her husband runs a hedge fund. They're major donors to the symphony and the school for the deaf. The woman in the dress is married to the owner of a construction company. We're talking serious fund-raising power here."

"Good for you," Lauren said. "And good thing there was a long line."

"We really had a wonderful conversation," Mia said. "There's such camaraderie in situations like this. It's really heartening. It's like our babies aren't in competition at all."

"So how was the competition?" Lauren asked. "How did Lyle do?"

"I think it went really well," Mia said. "The photographer said he had an extraordinary nose!"

Extraordinarily gnomelike, Lauren thought. But if Mia was happy, who could complain?

CHAPTER 10

GREAT, MORE KIDS in the office, Maisy thought. She was sitting at her desk, staring at a flier for the Motherhood Advisory Committee meeting that was scheduled to start soon. Since the MOMs had turned this into war, a string of new women had come by the headquarters, offering to volunteer or make a small donation, many of them with babies and toddlers in tow. Theoretically, this should have created an atmosphere of youthfulness and promise. Practically, it meant more noise and the ever-present, faint odor of poop. There was also the constant chance that a runaway tyke, whose mother was busy filling out a contact form, would knock over a stack of mailers or impale himself on a yard sign. Maisy had even discovered a couple of dirty diapers stashed in corners. She used a tissue to hold them as she carried them to the trash can, as if she were handling hazardous waste.

When the committee convened, there were certain to be more kids, along with brightly-colored slings, soggy cookies, and plush toys wet with baby drool. It would feel like a day care center—except louder, with more crumbs. Whatever time Maisy had spent with her nieces and nephews hadn't prepared her for this sort of mass invasion. Nor for the fact that, no matter how old any of these kids were, they would all be nursing. There was never a bottle in sight.

Maisy swiveled her chair around to face the window, reached her hand into the top of her shirt and tugged at her bra strap, which was digging into her shoulder. *You get what you pay for,* she thought. On a whim this morning, after her run and her shower, she had put on one of the Calloway for Governor bras the campaign had ordered after the debate. This was another one of Maisy's theatrical ideas, and she was proud of it: Remembering a cousin who had spent time in the Alabama women's peniten-tiary system, she had done a quick Internet search and found a wholesaler that made bras for American prisons. She had or-dered a few hundred, then made an awkward call to a silkscreen shop. Now, the campaign possessed several large boxes of pink bras, ranging in size from 36C to 38DD, emblazoned with "Cal-loway" on one cup and "Governor" on the other.

Maisy reached further into her shirt and adjusted a breast. It was large and heavy, a water balloon, and it hadn't been touched by anyone but her in quite some time. She wondered what her life would have been like if she had nursed a baby, if she had *had* a baby, if she had given herself some reason to abandon her itiner-ant ways and settled down in a town with nice parks and decent schools. Of course, to have a baby, you had to have a partner, and that was nothing Maisy had ever done well.

There had been men, some clumsy campaign trail ro-mances fueled by too much beer in dive bars late at night. More recently, there had been women, and one woman in par-ticular: a local political operative, self-confident and serene, whom Maisy had met during a stint in Minnesota. She had worked as a consultant for a rival Congressional campaign, and her candidate was a hard-line social conservative, so her trysts with Maisy were furtive in more ways than one: always late at night in the dumpy basement apartment where Maisy slept, sweaty fumbles on a lumpy plaid couch. When Maisy had left Minneapolis—victorious, in the political sense—she had cried, for the first time she could remember since college. There was talk of a rendezvous in Asheville, but it never happened. Sometimes in the middle of the night, if Maisy had campaign insomnia and wanted to clear her mind, she imagined a visit—the whole thing, from the greeting at the airport to the tour of her bungalow, the hand-in-hand walks through downtown streets, the late nights in Maisy's soft bed, her breasts in someone else's warm, sweet hands.

"You're staying for the meeting, too," said a voice behind her. Startled, Maisy swung around to find Candace. The candidate had changed into casual clothes, which, for her, meant skin-tight jeans, high wedge-heeled shoes, and a navy-blue silk blouse that showed a hint of cleavage. Her hair glistened with moisture. She had just been to the gym.

"Candace, you don't need to be here," Maisy said. "I'm not going to give you too many nights off, so take this one while you can. Read up on the position papers. Get some rest."

"I want to be here," Candace said. "These are my people. What about you?"

"I'm staying to make sure your people don't stray too far off the reservation," Maisy said. "It's not my ideal choice for how to spend an evening, but it's my job. And if you choose to stay, I'm going to warn you right now: There will be bare breasts. And probably some slurping."

"The sound of sustenance!" Candace said. "I want to see these mothers in action. I want to feel the aura of these babies. My future constituents."

This didn't sound like the jaded candidate Maisy had shepherded to the debate. Tonight, Candace's voice was different, uncharacteristically bright. Frankly, it made Maisy a little nervous.

"I realize you have to talk a good game about this breast stuff," she told Candace, "and I appreciate that you can. But don't worry, you don't really have to believe it."

Candace actually looked hurt.

"I find your cynicism disappointing," she said, and left the room.

A HALF HOUR LATER, the women, with babies and toddlers in tow, started filing into the conference room where the interns had set up a circle of folding chairs. Maisy stood in one corner and watched them. Mia Hastings Hoberman, holding a baby in one arm and toting a briefcase over her shoulder, was dressed elegantly in a sweater set and a pair of slim knit pants. The rest of the 15 or so women were dressed more casually, in jeans or long, shapeless skirts. One of them wore a T-shirt that said "Eat at Mom's." Several of them sat down and immediately started nursing. Maisy reached into her shirt again and adjusted her bra, not caring if anyone saw. She felt the urge to start and finish the meeting as quickly as possible, the sooner to get to a large glass of white wine.

But Candace seemed to have the opposite idea. With a broad smile and a look of determination on her face, she walked around to each of the women, shaking hands and exchanging enthusias-tic pleasantries. Maisy watched her nod vigorously at things the women were saying and grasp some of their hands with both of hers. She couldn't make out many of Candace's words over the buzz of conversation, punctuated by baby fusses and the occa-sional toddler's shriek. But at one point, she thought she heard the candidate say "vaginal."

Maisy made eye contact with Mia, then beckoned her to the empty chair beside her. Mia swiftly came over and sat down, bouncing Lyle on her lap as she reached into her briefcase and pulled out several sheets of paper. Lyle was wearing a white cot-ton onesie that said "I have a PhD in Poopology."

"Hi, Maisy," Mia said breathlessly. "I've got the list of mother's

venues you asked for right here. Also, I took the liberty of looking up the names of some booking agents for daytime talk shows.
One of my old clients was a stylist, and she did the rounds."

"Fantastic. I'll take a look," Maisy said, thinking that Mia was
already more on the ball than Chip, and had the added advantage
of being free. She took one of the papers from Mia and glanced
at it briefly. It was color-coded: the names of talk shows in black,
the names of booking agents in blue, telephone numbers in red.

"Mia. Hello! You look lovely." Candace was suddenly hovering over them. She had pulled an extra folding chair from the
side of the room and now squeezed it between Mia's and Maisy's.

"Senator Calloway!" Mia said. "I had no idea you'd be here
tonight!"

"I wouldn't miss it," Candace said, glancing quickly at Maisy, who
sat watching, poker-faced. "And I'm so glad you brought…Lionel?"

"Lyle," Mia said, smiling.

"And he's…six months?"

"Five," Mia said. "Though he is 80th percentile on the
growth chart."

"He is just so handsome," Candace said, looking at him lov-
ingly. "May I hold him?"

"Oh, of course!" Mia said. "I'd be honored."

Candace lifted Lyle gingerly into her lap, holding the baby as
far as possible from her torso, as if he were an uncooked chicken.
She perched the baby on her knee and bounced her leg up and
down. Lyle looked up at her and smiled. Candace smiled back.

"Goo?" she said tentatively. Lyle smiled again.

"Goo!" Candace said, sounding more confident. "Goo goo
goo goo goo!" Mia looked on, beaming.

Maisy felt increasingly itchy around her chest. She cleared
her throat, then stood up. "Ladies," she said. A couple of the
women emitted loud shushes, trying to quiet their toddlers.

"Thank you so much for your continued support," Maisy
went on. "As you know, this has been an exciting and challeng-

ing week for the campaign, and we're going to need your help now more than ever."

The women who weren't tending to their children looked up at Maisy expectantly. Maisy looked over at Candace to see if she wanted to say anything, but she was too busy whispering "goo" to the baby.

"You are our best ambassadors," Maisy continued. "We need to keep explaining that Candace Calloway is the best friend women can have in this race. And I'm happy to announce that we have some tools to help you spread the word."

She turned and headed for the cardboard boxes by the wall, which held the campaign's new cache of uncomfortable bras. Two toddlers, it turned out, had found the boxes already and were rooting through one of them, tossing bras onto the floor. Another was sitting cross-legged with a bra in his lap, sucking away happily at one of the straps.

"Excuse me," Maisy said quietly, reaching past four small, dirty hands to grab another bra out of the box. She held it up and showed it to the room. "I've learned, over the years, that it helps to have props. When you go door to door or visit groups, you can hand out these."

A scattering of applause went up, though Maisy was surprised, and a little perturbed, at how unimpressed the women seemed. "Is that a nursing bra?" she heard one of them ask, *sotto voce*, to the woman next to her. "It doesn't look like a nursing bra."

Maisy looked at the candidate again. But Candace's gaze remained on Lyle, who was reaching out to try to grab her necklace, a choker of chunky white and aquamarine beads. Instead, Maisy made eye contact with Mia, who was looking up at her eagerly, both hands on her briefcase.

"Now, let me turn things over to Mia Hastings Hoberman, the chair of this committee," Maisy said.

Mia stood up quickly. "Thank you, everyone, for serving on this very important board," she said. "I'd first like to pass this sheet around the room so we can make a telephone and e-mail tree." She handed the paper and a ballpoint pen to the woman on her right.

"Next, I'd like to talk about our outreach project," she went on. "I've compiled a list of places we can visit to talk to new mothers about their choices. I've put together a list of mommy-and-me groups, toddler gyms, and music classes. And—" she reached into her briefcase and pulled out another piece of paper—"I've compiled a list of yoga studios across the state. Will someone volunteer to call and find out which of them offer prenatal?"

A woman in long brown braids, a baby at her breast, raised her hand. Mia walked across the room to hand her the list. Lyle, still reaching for Candace's choker, let out a yelp. Candace kept smiling, but arched her back in an effort to avoid his tiny hands.

Mia swooped over and picked Lyle up. He immediately started rooting, rubbing his head into her shirt and trying to chew on her shoulder. "I'm sorry," Mia told Candace. "I think he's hungry." Candace smiled and mouthed, "It's OK."

"Thank you, Mia," Maisy said. "Now, let's talk a little bit about what to say at these groups. Make it personal, of course. Explain what breastfeeding means to you. But also lay out the differences between Senator Calloway and her competitors. Talk about the story of the Stonewall Museum, and how Senator Calloway was the first to take a stand."

"Come talk to me about it if you want details. I was there!" Mia interjected from her chair, where she was adjusting a blanket over her shoulder, preparing to feed Lyle.

"Mia? Mia!" Sheila McDonough interrupted. Her toddler son, Sampson, was lying in her lap, his head buried beneath her shirt. His legs were kicking rhythmically back and forth.

"Mia, don't bother with the blanket, hon," Sheila said. "We've got to end this idea that nursing mothers have to hide. Look! Breastfeeding is a natural act. It deserves to be out in the open."

"Hear, hear," said the woman in the brown braids, who was

still nursing her baby, no blanket involved. "I'm sure Senator Calloway agrees."

"Out in the open," Candace said, sounding far less uncertain than Maisy thought she would. "Definitely."

"That's what we should be talking to these mothers' groups about," said another woman, with short hair and horn-rimmed glasses. Her baby let out a squeal from her lap. "This is our chance to spread the word about the beauty of nursing. There are too many women—Delilah, Mommy's talking now, please wait—there are too many women who have been brainwashed by society."

"Maybe instead of bras, we should hand out T-shirts with pictures of babies on the breast," said the woman with braids. "I've got one on my Facebook page. I had a professional photographer take it."

"I've seen that picture, Sarah. It's beautiful!" Sheila said, laying an arm on Sampson's legs, which were still chugging vigorously. "I can see it on T-shirts. And maybe billboards!"

"It's too bad Calloway has only one 'o' in it," said the woman next to her. "If there were two, we could make them look like two little breasts on the signs."

"Couldn't we put two 'o's in it anyway? Just for the posters?" another one asked. The little boy in her lap started to cry.

"Hold on now," Maisy said, trying to keep smiling. She raised her voice above the din. "We're fine with the metaphors. Bras. Doughnuts. But I don't think we want to go too far with breasts in people's faces. We don't want to alienate anyone."

"How could anyone be alienated by a breast?" said Sarah, the woman in the braids.

"You shouldn't be a mother if you don't want to breastfeed," another woman piped up from the side of the room, where she was pulling one of the toddlers away from a box of bras. "How about a law saying it's child abuse to feed your baby formula? You'd stand behind that, wouldn't you, Senator?"

"How about a sin tax on formula?" another woman said. "Twenty-five percent!"

"Well…" Candace began.

"Look," Maisy said quickly. "These are ideas worth considering. But we don't want to expand the senator's platform too much."

"I'm sorry," Sarah said. "I thought we were an *advisory* committee. If you're not going to take our advice, what's the point?"

"Yeah, why shouldn't I just go back to supporting Lois Manson?" said the woman by the bra box.

"Because Lois Manson doesn't stand a snowball's chance in hell of getting elected," Maisy said.

"Language!" the woman by the bra box shouted, putting her hands over her toddler's ears.

"I'm sorry," Maisy said, clenching her teeth. "Lois Manson doesn't stand a snowball's chance in *heck* of getting elected. The point is, your candidate can't do anything for you if she isn't in office. And Candace Calloway has a chance to win, provided you people don't freak out half the women in the state."

"That's called compromising your principles, if you ask me," Sarah said.

"That's called politics," Maisy shot back.

"Let me step in here," Candace said, suddenly looking engaged. She stood up and patted Maisy on the shoulder condescendingly. "Ladies, thank you so much for being here. And for bringing your beautiful children. Like this one! Little Lionel!" She turned to Mia and reached out her arms to pick up Lyle again.

"Lyle," Mia said, smiling, as she extricated Lyle from her lap and handed him over to Candace.

"Lyle!" Candace repeated. She hoisted the baby onto her shoulder, arching her back again to keep him from touching her necklace. "For this guy's sake, I promise that I will always listen to everything you have to say. But you have to understand where Maisy is coming from here. She is not a mother, I know, but she is a skilled campaign manager. We have to trust her, as hard as that might sometimes be."

Maisy sat down glumly and adjusted her bra again, trying

to remind herself what she ever found attractive about women.

"I see what you're saying," Sheila McDonough piped up. "This is a stealth campaign. We hold back now, and once you get in office, it's a whole new day for the breast."

"A whole new day," Candace said confidently, as Lyle started to whimper. She pulled him toward her body and bounced him up and down. He squealed and smiled. Then he opened his mouth wide and a stream of spit-up poured out, tumbling down his chin and onto Candace's dark blue shirt.

"Oh!" Candace said, looking down at the curdled milk that was staining her blouse and dripping into her cleavage. She extended her arms and held Lyle as far from her body as she could.

Mia gave a horrified gasp, leaped from her seat and grabbed Lyle, who was gurgling and smiling. "I'm so sorry, Senator! He never does this! It's my fault. I put a slice of cheese on my sandwich at lunch today."

"Is that silk?" the woman on the other side of Mia piped up. "If so, it's gonna stain."

The room erupted into pandemonium. Several women started rummaging into their diaper bags for wipes. Sheila was the first to produce them, waving a white rectangular package triumphantly into the air. Sampson, detached from his meal, let out a shriek of protest and then started to whine, "Ma-ma. Ma-*ma!*"

Sheila ignored him and jumped up to Candace's aid. "These are completely organic and perfume-free," she said as she dabbed at Candace's blouse and skin.

"That's nice," Candace said dully, looking shell-shocked.

"I'm so sorry," Mia said again. "I should have given you a burp cloth, just in case. I have wipes, too."

"Seltzer!" one of the women shouted. "Seltzer will get it out!"

"Seltzer gets out red wine," another woman corrected her.

"I'm fine," Candace said. "It's milk. It's a beautiful thing." She turned to the assembled women and raised her voice to address them all. "Thank you again for coming, and for your continued support." Then she left the room.

AFTER THAT, it was hard to get the meeting focused again. First, the BOOBs started whispering about Candace: "I don't know how she'll get that off her shirt," said one, and another asked, "Doesn't she know not to jiggle a baby who just ate?" Before long, they had broken into small groups, vigorously arguing the merits of a tax on formula or lamenting the fact that "new baby" wrapping paper bore pictures of bottles instead of tiny breasts. A few of them gathered around Sheila McDonough's iPhone, evaluating photos of babies at bare breasts to find the one that would look best on the side of a bus. Mia, looking ashen, circulated another sign-up sheet. Lyle, his work for the evening done, fell asleep on his mother's shoulder. Three toddlers ran in circles around the room, each of them waving a Calloway bra and shrieking, until their mothers finally corralled them and carried them out of the headquarters.

Once the women and babies had finally gone, Maisy cleaned up the room herself, throwing out the trash and stacking the chairs against one wall. She tossed a granola bar wrapper, several crumpled tissues, and a small, wet plastic bird into the trash. When she got back to her office, Candace was lying on the couch, her shoes off, her feet crossed, her toes perfectly manicured as always. She had changed from her silk blouse into a tight-fitting sweatshirt from her gym bag. Her eyes were open. She was staring at the ceiling.

"You did a nice job in there," Maisy told her. "I have to hand it to you. That little speech you made was very...politic."

"It's the same thing I do at Chamber of Commerce meetings, when they're asking me to commit to no-new-taxes pledges,"

Candace said, slowly pulling herself upright. "Except that instead of holding a baby, I grab one of the businessmen's hands."

She got up from the couch and clasped one of Maisy's hands between her own.

"I'm here because of Richard," she said, her voice growing husky as she peered deeply into Maisy's face. "I am committed to making sure his business succeeds, because his businesses makes him strong. It makes all of us strong."

She dropped Maisy's hand and turned away. "Usually, the guy gives me a campaign donation afterward, even if he's a Republican," she said. "And usually he doesn't spit up on my shirt."

"Imagine that," Maisy said. "A Republican who's better-behaved than a baby."

Candace emitted a laugh that sounded more like a choke. When she turned back around, her eyes were red and glistening with tears.

"Oh, Candace. Look, I'm sorry about the shirt," Maisy said. "I'm sure we can get you a new one. We'll find a way to charge it to the campaign."

"It's not the shirt," Candace said, starting to cry audibly. "It's my *life.*"

"Your life is fine," Maisy said. "It's better than fine. You'll probably win this election. You'll be the governor of a major state. And even if you don't win, your profile is higher, you're in line for a Cabinet position—"

"I don't care about my career!" Candace wailed. "I want a baby!"

"Oh, God," Maisy said.

"I want a baby," Candace repeated, sniffling. "I want my own baby to spit up on my shirt. I want to buy baby clothes. I want to know what it feels like to feed a baby from my breast."

"OK," Maisy said. "Let's take a deep breath here."

"All this time I've been spending in the State House, and what do I have to show for it?"

"Are you even asking me this question?" Maisy said.

"I've wasted my childbearing years!" Candace said.

"Candace," Maisy said. "Come on. Not everyone has children. Not everyone wants children." She pulled a tissue from a box on her desk and handed it to Candace, who blew her nose delicately, with a barely audible snort.

"Those babies are so beautiful," Candace said.

"Sure they are, for a few minutes," Maisy said. "But they poop, they burp, they puke all over you. They keep you up all night. They make you feel guilty for every minute you spend away from them. And then they turn into teenagers and blame you for everything."

"How would you know?" Candace said, her voice still wobbly. "You've never had a kid."

"I was a kid," Maisy said. "And then I was a teenager. And then I got nieces and nephews, and I see what they do to their parents."

"I wish I'd thought of this before," Candace continued. "Maternity clothes are so stunning these days."

"Candace, I've seen a lot of women in politics," Maisy said. "Here's how it works. Either they wait till their kids are grown, or they're racked with guilt for ignoring their kids while they work 18-hour days."

Candace blew her nose again.

"Here's my recommendation to you," Maisy said. "Get a cat. It'll sit on your lap when you're home and fend for itself when you're not. Be all maternal with that cat and concentrate on your career. You can help as many kids as you want when you're governor, and they won't be bitching about you in therapy for the rest of their lives."

Candace sighed.

"Besides," Maisy said, looking down at Candace's impeccable cleavage, allowing herself, for the first time, to feel a stir of interest. "You do know what nursing does to your breasts, right? Deflates them. You get pregnant, and two years from now, you'll be looking down at some seriously saggy balls of flesh. Wouldn't that make you sad?"

"Oh, Maisy," Candace said, sounding agitated again. "That's what plastic surgery is for."

Chapter 11

LAUREN KNEW it was crazy, some side effect of stress and sleep deprivation, but the day after the photo shoot, she started to imagine that her breast pump was sending her messages. She had decided to pump early in the mornings, just like Mia did, to build up a supply of milk in the freezer for emergencies. So at 7 a.m., she put Rory in her bouncy chair, set up the apparatus on her bed, and experimented with speeds on the dial. At a low-speed setting, the machine told her to "*wank off.*" But when she cranked it higher, the pump started saying, "*Food at home.*"

"*Food at home. Food at home.*" The pump blathered on as the bottles slowly filled with milk. But what did it mean? That she should leave Rory behind with a sitter and a bottle and join Mia on the campaign trail? That she should ignore the campaign, forget about leaving the house, and stay home to breastfeed forever?

Somehow on this morning, drizzly and cool, staying in her house seemed like a reasonable idea. Lauren had promised to accompany Mia to some new-mommies' groups, but nothing was scheduled for today. She was free to adjust to her new life as a stay-at-home mom. When her pumping was done, four ounces of breastmilk poured delicately into a freezer bag, she drank a mug of coffee, fully aware that Mia would disapprove of caffeine intake while nursing. She flipped through the newspaper absently. She watered the houseplants with one arm, holding Rory in the other. And when Rory started to fidget, she settled down on the sofa in front of the television. She laid the baby on her U-shaped lap pillow, which was decorated with smiling ladybugs, grinning ants, and eerily happy little spiders.

Rory ate voraciously as usual, making little mumbling and slurping noises. As she grew sleepier, her suckling slowed down and her grip grew weaker, but she still stayed attached to Lauren's breast, stuck there by inertia and the occasional sleepy pull. Lauren gently stuck her pinky into Rory's mouth to release the suction. The baby stirred, then relaxed again, fast asleep.

Her mother had always advised her against holding Rory in her lap during naps. "You're going to train her to need you all the time," she had said a week after Rory was born. She had traveled up from Virginia, staying nearly three weeks to help around the house, and while she had been greatly useful in matters of laundry and dishes, she had been rigid and judgmental on the subject of baby care. She frowned on the fact that Rory slept at night in a bassinet beside Lauren's bed, rather than in the crib in her designated room, a tiny bedroom scarcely larger than a closet that Rob and Lauren had once used as a home office. "That room is so lovely," she had said. "It's a shame that Rory can't enjoy it."

The room was pretty, Lauren had to admit. Almost too pretty. They had known that Rory would be a girl since the eighteen-week ultrasound scan; Lauren had toyed with keeping the gender a surprise, but Rob had insisted that a secret was absurd. So with ample and competitive assistance from Rob's and Lauren's mothers, they had turned the tiny room into a frilly getaway. The white-painted crib was outfitted with pink toile bumpers. The wall art was comprised of kittens and bunnies. The curtains were pink, with cascading ruffles. Lauren had wondered what would happen if the baby grew up to be a tomboy who loved superheroes. Or, worse yet, if the ultrasound was wrong and the baby turned out to have a penis.

Rory was born with girl parts as expected, but Lauren wasn't ready to turn her over to that pink space. "She'll get there soon enough," she had said to her mother. "I'm not sure she'd enjoy it at this point, anyway. Apparently, newborns only see red, white, and black."

Lauren's mother had snorted. "Don't believe everything you read."

"Besides," Lauren had said, "it's so much easier to feed her at night this way. I don't have to get up."

"You know, when you were a baby, you slept through the night right away," her mother had said. "That formula filled you up."

Lauren had responded by placing breastfeeding brochures pointedly on the kitchen table. She printed out a page from a parenting website with the title "You Can't Spoil a Newborn" and stuck it on the refrigerator, using a "Don't Like My Cooking? Dial 1-800-EAT-SHIT" magnet that Rob had gotten her once as a Valentine's Day joke. She held Rory during every nap, staring at her tiny puffed-out lips and her awkwardly bent neck, even when her mother sat beside her, crocheting a blanket and emitting an occasional sigh.

The truth was, Lauren liked holding a sleeping baby, feeling Rory's deep, rhythmic breaths, watching the range of human emotions pass over her tiny face. Often, the baby was more interesting than anything Lauren could find on TV, as she absently flipped channels through the daytime fare of soap operas, talk shows, and decades-old movies. Today, she stroked Rory's hair and fiddled with the remote. Baseball scores…a telenovela…an earnest hostess pitching mascara on a home-shopping channel. She came across the "Polly Park Show," heard the words "pregnant women," and stopped.

Polly Park was a half-Korean supermodel with a potty mouth and a popular Los Angeles-based talk show, which featured the standard range of bickering spouses, relationship experts, and makeover challenges. Her claim to fame was the number of times the censors had to bleep her utterances and the way the audience howled and cheered after each bleep, pleased that they knew a secret that was being kept from the rest of the nation.

"...so we've filled our entire audience with these gorgeous mamas-to-be," Park was saying, her mouth moving in exaggerated stretches beneath pink lip gloss. "Look at these knocked-up ladies! Girls, hang on to your BLEEEEEEEEEEEEP." Her mouth kept moving. Then the camera shifted to the audience, rows of women with burgeoning bellies, applauding wildly.

"We've also brought in some experts on S-E-X!" Park continued. "Give it up for our good friend and sex therapist Dr. Richard Cummings. You sir, have a dirty name! I can't believe these BLEEEEEEEEP aren't going to bleep it out!"

A very tan man in a shiny grey suit grinned and waved from his chair. His teeth shone brightly in the television lights.

"And please welcome Nancy Nathanson, licensed clinical therapist, mother of five, and author of the new book, "Mama Needs Some, Too." The camera panned to a thin bleached-blonde whose skirt was short enough to showcase a pair of long legs.

"Let's get started right away with the ladies in the crowd," Park said. "Do I have any questions from my hot mamas?"

A heavyset woman in a tight magenta shirt was already standing at a microphone. The camera zoomed in to her face, dipped down to her cleavage, and rose again.

"Hi, Polly! I'm seven months pregnant," she said. She was chewing gum. "My question is, my boyfriend and I like to, um, make love a lot." She giggled. "And we want to know, like, is that gonna hurt the baby?"

"Oooh, wait! Tell me more. How often, girl?" Polly cooed.

"Like, I don't know, like once or twice a day," the woman said, blushing slightly. The audience cheered.

"I can assure you that it's fine," said Dr. Cummings. "We encourage pregnant women to keep up with their sex lives. The baby will be fine. And you will be relaxed and ready for the next stage in your life!"

"You'll be better than relaxed!" Polly said. "You do it right, girl, and you'll be BLEEP BLEEP BLEEP BLEEP."

As the crowd cheered again, another woman made her way to the microphone. She scarcely looked older than a teenager, with long straight hair that fell down to the middle of her back. She wore a loose-fitting shirt with an empire waist that made it hard to tell that she was pregnant at all.

"Sweetheart, are you really pregnant?" Polly asked her. "You look so teeny!"

"Three months, Polly," the woman said.

"How ya feeling?" Polly asked. "Are you puking a lot?"

"I'm good," the woman said. "I puked earlier. But here's my question. My husband really likes oral sex. Like, giving it to me. He says it's good for the baby. Is that true?"

"Polly, I just want to tell you how proud I am that your audience has its priorities straight," Nancy Nathanson said. "Sex is such an important part of everyday life. So, sure, in this case, I'd say what's good for the mother is good for the baby."

"Awwww, good," the young woman said. "I was hoping you'd say that."

As the show went to commercial break, Lauren tried to think back to the last time she'd had sex with Rob. The months after she'd gotten pregnant had been strangely libidinous; she was growing larger than she'd ever been, but she felt beautiful, womanly, and Rob seemed to agree. For awhile, they had wound up having sex nearly every night, adjusting their positions in creative ways as Lauren's belly swelled. And then, at around the point when she started feeling strong kicks from within, Lauren had realized that she had a witness. From then on, when Rob had nestled up to her in bed, burrowed his lips into her neck and edged her panties down her hips, she had rolled over and claimed, fairly accurately, to be tired.

After Rory's birth, sex was a distant memory. Rob was usually exhausted by the time he got home. Rory woke up several times a night. And since the delivery had required a fair amount of stitches, Lauren pictured her vagina as something delicate and damaged, a bruised piece of fruit, not ready for human touch.

It wasn't that sex never crossed her mind. Every once in awhile, her memory would drift far, far back to the early days when she and Rob had just started to date, when they'd spend entire Sundays in bed. Sometimes, she'd drift into a reverie at traffic lights, remembering his warm breath against her face, his fingers on her skin, his tongue exploring...

The sound of raucous applause jolted her back to the "Polly Park Show," which had returned from commercial break. Another woman stepped to the microphone, wearing tight jeans and a tank top that showed off a burgeoning belly.

"Hi, Polly," she said with a Spanish accent. "I'm seven months pregnant, and my husband and I work different shifts, so I don't get to see him that often. So what I do is, I masturbate. My question, you know, is, will that hurt the baby?"

"No!" Richard Cummings said. "Heavens, no! Have fun with yourself, my dear!"

"Way to show yourself a good time while your husband's out, girlfriend!" Polly Park squealed. "While the cat's away, the mice will BLEEEEEEEEEP."

ROB DIDN'T COME HOME for dinner that night; he was stuck in long meetings about the upcoming trial. So Lauren dined on a large bowl of cereal while holding Rory in one arm. She gave Rory some of the "tummy time" her doctor recommended, watching her grunt and whimper and try to lift her head. She gave the baby a tour of the kitchen for the umpteenth time, pointing out the stove and saying, "Hot. Don't ever touch." Rory looked at the burners blankly. She still had no control over her arms and legs.

There was still time to kill before Rory's bedtime, so she gave the baby a bath, singing gently as she lathered each tiny body part, hoping Rory wouldn't care that she was slightly off-key. She dried Rory off on the changing table in her ultra-pink room and struggled to fit her into a pair of pajamas. It took Lauren nearly ten minutes to line up the snaps correctly. She wondered if some baby clothes were specially designed to make mothers feel incompetent.

Once she'd finished, she brought Rory into her and Rob's bedroom, leaned against the headboard, and read "Goodnight Moon" with as much dramatic flair as she could muster as Rory stared intently at the wall. She nursed Rory one last time, wrapped her in a tight swaddle, and placed her gently on her back in the bassinet. She turned off the light and lay down on top of the bed, intending to close her eyes for only a minute.

She opened them again when she heard the front door shut. An hour had passed, according to the bedside clock, and Rob was home. Awake again, Lauren listened to him making his way through the apartment, rustling the newspaper on the kitchen table, opening and closing the refrigerator, running the water in the bathroom. Eventually, he opened the door to the bedroom and began to undress in the dark.

"Hi," Lauren said quietly.

"You're awake," Rob whispered, startled.

"Didn't mean to scare you," Lauren said. "Yeah, I'm up."

"Is Rory asleep?"

"She should be out for another hour at least," Lauren said. "How was work?"

"Ugh. Spent the whole day and night pouring through depositions," Rob said. He walked over to Rory's bassinet, and softly stroked the baby's head. "She looks so sweet when she's sleeping."

"She is sweet," Lauren said. "Except when she's hungry. Then she's kind of pushy." She sat up, leaning against the headboard, and pulled the quilt and sheet out from beneath her. "What did you do for dinner?"

"We brought in," Rob said. "If I have any more Chinese take-out, I'm going to turn into a chopstick. And not a nice plastic one like you find in restaurants. One of those chintzy wooden ones that you have to pull apart."

"The kind that give you splinters," Lauren said. Rob bent down to give Rory a kiss, then stripped to his underpants and climbed into bed beside her.

"I was thinking of you all day," Rob said.

"That's sweet," Lauren replied.

"Well, it's partly because the partners are still talking about your breasts."

"That's not as sweet," Lauren said.

"It's OK," Rob said. "Apparently, you've got their wives talking, which isn't bad. Takes the pressure off when they decide to donate more to the Winkle campaign."

"They're really still donating to Winkle?"

"That train has left the station," Rob said. "But now, the wives want to make their own donations. Apparently this 'MOM' thing has them all excited. So I guess they have you to thank."

"You're welcome," Lauren said. "From the bottom of my heart."

They lay there silently for a minute, listening to each other's breathing. Then Rob reached out an arm and stroked Lauren's hair. A minute later, he moved it again, down her cheek, along her chin, gently down her neck, with a light, familiar, knowing touch that made her heart beat faster. When he reached Lauren's chest, he laid his fingers tentatively on her right breast, jolting her back from the faraway place she was headed. Now, she was back in the bedroom, and her nipple hurt.

"Ouch," Lauren said, sitting up.

"Ouch?" Rob asked.

"They're sore," she said. "I told you they were sore."

"So I can't touch them?" Rob said.

"They already get touched so much," Lauren said. "I'm not sure I want them touched any more."

"I like your breasts," Rob said, propping himself on an elbow. "I miss them. I want them back."

"You talk like you own them," Lauren said. "They're mine."

"They're community property," Rob said. "Before Rory, you always let me touch them whenever I wanted. And you seemed to like it."

"Even when it was totally inappropriate," Lauren said with a snicker.

"Remember when I was a first-year associate, and I felt you up in the corner of the company party?" Rob said.

"At Maison Robert," Lauren said. "A five-star restaurant. I can't believe I did that."

"It was a four-star restaurant by that point," Rob said. "It had seen better days. But that was still hot."

"I don't know if I'll ever be hot again," Lauren said.

"What are you talking about?" Rob said. "You're as hot as you ever were."

"I've got a roll of flab on my belly," Lauren said.

"You can't tell," Rob said.

"I can tell," Lauren said. "I think my butt is still big, too."

"And your breasts are bigger," Rob said. "That is hot."

"You noticed," Lauren said.

"How could I not notice?" Rob said.

"You're not supposed to notice," Lauren said. "I said they were mine, but I feel like they actually aren't mine anymore. I feel like they belong to Rory."

"That's what the BOOBs want you to think," Rob said. "But I know better. I studied property law. How about this: Your body is yours, but you've granted a temporary easement to your daughter. And a permanent easement to me."

"Permanent?" Lauren said.

"'Til death do us part," Rob said. "I studied contract law, too."

He lifted himself up, leaned over Lauren's face, and gave her a long, slow kiss.

"How about I concentrate on your lips?" he said. "And some of your other parts?"

Lauren thought about it. She was as tired as ever, hopelessly tired, and she knew that if she stayed up too much longer, she'd feel even worse the next day. But for the first time since Rory's birth, she didn't really care. She needed to keep up with those women on the "Polly Park Show."

Then she remembered that Rory was still a foot away, sleeping soundly in her bassinet.

"What about the baby?" she whispered.

"She'll sleep through it," Rob said.

"What if she doesn't?"

"Then she'll have no idea what we're doing," he said.

"I can't do it in front of her," Lauren said. "It's too weird."

Rob sighed. "The bassinet is on wheels, isn't it?" he said. "Let's get it of the room."

"Temporarily," Lauren said.

"Temporarily," he repeated.

"Just be fast," Lauren said. "She's going to wake up soon."

"I think I can be relatively quick," Rob said.

"I know you can," Lauren said. "From experience."

She watched as Rob got out of bed, gently wheeled the bassinet into the hallway, and slowly closed the door until it made a barely audible click. She closed her eyes and felt him approach the bed.

"Rob…" she said quietly as he leaned in for a kiss.

"Mmm?"

"Don't touch the breasts."

"Mmm."

"Anything else, you can touch."

"Mmmmm."

She lay back in the pillow and tried to clear her mind. *Forget that you have a baby,* she thought, willing herself to believe it.

CHAPTER 12

AFTER A MISERABLE rainy day and a stormy night, the weather in Boston suddenly shifted to October perfection. By morning, the clouds had blown away completely, the sky was a vibrant blue, and the forecast promised a gentle breeze. Maisy awoke to the sun pouring in around the corners of the shades and the sound of Claire Langoon's voice. The alarm clock was set to the public radio station, and Claire was talking excitedly to the morning show host, sounding entirely too lucid for 6:20 a.m.

"...so it was the worst experience I'd ever had with my body," she was saying. "And when I gave my son a bottle, I finally felt free."

"But what about the people who say breastfeeding exclusively is healthiest for babies?" the host said.

"It's hogwash," Claire said. "That's the strongest word I can use on the radio, but I put some stronger words on my blog. There are no good studies that say for sure that breastfeeding is better. Because they can't control for everything, right? The people who breastfeed are people like my friends, who are educated and kind of crazy-intense. They're also more likely to take their kids to the doctor and read to them, and they're less likely to live near toxic-waste dumps. It stands to reason that their babies would be healthier, no matter what they eat."

"Why do so many of your friends refuse to use formula, then?"

"Because they've been brainwashed," Claire said. "For some reason that I have yet to figure out, smart career women really, really want other people tell them how to raise their kids."

"And what are people saying about your blog?"

"You would not believe the response I've been getting," Claire said. "A lot of women out there are ready to be free."

Maisy pulled herself out of bed and went to the bathroom to wash up. Clearly, another publicity blitz was in order.

ONCE SHE HAD gotten to the office and gulped down a large cup of coffee, Maisy looked through the schedule for the day. There was a meeting with Leroy Mason, some time blocked out for Candace to make fund-raising calls, a visit to a nursing home in the afternoon. And at 10 a.m., a conference call with the Pep Boys to discuss the latest round of campaign ads. The boys had promised to work their questionable magic on the breastfeeding issue.

Maisy picked up the phone and called the intern who was serving as the front-desk receptionist. Was it Rachel? Rebecca? Robin? It was hard to keep track of the college girls' names as she moved from state to state. They all seemed to look alike, too, with long brown hair, tanned skin, and mouths that were always slightly open—as if they had a snide comment to make, or a lollipop, or something else, to suck.

"Can you send Chip Osterville in to me?" Maisy asked. Visits with Chip had become one of the small, sadistic pleasures of her day. A week of breast obsession had left the once-confident frat boy at a loss. He was unjustifiably comfortable churning out bland press releases on policy statements, but he seemed ill at ease writing anything about lactation.

"Can't someone with breasts write this?" he had whined a

day earlier, when Maisy had ordered him to draft a release on the Calloway bras.

"Four years of college and you can't get excited about unbuckling a bra strap?" Maisy had replied. "What's wrong with you, Chip? You should be able to do this in your sleep. 'Candace Calloway supports women where it really counts.' 'They already wear their love for Candace Calloway on their sleeves; now they can wear it on their chests.' Do I have to do everything around here?"

At the time, Chip had skulked back to his office with a glum look on his face. This morning, he appeared in Maisy's doorway looking cheerful. He cleared his throat with fanfare and started to read statistics off a legal pad.

"I sent the release about the bras to 27 media outlets and 35 political blogs yesterday," he announced. "We got pickup in six newspapers and seven TV newscasts. Also, 12 blogs. Except that some of them were kind of mean."

"They're bloggers," Maisy said. "By definition, that means they're assholes. This just shows that they're paying attention."

"This morning, I'm having the interns watch the cable channels," Chip continued. "We already got mentioned on the Fox News morning show. That's pretty good, I think." He gauged Maisy's expression. "So why do you look mad?"

"Claire Langoon was on public radio this morning," Maisy said, trying to fix him with an intimidating stare. "Why wasn't one our surrogates on to rebut her?"

"Uh, they didn't call us to ask for anyone?"

"That's not balance," Maisy told him. "That's bullshit. Call up the producer over there and rip him a new one. If you can't handle it, let me know his name and I'll do it. It's crunch time, baby. We've got to be out there, everywhere Winkle is."

She fiddled on her desk until she found the color-coded sheet of paper Mia Hastings Hoberman had presented, listing the booking producers for daytime talk shows. She scanned it, then scratched a name and number on a Post-it note.

"We can't afford to sit around waiting for CNN to call," she said. "Here's the contact for a producer there. And here..." she scrawled another number "...is MSNBC. Actually, why am I doing your job for you? Take this whole thing back to your hole. Check into the talk-show circuit. Pitch some of our people. It's time to take back the message here."

Chip grabbed the paper glumly and headed out of the office.

"But be careful who you book," Maisy called after him. "I don't want one of those die-hard BOOBs talking crazy shit on TV."

ONCE CHIP WAS gone, Maisy read through the papers herself, trying to get a firm sense of where to go next. The bra story was mostly mentioned in political roundups, as intended; it had been a small publicity stunt. But the op-ed columnists were starting to focus on Claire Langoon and her challenge to the breastfeeding orthodoxy.

"Breast is best for babies, but how about mothers?" read the headline on a piece from one of the boomer feminists in the Globe. A columnist for the Cape Cod Times wrote, "I never enjoyed feeding my kids. Not until I could take them out for sushi."

Maisy thought about the "Got Milk?" photos that were showing up on billboards and the sides of buses, the toddlers spitting up and wreaking havoc on her headquarters, Candace's sudden embrace of her biological clock. All of that talk about babies suddenly felt wrong. Maisy had a feeling the Pep Boys might agree. They liked to think of Candace as a sexpot, not a frustrated would-be mommy. And lust was about the only thing that motivated them to do good work.

At 10 a.m. precisely, Maisy dialed the pre-arranged conference number and waited for the Pep Boys to come on. The on-hold music was an instrumental version of "Who Let the Dogs

Out," played at a light-rock tempo. It continued for a good five minutes before Bob Brooks came on the line.

"Hello there, Maisy," he said. "Breast storyline is still going, I see."

"Like I told you it would," Maisy said.

"Well, we've been drafting some ads," Brooks said. "We think it's time to go negative."

"You'll get no complaints from me," Maisy said. "Let me have it."

"Mike?" Bob said. "Take it away."

"Thanks, Bob," came the voice of Mike LaDuke. "Here's one we think you'll like. Standard negative ad. Mwwaa-mwwaa music. Female voice. Picture of a cute baby. Cue narration." He shifted his voice higher to approximate a woman's, and spoke in the familiar negative-ad intonation.

"*This* is Baby *Ryan*," he said. "He's out *shopping* with his mother, and he *needs* to *eat*. But Ron *Winkle* wants him to *wait*. How *long* should he wait? An *hour*? *Two* hours? Will he get *dehydrated*? Will he *starve*? Ron Winkle says he doesn't *care*—as long as the *men* around him don't feel *uncomfortable*.

"Cut to a picture of Candace holding the baby," LaDuke continued, in his normal voice. Then he shifted to an even higher falsetto. "I'm Candace Calloway, and I approve this message because I want babies to eat whenever they need to. Calloway for governor. Feed the children."

There was silence on the other end of the line, as the Pep Boys awaited Maisy's reaction. She cleared her throat.

"It's very baby-centric," she said.

"It's direct," Albee said. "Hammers in the message."

"I think the message is changing," Maisy said. "It's not about feeding babies anymore. The base cares about that. But if we want to get the swing voters, we need to make this a women's issue. It's about empowerment, you know? How nobody should tell you to hide your body. That kind of thing. Winkle's not the enemy of babies. He's the enemy of women."

"Ron Winkle *says* he *cares* about *women*," LaDuke offered, in his faux-female voice. "But he wants them to *hide* from view when they're *feeding* their *babies*. Ron Winkle, *what* are you *ashamed* of?"

He shifted to higher falsetto again. "I'm Candace Calloway, and I approve this message because I think our bodies are beautiful."

"That's closer," Maisy said. "Much closer."

"Our bodies are beautiful," Steve Albee mused. "How's that for a tagline?"

"A little too 'Summer of Love,' don't you think?" Brooks said.

"Don't be ashamed?" Albee tried.

"Set yourself free," LaDuke suggested.

"Hear me roar!" Albee offered.

"Be proud," Maisy said.

"Hmm," LaDuke said. "I think I like that."

"It's empowerment," Albee said. "Women at work. Be proud!"

"Girls achieving anything. Be proud!" LaDuke said. "Implants if you want them. Be proud!"

"It's not quite there," Brooks said. "The right idea, but too flat. We need to make it more visual." He paused for a few seconds. "How about, 'Chest in the air'?" he said.

"Chest in the air?" Maisy said.

"'Chest in the air.' A double meaning!" Albee said.

"It's brilliant!" LaDuke said. "It's visceral!"

"It's immediate," Brooks said. "It's palpable."

"It makes me think 'naked,'" Maisy said.

"A *triple* meaning!" Albee cried.

"Well…" Maisy said.

"Gotta go!" Brooks said. "Back to the salt mines. We'll write up three scripts and check in with you again tomorrow morning." The dial tone rang loudly in Maisy's ear.

Maisy sat still at her desk for a few minutes, repeating "Chest in the air" in her head a few times, visualizing the words on bumper stickers and yard signs. She reached into a bottom desk drawer and pulled out the forbidden pack of cigarettes and the vintage "Kennedy '60" lighter she had stowed in there for moments of high stress and indecision. She grabbed one cigarette, then two, shoved them in her pocket with the lighter, then headed out the door to take a walk.

When she passed Candace's office, she was surprised to see the light on and the door ajar. She could hear the sound of female voices. She pushed the door slightly and looked at the desk, but Candace's chair was empty. Then she opened the door wider and looked on the floor. Candace was there, wearing a powder-blue tailored suit, her long legs folded beside her, her bare feet resting on the dingy carpet. Beside her was Sheila McDonough, wearing a flowered dress with a Peter Pan collar and holding a blue metal Thermos. Little Sampson was there, too, in a matching shirt-and-pants set covered with sea turtles and small birds. He was stacking some wooden alphabet blocks into a wobbly tower.

"Sampson, can you show me an S?" Candace said. "S for Sampson! S for smart!"

"S for species," Sheila added. "Endangered species. Like the ones on your outfit."

Sampson looked at her quizzically, picked up a block, and chucked it against his head.

"No, that's a T," Sheila said. Maisy cleared her throat.

"Maisy!" Candace said cheerily. "Good morning! Come in!"

Maisy stepped inside tentatively. "Nice to see you again, Sheila," she said. "I hadn't expected you back here so soon."

"I e-mailed Candace this morning," Sheila said. "I hope you don't mind. I had something I wanted to share with her."

"She had a brilliant idea, if you ask me!" Candace said, lifting a small disposable paper cup from the coffee table beside her. "Here, Maisy, pour yourself a cup. You look like you could use some morning sustenance."

"I already gassed up, thanks," Maisy said.

"Oh, it's not coffee," Candace said. "It's a banana smoothie. It's *extremely* healthy."

"Treat yourself," Sheila said. "You'll be glad you did."

Maisy picked up the Thermos and poured some yellowish liquid into one of the cups. She took a large sip. It was thin and sweet.

"Pretty good," she said. "Your own recipe?" She took another sip.

"Not just my own recipe," Sheila said proudly. "My own ingredient. It's made with breastmilk!"

Maisy spit the liquid back into her cup.

"Maisy!" Candace said. "It's all natural!"

"I had so much stored milk in my freezer," Sheila said. "I've always been very productive. But it only lasts so long, and I didn't want it to go to waste."

"Forget about cream-filled doughnuts," Candace said. "Let's hand this out at South Station!"

"Absolutely not," Maisy said. "And for the love of God, don't let any newspaper reporters see this."

"Let any newspaper reporters see what?" Chip had poked his head in the door.

"Chipper!" Candace said.

"Chipper?" Maisy said. "You're calling him Chipper?" To Chip, she said, "You'd better not have that goddamned Herald reporter with you."

Sheila gasped and threw her hands over Sampson's ears.

"I'm sorry," Maisy said with a sigh. "That unpleasant Herald reporter."

"McFeeney's not here," Chip said. "And I have some good news."

"Well, then, come in and have a drink," Candace said.

"Do *not* drink anything," Maisy said. "That's an order. You will thank me for it, I promise."

"Um, OK," Chip said. "So, anyway, I just got off the phone with the booking manager of the 'Polly Park Show.' They're going on the road for a week, and on Thursday, they're taping in Boston. They were planning to have on some witches from Salem to talk about voodoo dolls. Now, they're switching gears because of this whole breastfeeding thing. And they want Candace."

"You pitched the 'Polly Park Show'?" Maisy said. "Chipper, I think I underestimated you."

"Well, um, they called me," Chip said. "They're having Ron Winkle on, too. And Claire Langoon. But I told them 'yes' right away."

"Claire Langoon? Crap," Maisy said.

"Language!" Sheila said, lunging toward Sampson again. The toddler began to cry and pull at the top of Sheila's dress. "Nummers," he said. "Nummers *now*."

"We'll have to send a supporter on with Candace," Maisy said.

"I'll do it!" Sheila said as Sampson clawed at her collar, whining wordlessly. "Sampson, hold on, honey. Give Mommy a chance to set up."

"No BOOBs," Maisy said quickly. Sheila looked up with a shocked expression.

"I think we should get Lauren Bruce to come on," Maisy continued. "She can tell her story in first person. It will be dramatic. And sensitive. And she'll make Claire Langoon look mean."

"Is Lauren Bruce committed to the cause?" Sheila said. "I didn't even see her here last night," She had unbuttoned the top of her dress and was starting to fiddle with her nursing bra.

Maisy turned away so that she wouldn't see anything more. "She's as committed as she needs to be," she said. "Now, if you'll excuse me, I'm expecting a call. Enjoy your drinks. All y'all."

DOWN ON WASHINGTON STREET at last, Maisy sucked on a cigarette, then another, watching the people walking by in Downtown Crossing. This section of the city sat in the shadow of historic Boston—steps from the State House, the Old South Church and the site of the Boston Massacre, which was occupied now by an unmarked traffic island. It was a busy shopping district, but also a perpetual disappointment, filled with discount shoe stores, drugstores, and teen-oriented sportswear shops. The passers-by didn't dawdle or browse; they all seemed to have clear destinations. Some were dressed in work clothes and headed to early lunches, taking swift, productive strides. Some were teenagers whose sagging pants threatened to expose their nether regions. They pouted under sunglasses and baseball caps, not appearing to enjoy their freedom.

Dotted among them were mothers pushing babies, struggling to lift their heavy strollers over curbs or squeeze them through storefront doors. They looked purposeful, these women, and slightly voluptuous. *Chest in the air,* Maisy thought to herself.

"Maisy Street?" said a voice beside her. Maisy spun around to see a tall, heavyset woman. She had an apple-round face, wire-rimmed glasses, and brown hair. She looked serious, intense, and slightly out of breath.

"Jean Thompson," Maisy said, looking into the eyes of the woman who might—might—have resurrected her campaign. "It's nice to finally meet you. What brings you to beautiful Downtown Crossing?"

"Actually, I came to see you," Jean said. "I hoped you might have a few minutes to talk."

Maisy glanced down at her watch. "I have a call to take in 45 minutes," she said. Over Jean's shoulder, she spied a woman struggling to fit a double stroller into the revolving door of Macy's. "Do you want to grab a cup of coffee? All I had this morning was the office swill, and I could use a dose of Starbucks to get me through the day."

"I'd like that," Jean said.

They walked silently down the street, past a homeless man sitting on a corner surrounded by shopping bags and piles of books. Jean reached into her pocket, pulled out some change, and dropped it into his cup. "There you go," she said, looking him in the eyes.

"God bless you and your children and your children's children," he said. Maisy and Jean kept walking.

"I spotted you at the MOMs rally," Jean said. "You were hiding behind a tree."

"Busted," Maisy said. "So to speak."

"What did you think of the event?"

"It wasn't quite what I expected," Maisy said.

"Me neither," Jean said. "That's why I came by."

They reached the Starbucks and pushed in the door. "I have a confession to make," Jean said as they neared the counter. "I feel bad about saying it. I usually don't feel so strongly about things like this. But I'm developing some kind of deep-seated hatred for Claire Langoon."

"Hatred can be a very productive emotion," Maisy said. "Extra-large dark roast," she told the barista, a wispy young man with faint stubble on his upper lip. She refused to use the word "Venti" or any other retail terminology.

"A tall Chai," Jean told the man, reaching into her pocket. "It's on me."

Maisy didn't protest; her wallet was back at her desk. She grabbed her coffee from the counter as Jean paid, then headed to a table in a corner, as far from the entrance as she could get.

"I don't generally hate people," Jean said when she had settled into the seat across from Maisy. "It's a principle of mine. Even politicians. For all the activism I used to do, I never hated anyone. Not even Nixon. I pitied him, but I didn't hate him. I see people getting so angry, and I've never understood it. Especially now, with the Internet. So many people, riled up, all the time. It's like there's something new afoot, this viciousness I've never seen before."

"People have always been this angry," Maisy said. "Human nature has a mean streak. It's just that now, everyone can share it on Twitter."

"It's a dangerous game," Jean said. "It gets ugly. Did you know that someone wants to burn me in effigy?"

"You're kidding," Maisy said.

"I read it on a blog," Jean said. "A woman proposed a midnight rally to exorcise the anti-breastfeeding demons."

"People take breastfeeding pretty seriously around here."

"So do I," Jean said. "Breastfeeding used to be my life. I held meetings in my living room to teach women how to do it. I led training sessions for maternity ward nurses. I wrote to toy companies, asking them not to sell bottles for baby dolls. That's what scares me so much about Claire Langoon. She's sending the same message we were trying to fight 20 years ago. She's trying to erase our progress."

"She's a good messenger, I've got to hand it to her," Maisy said. "She gives great quotes."

"She's a demagogue," Jean said. "Mussolini with a baby bottle. She's picking up followers. And you're the only people who can stop her."

"What about Stuart Winkle? I thought you were his mascot."

"Stuart Winkle chose me," Jean said. "I didn't choose him. I can do what I want. And if he's bringing people to Claire Langoon, he has to be stopped."

"Look," Maisy said. "You know I've got no dog in this hunt. I might have the BOOBs on board, but I don't care about breastfeeding, one way or another. I'm just in it to beat Stuart Winkle."

"I know," Jean said. "I'm not naïve. But I still want to help."

CHAPTER 13

THE DAY AFTER her late-night tryst with Rob—an act that had done good things for her marriage, but bad things for her daytime state of consciousness—Lauren decided she was getting a new message from her breast pump. *"Booty call,"* it said. *"Booty call. Booty call."* No matter how much Lauren changed the speed, the low, deep voice still sounded basically the same. Lauren couldn't tell if the pump was trying to register approval, jealousy, or grumpy resignation.

When the telephone rang, she ignored it and kept pumping. A few minutes later, it rang again, then again, and her cell-phone jingled on the coffee table. Lauren finally turned off the pump, deposited six ounces of milk into a freezer bag, and went to the bedroom to retrieve the cordless phone. She glanced at the bed, unmade and still rumpled from last night's adventure. She smiled, then picked up the receiver.

The caller ID showed one call from Mia and two from the Calloway campaign. Lauren dialed Mia first.

"Thank God, it's you," Mia said. "Get dressed. We have to get to a mothers' group at 11. But I need to come over and show you something first." Her voice quavered slightly.

"What's wrong?" Lauren said. "Did you read another study?"

"I'll be there soon," Mia said. "It's something you have to see."

The doorbell rang fifteen minutes later; Mia had arrived in record speed. She looked deeply serious as she waited on the porch, holding Lyle, whose onesie said, "Room Service, Please." Lyle stared into the distance and cooed in long, luxurious phrases, as if he were singing in a language all his own. "Aaaaah," he said. "Aaaaah, aahhhh."

"Hi, Lyle," Lauren said sweetly, tickling his belly. "Are you OK? Are you still illiterate?"

Mia cracked a wan smile. "I need your changing table," she said, brushing past Lauren and making a beeline to Rory's bedroom. She lay Lyle onto the pink terrycloth changing pad, unsnapped his onesie, and took off his diaper. Lyle's small right hand moved immediately to his penis, a circumcised stem that looked sturdy and squat, like a tiny pink stalk of asparagus. Lyle took hold of it, grinned toothlessly, and started to squeeze. Lauren and Mia stared at him, speechless.

"Wow," Lauren finally said. "It starts early."

"He did it for the first time in the bath last night," Mia said. "It was like he had discovered fire. Now, every time I take his diaper off, his hand goes right there. He can't seem to stop himself."

Lyle was still smiling. His hand kept squeezing and unsqueezing, leaving a bright red mark on his little scrotum.

"I guess now we know he's right-handed," Lauren said.

"This is serious!" Mia said. "I'm afraid he's going to hurt himself. Plus, I'm representing the campaign here. I'm trying to be dignified. I can't show up to a new mother's group with a masturbating baby."

"I don't think anyone is going to blame you," Lauren said. "Most of these women have husbands, right? It's not like they don't know this happens."

"What is it with the males of this species?" Mia cried. "Why is everything always about sex?!"

"It's evolutionary," Lauren said. "So we can have these babies." Her cellphone rang again. She ignored it.

"So," she said to Mia, her eyes still on Lyle. "Where are we going today?"

"A breastfeeding drop-in group in Weymouth," Mia said. "And we've got a new message. We're not supposed to talk about nutrition so much. Now, we're supposed to say that breastfeeding in public makes women proud. We're supposed to say, 'Chest in the Air.'"

"'Chest in the Air?'" Lauren repeated. "That's our slogan?"

"It's a statement of confidence," Mia said.

"I see," Lauren said. "I think maybe I'd feel more confident if I weren't wearing sweatpants."

She changed into the roomiest skirt she could find and loaded Rory's car seat into the back of Mia's Volvo, next to Lyle's. As they wound through Jamaica Plain toward Mattapan, passing a mix of regentrified blocks and gritty urban stretches, they stared at the political signs that filled the storefront windows.

Loyalties seemed equally divided between Calloway and Winkle, with Calloway dominating the secondhand clothing boutiques and fair-trade coffeehouses, Winkle taking the convenience stores and doughnut shops. Some of Winkle's signs bore his campaign logo, his name in crimson letters beside the slogan, "Vote Smart." But there were also some new ones, with purple cursive lettering on a baby-blue background. "Women for Winkle," they said. "Break These Chains."

Chests. Chains. Lauren was already tired of metaphors. She pulled out her cellphone and called up her voicemail, hoping for a distraction from the campaign; maybe her mother had called to share some family gossip, or Rob had dialed urgently to tell her he'd made partner. But no. It was Chip Osterville, and he had left three messages.

The first was, "Lauren! I've got great news! Please call me right away." The second was, "Lauren? It's Chip again. I have something exciting to share with you!" The third was, "Lauren, Chip. Please call me back. Please." She called the campaign switchboard and asked to speak to him.

"Lauren! You're alive!" he said.

"I am," Lauren said. "So far."

"So," Chip said, "Have you ever seen the 'Polly Park Show'?"

"I have," Lauren said, thinking about the oversexed pregnant women.

"Great," Chip said. "Guess what? On Thursday, you are going to be *on* it."

"What do you mean?" Lauren said, alarmed.

"She's broadcasting from Boston," Chip said. "She's doing a whole show about the campaign. And she wants you on with Senator Calloway, to talk about the whole...you know. Thing."

"Oh," Lauren said. "Oh, my."

"What?" said Mia. "What is it?'

"Polly Park," Lauren whispered.

"What about her?"

"They want me to go on 'Polly Park,'" she whispered.

"You?" Mia said.

"Me?" Lauren asked Chip. "Are you sure they want me?"

"Yes, definitely you," Chip said.

Lauren sighed. "Can I get back to you on that?" She promised to call Chip after the breastfeeding class.

"That's interesting," Mia said slowly after Lauren hung up, "that the campaign would still choose you for the 'Polly Park Show.' I mean, you're a wonderful spokesperson and everything, but I really thought the campaign had moved onto other messages. That we aren't supposed to be victims anymore."

"You think I'm a victim?" Lauren said. Then she let out a gasp.

They had approached the intersection of Blue Hill Avenue and Morton Street, where, towering above the convenience stores and delis, Rory's face covered the bulk of a giant billboard. Her blue eyes were open wide, her mouth puckered into a perfect "O." A string of white Fluff was stretched across her upper lip. Her eyebrows were raised slightly, as if to say, "Are you sure you did the right thing here, Mommy?"

"She's a star," Mia said matter-of-factly. "A victim, but a star."

"She's pretty cute," Lauren said. She glanced at the cars idling beside her to see if anyone was looking at the sign. That's when she spotted something pink, moving amid the traffic. "Oh!" she exclaimed. "Oh, my."

Mia spotted it, too. "Oh my God," she said. "Who is that?"

"That," Lauren said, "is Blue Hill Mel."

She'd been to this intersection many times before on the way to visit Rob's great-aunt in Milton, so she recognized the panhandler slowly making his way through the intersection. He was here every day regardless of the weather, weaving awkwardly from car to car. One of his hands was locked to his side, the apparent consequence of an old war wound. His beard was perpetually scruffy, his hair unkempt. But his face always looked serene, as if the act of passing cars fed something deep in his soul. It was clear that someone looked after him, since he wore a warm coat in the wintertime and a slicker on rainy days. Today, he was wearing jeans and a T-shirt—and over his shirt, a massive, cotton-candy pink "Calloway for Governor" bra.

Lauren and Mia stared at him wordlessly until the light changed.

"Well," Mia said when they started moving again. "Better that he's with us than against us."

"True," Lauren said. "I guess everyone's taking sides."

A HALF-HOUR LATER, they had turned onto an industrial road in the coastal suburb of Weymouth. They passed aging strip malls, industrial parks, and a decaying former Navy yard before they reached a tan building set far back from the road. A giant inflatable pacifier was tethered to the roof, and swayed gently in the breeze. The sign out front read, "Babies 'n Stuff: Your New Maternity Superstore." The parking lot was vast, and it was packed.

"It's the latest wave in maternity retail," Mia said, as she pulled into a space in a far corner of the lot. "They carry everything you need for your baby, and they offer classes, too. It's one-stop shopping!"

"With an emphasis on the shopping, I'm sure," Lauren said. She and Mia unhooked their infant car seats, with Rory and Lyle asleep inside. Mia hoisted a tote bag full of bras and campaign literature over her shoulder. They limped toward the building with their heavy loads.

Inside, a gentle instrumental version of "Polly Wolly Doodle" wafted through the loudspeakers. Behind a glass wall, some women were taking a prenatal yoga class, doing the downward dog with bellies bulging toward the ground. In one corner was a jumble of parked strollers, most with titanium frames and egg-shaped seats that looked ready to blast into orbit. In front of them were rows and rows of merchandise, in aisles that seemed to stretch on forever, perhaps to the sea.

Mia headed straight to a Customer Service sign. "We're here for the breastfeeding drop-in group," she told the clerk.

"Door 3A, right-hand side," the clerk said, without looking up from a teetering pile of receiving blankets.

Lauren and Mia trudged across the store, past a display of leather upholstered bouncy chairs, a car-sized model of Thomas the Tank Engine, and a towering plush Dora the Explorer. They wove through a labyrinth of bath and potty-training paraphernalia, turned right at a floor-to-ceiling display of diaper-rash ointment, and finally reached the opposite wall. They walked past several doors before they came across one marked "3A." A piece of paper, taped to the front, said "Lactation Support."

From outside, they could hear the buzz of conversation and the high-pitched hum of infant whimpering. When they pushed the door open, the noise was overwhelming. The windowless room, roughly ten feet square, was filled wall-to-wall with women and their babies. Some of the women were in the act of nursing. Others were hovering over diapers or bouncing infants in their arms. They wore trendier clothes than the BOOBs, and more makeup, and they didn't look nearly as blissful. They looked exhausted, like the women in Lauren's original breastfeeding class.

A woman with close-cropped white hair was scurrying among them, peering down at babies and breasts. "Looking good, Charlotte!" she said to one woman, before turning to the next. "Do you need me to show you the football hold *again?*"

Mia cleared her throat. No one seemed to notice. "Excuse me?" she said, in her normal speaking voice. Then she tried a little louder. Then she shouted, "HELLO?"

The room got marginally quieter and the white-haired woman looked up. "Can I help you?" she said.

"We're here from the Candace Calloway campaign,' Mia said. "We wanted to—"

"Oh, yes," the woman said. "They said you were coming. Just go ahead and tell the girls whatever you'd like." She returned her attention to the breast nearest her face.

"OK then," Mia said, setting Lyle's car seat on the floor. "Hello, everyone! I am Mia Hastings Hoberman, and I would like to tell you about how confident I feel when I'm nursing my child! We have a little saying around the Calloway campaign: 'Chest in the Air.' Senator Calloway knows how proud we all feel about our bodies and our..."

She trailed off. It was quite apparent that no one was listening. The women were either focused on their babies or locked in quiet conversation. Lauren could hear snippets if she strained her ears.

"...and he has the most terrible gas."

"Maybe it's the broccoli."

"No, Calvin, you can't eat yet. Your next feeding isn't till noon."

Lauren turned to Mia. "They're in no state for a speech," she said. "Why don't we just pass around the bras and let them think about it at home?"

"Fine," Mia said. "Or maybe they'll focus if we get them one-on-one." She dug into her bag for a stack of brochures and a handful of Calloway bras and started working her way through one side of the room. Lauren took the other side, quietly placing pamphlets and bras on top of diaper bags, smiling at anyone who looked at her strangely.

Eventually, she made her way to a woman whose shirt was completely off. A thin strand of translucent tubing was strung up her chest, over her shoulder, and down one breast, and attached to her nipple with surgical tape. The woman was Caucasian and held an Asian baby, whose lips she was trying to force near her breast.

"Here's some information for you, and a souvenir," Lauren said, setting down a pamphlet and a bra.

"Thanks," said the woman, looking up from her breast. "Sorry for the display."

"You definitely don't have to apologize to me," Lauren said with a laugh.

The woman looked at her more closely. "Wait…I know you," she said. "Are you the woman who fed your baby in the museum?"

"I am," Lauren said, feeling a little embarrassed to be recognized. "I'm Lauren. Nice to meet you."

"Oh my God!" the woman said, her eyes lighting up. "It's you! I want to thank you! You're the reason I'm doing all this."

"What is all this?" Lauren asked, looking at the pile of tubing on the floor.

"It's an adoptive mothers' breastfeeding kit," the woman said. "Chloe isn't my biological child, obviously. But this way, we get to bond, at least, and she gets human milk."

"That's not formula?" Lauren asked, glancing at the bag.

"Oh, God, no," the woman said.

"Where did you get it?" Lauren asked.

"Black market," the woman said.

"You're kidding."

"Believe me, if they sold it at Stop 'n Shop, I'd buy it there," the woman said. "But you can find it on Craigslist, if you know the code words."

"Wow," Lauren said. "You're really dedicated."

"No, *you're* really dedicated. You're my inspiration, too," said another woman nearby. She had red hair and dark bags under her eyes, imperfectly covered with foundation. She looked as if she were about to cry.

"Are you OK?" Lauren said.

"I'm fine," the woman said, sniffling. "Just tired. My baby wakes up every hour to feed, all night long." She looked down sadly at a tiny redheaded baby, wrapped tightly in a yellow blanket.

"My doctor said he's having a reaction to my milk," she continued, "so I can't have any dairy or wheat. I don't even know what to eat that doesn't have dairy or wheat. But when I start feeling bad for myself, I just think about you. How brave you were. How hard that must have been. It keeps me going."

"Oh, my," Lauren said. "I mean, I'm flattered. Really. But I don't want you to suffer." She paused. "Have you thought about using formula?"

"Isn't that bad for your baby?" the woman said, looking shocked.

"Shhhh!" said the woman with the tubing, cocking her head to indicate the white-haired woman across the room. "Don't let her hear that word. She'll bite your head off."

"Have you given *your* baby formula?" the redhead asked Lauren.

"No," Lauren admitted.

"I knew you wouldn't," the redhead replied. Then she lowered her voice to a whisper. "But I have a confession to make," she said. "For a shower gift, one of my friend's mothers got me this machine. It's like one of those single-shot coffee makers, but it dispenses formula. At just the right temperature. With the press of a button. They only sell it in Sweden. It's gorgeous. And it looks so easy. And sometimes, I'm so tempted…I just don't know what to do."

Lauren didn't know what to say. On one hand, the answer

seemed obvious. Breastmilk couldn't possibly be worth this sort of trauma. On the other hand, she was here representing the Calloway campaign. She was supposed to be confident of her choices, proud of her breasts. A leader, not a victim. To recommend formula—outright, at least—would be a betrayal. Of someone.

"You need to do what feels right," said tentatively.

The redhead gave a heavy sigh. "I can tell what's right by looking at your baby over there," she said, gazing across the room at Rory, who was sleeping in her car seat. "She's so beautiful."

"And so healthy," said the woman with the tubing. "I want my baby to be just like yours."

Lauren felt a gush of pride, but it was tinged with other emotions. Doubt, for one. And guilt. No matter what she said or did, these days, there was always guilt.

CHAPTER 14

WOMEN RESPOND TO guilt. That was one of Maisy's long-held tenets, which had served her well in many a campaign. If you wanted to convince a man to do something, you flattered him, cajoled him, made him feel like the only capable person in the world. If you wanted to convince a woman to do something, you made her feel like she would be an awful person otherwise.

That was how she finally got Lauren Bruce to agree to go on the "Polly Park Show." Chip came into her office in a panic to tell her that Lauren had said no, and maybe they should call Sheila McDonough after all. But Maisy wasn't about to give up so easily. The show was another one of those campaign gifts, a way to reach the stay-at-home mothers who paid no attention to the news, the hipsters who watched the show late at night off their DVRs with a glass of wine, the pop-culture junkies who caught up with the buzz via YouTube clips. Women loved to watch Polly Park talking about breasts. And they needed to see her talking about Lauren's breasts, not Sheila's.

"Stay in the room here, Chipper," Maisy told Chip as she dialed Lauren's cellphone. "Observe."

Lauren answered the phone on the second ring. "I'm sorry, Chip. I just can't do it," she said, without saying "Hello."

"It's Maisy Street here, Lauren," Maisy said. "And here's the thing: You *can.*"

"That's nice of you to say," Lauren said. "I mean, Polly Park. It's big. But I'm not sure I'm the best person to speak for your cause. Maybe you should ask Mia. Or someone else who's more of a true believer."

"The BOOBs," Maisy replied. "You're talking about the BOOBs. And God bless those BOOBs. But you've got it exactly wrong. We need someone who's *not* a true believer. Or, I should say, that's what other women need."

"What do you mean?" Lauren asked.

"I mean, you should think about the mothers out there who are just like you," Maisy said. "They've just got these babies, they're trying to live their lives, and somebody comes and tries to make them hide. And because they're not BOOBs, they might get cowed. They're not going to just whip up a boobie milkshake and throw it in somebody's face."

"A boobie milkshake?"

"Never mind," Maisy said. "The point is, you've seen the MOMs. They're mean. And maybe a little jealous that they don't have babies, too. They're going to make new mothers feel bad for breastfeeding outside, and maybe those mothers will decide to stay home and just be unfulfilled. Unless...unless they see some-one like you on TV, someone they can relate to. Maybe then they'll say, 'If she can do it, I can do it. I'm not going to let those MOMs keep me indoors.' That's how progress happens, Lauren. And honestly, I thought for sure you'd want to help with that."

"I do want to help," Lauren said. "It's just that..."

"No, don't worry," Maisy said. "I understand. We'll find some-one else...I'm looking down this list..." She let out an audible sigh.

"OK," Lauren said. "OK. I'll do the 'Polly Park Show.'"

"I knew you would," Maisy said. "Because you're a real wom-an, and you know what's important."

When Maisy hung up the phone, Chip stood up and ap-plauded. "Wow," he said. "You're like my mom."

"I'm going to take that as a compliment, Chipper," Maisy said.

The door opened slightly and Candace poked in her head.

"When am I supposed to do that fund-raising call?" she asked.

"There you are," Maisy said. "Where have you been? Jodi was looking for you all morning. She kept trying your cell."

"I've been in my office," Candace said. "Working."

"Working on what?" Maisy said.

"Research." Candace glanced over at Chip and looked at him curiously. "Hi, Chipper," she said. "You look good today. That's a very nice shirt."

Chip was wearing a cotton, plaid button-down shirt that looked almost identical to the shirt he wore every day.

"Thank you, Senator," Chip said, blushing a little bit.

"I've been wanting to buy a shirt like that for my nephew," Candace said. "Could you stop by my office when you get a chance? Tell me where you got it?"

"I got it at the Gap," Chip said, looking confused.

"Very interesting," Candace said. "I'd love to know more." She disappeared.

"That was weird," Chip said.

"Sure was, Chipper," Maisy replied, replaying Candace's behavior from the past two days. When she made phone calls to potential donors, she asked them detailed questions about their kids. When she chatted up voters in restaurants, she lingered near the babies and toddlers. She had a strange, obsessive glint in her eye that reminded Maisy of a senatorial candidate in Kentucky, a few years back. Running on the fumes of a midlife crisis, he had refused to trim his beard midway through the campaign. Then he had started showing up at open mikes with an electric guitar and playing psychedelic versions of "Starry, Starry Night." The campaign had not ended well.

This time, Maisy resolved to watch Candace as closely as she could. So at the end of the day, she was keenly aware when Candace strode past her office door in a different outfit than she had worn to work: a low-cut sweater and skin-tight jeans that fit her contours perfectly, even if they were intended for a woman ten years younger. The senator walked with resolve toward the ladies' room, clicking down the hallway in high-heeled boots. Something about her gait made Maisy realize that tonight, she would be going undercover again.

Maisy positioned herself just inside her office doorway so she could spy on Candace, unnoticed. She watched the senator strut back from the bathroom, stop back into her office for her tailored hound's-tooth coat, and head toward the front door. Maisy grabbed her own jacket, a North Carolina-bought windbreaker that was a little too thin for the New England nighttime air, and counted to ten. Then she followed Candace's path, waving goodbye to the Rachel/Rebecca/Robin at the front desk and heading for the stairs. At the bottom of three flights, already short of breath, she caught a glimpse of Candace leaving the building and stepping into the cool air on Washington Street.

Candace turned right and headed toward the Theater District. Maisy kept an eye on the hound's-tooth coat as she dodged a set of loud teenagers in Red Sox caps, play-fighting in the sidewalk. She wove her way around the people headed toward the T: business types in leather jackets, state bureaucrats in utilitarian trench coats. Ahead of her, the hound's-tooth coat moved ahead swiftly, with purpose, then hung a sharp right on Temple Place. Maisy followed, rounding the corner just quickly enough to spy Candace pushing through the door of a restaurant and bar. The name on the doorplate was "Ennui."

Maisy counted to ten again and watched a group of twentysomething women enter the bar. They had identical straight blonde bobs, and wore similar pea coats in varying shades of beige. Maisy followed them inside and blinked a few times. Ennui was nothing like the restaurants in Asheville, and nothing like the grimy political-insider bars that she tended to frequent on mid-campaign nights. It was as if a bomb labeled "baroque" had exploded and left its debris scattered randomly. The walls were covered with textured silver paper, elaborate sconces, and strips of mirror. The bar was topped with marble. Ornate crystal chandeliers of varying lengths hung from the ceiling. In the middle of the room was a huge cylinder draped with brocaded fabric, with a tent-like opening through which a patron occasionally entered or exited. Maisy stared at it, confused.

"What is that?" she asked a waitress brushing by.

"It used to be a hookah bar," the waitress said. "But the fire inspector shut it down. Now, people use it to send videos from their phones."

Maisy sighed and scanned the room, looking for the hound's-tooth coat or some glimpse of Candace's flowing hair. She hoped the light was dim enough that the senator wouldn't be recognized—or that the bar-goers were young and vapid enough that none of them followed politics. She saw the blondes in pea coats eyeing a group of men, their ties loosened and their hair slicked back as they sneered over highball glasses. Maisy figured they were financial services workers; they had that money-loving look. She tried to make out what they were saying, but trance music was playing too loudly in the background. The drum machines made a steady rhythmic ticking sound, *TOO-too-too-too-TOO-too-too-too.*

At last, to one side, near a shiny silver wall, Maisy spotted the back of Candace. She had taken off her hound's-tooth coat and was standing in front of a man. Maisy couldn't make out his face; Candace was tall as he was in her stiletto heels, and her hair had enough volume to block his head completely. His back was against a wall, and he held a bottle of Sam Adams in his right hand.

Maisy didn't want to venture any closer, for fear of being detected. So she found an empty table with a clear view of the wall, and hid behind a fancy metal picture frame. The frame, it turned out, held the cocktail menu. The signature mixed drinks, mostly concoctions made from vodka and absinthe, had names like "The

Middle Manager," "The Bad Hair Day," and "The Tax Return."

Maisy looked back up at Candace, who had cornered the man gracefully and deliberately, the way a cat surrounds a bug and prepares to bat it with her paws. She was talking emphatically, waving her hands to make some sort of point. The man still clutched his beer in one hand and held the other hand limply at his side.

"Drink?" said a voice in Maisy's right ear. She turned to see a waitress with a harried expression.

"I'll take a Miller Lite," Maisy said, annoyed that her concentration had been broken.

"We don't carry Miller Lite," the waitress said condescendingly.

"Of course you don't," Maisy said. "Why don't you bring me whatever beer you have that tastes the most like piss."

The waitress sniffed and spun away. Maisy turned back to Candace, who had placed her hands on the man's shoulders and was swaying back and forth, matching the rhythm of the *too-too-TOOs*, trying to coax him into dancing. She shook her head suggestively, her thick blonde hair cascading like a horse's mane. The man placed his hands between Candace's shoulder blades, then slowly moved them downward, to the middle of her back, the small of her back, and finally to her rear end. He held them there a moment, hesitating, then gave Candace's butt a tentative pat.

Maisy shifted to try to glimpse the man's face, knocking over the menu in its picture frame. As she struggled to set it right again, the waitress reappeared.

"I've brought you a Pilsner Urquell," she said in a haughty monotone. "It's light."

Maisy pulled a ten-dollar bill from her wallet. "Thanks," she said. "Keep the change."

"The beer costs $12," the waitress said without moving her arm. Maisy withdrew her ten and dug into her wallet for a twenty. "Keep this, too," she said. "You can buy yourself a six-pack of Bud."

When she returned her attention to Candace, she saw that the pair was dancing close, bodies pressed against each other, slowly revolving as one. As they turned, Maisy could finally make out the man's face. It wasn't a man, it turned out. At least, not in Maisy's book. It was a boy. It was Chip.

Maisy tried to duck further behind the picture frame. But Chip wasn't looking around the bar. As he spun around again and again, his eyes shifted down Candace's body, then back up, then down again. He appeared to be in a trancelike state, his face a mix of lust and abject terror.

MAISY BARELY SLEPT that night, wondering where Candace had taken Chip. Despite her best intentions, she had lost them at the bar; the waitress had come to ask if she wanted another drink, and by the time Maisy had looked back up, Chip and Candace were gone. She had wandered up and down the short blocks between Tremont and Washington streets, to no avail. Now, lying in bed, she tried in vain to come up with a theory that didn't involve anyone getting undressed. By 3 a.m., she decided to just ask Candace directly what had happened. By 4, she realized that she couldn't tell Candace she had followed her. By 6, she had come up with a scheme.

At campaign headquarters later that morning, she told the Rachel/Rebecca/Robin to buzz her when Candace had arrived. When she got the buzz, she let five minutes pass, then went into Candace's office and closed the door.

"What were you doing with Chip last night?" she demanded.

Candace looked up from her laptop, stunned. "He didn't talk to you, did he? He promised. The little snitch."

"He hasn't said a word, and he'd better not," Maisy said. "One of the interns asked me about it. She said she saw you together dancing at some bar. Entrail, or something."

"Ennui," Candace said. "In the Ladder District."

"Candace, what were you doing?" Maisy said.

"Seducing Chip," Candace said, matter-of-factly.

"Why?" Maisy said. "Are you insane?"

"Because he has something I need," Candace said. "Sperm."

"Oh, God," Maisy said.

"I've been doing research," Candace said. "Yesterday afternoon, I talked to a sperm bank. I was all set to go in and look through their catalogue, check for family history and education. And then I thought, 'Why should I spend all this money when I have a perfect specimen right here?' Chipper is smart. He comes from a good family. He's tall and he has good hair. And since I'm ovulating right now, I figured I should act fast."

"Candace," Maisy said. "Tell me you didn't."

"He's a 24-year-old boy," Candace said. "Of course I did. It didn't take a lot of time."

"Where?" Maisy said, looking down at Candace's couch in horror. "You didn't bring him back here, did you?"

"I got a hotel room," Candace said, as if Maisy were an idiot. "They have beautiful sheets at the Ritz. And I have to tell you, it was fleeting, but it was amazingly erotic. I felt self-actualized, you know, just truly in the moment, knowing I was using my body to create another life!"

"OK," Maisy said, conscious of her breathing and her efforts to stay calm. "Let's talk about the lives we've already got here. The lives that would like to win this campaign. You realize what's going to happen now. Chip is going to tell every frat boy he knows what just happened."

"No, he won't," Candace said confidently.

"And his parents. He'll tell his parents," Maisy said. "Shit, Candace, you *know* his parents. They're huge fund-raisers."

"Another example of his fine genetics," Candace said. "They have money and the right politics. I think all of his grandparents are alive, too. But don't worry. I know he won't tell a soul."

"What makes you so sure?" Maisy said.

"Let's just say that I now know some fairly embarrassing details about him, which I have threatened to share if he ever goes public. He has this incredibly tiny little…"

"Stop right there," Maisy said. She rubbed her temple. "What are you going to tell him if you actually get pregnant? What are you going to tell everyone?"

"Obviously, I thought of that," Candace said. "Chip will never know it was him. I told him I was on the pill. I'm going to say I froze John's sperm. It's perfect, isn't it?"

"It is far from perfect," Maisy said. "It is extremely imperfect. It's a lawsuit waiting to happen. It's bad karma. It's bad family planning. It's bad campaigning. You can't do this, Candace. I forbid you to lay another hand on that boy."

Candace looked back at her laptop. "Ah, well," she said, addressing the computer more than she did Maisy. "I have other options."

CHAPTER 15

MAISY BARELY SLEPT again that night. Her mind kept drifting from Chip to Chip's parents to Chip's frat-boy friends to what Candace might have meant by her "other options." She pulled herself out of bed at 5:30, smoked three cigarettes, took a shower, then got dressed. She had said she would get to headquarters at 7 to meet Lauren, Rory, and Christopher, who were getting ready for the "Polly Park Show."

When she arrived, the rest of them were already there, using Maisy's office as a dressing room. Christopher used a curling iron to arrange Lauren's hair in a loose helmet of tousled cork-screws. He applied the tiniest amount of rouge to Rory's cheeks. He had instructed Lauren to bring three outfits, and he mixed and matched from her choices, dressing her in a scoop-necked pink maternity shirt, a black skirt with an elastic waist, and a pair of kitten-heeled pumps. Around her neck, he arranged a blue and green scarf he had brought himself. Then he dug into his bag and produced a pair of plastic-framed glasses.

"I don't wear glasses," Lauren said.

"Oh, honey, that doesn't matter," Christopher said. "These have clear lenses. They're just for show. But they'll make you look sexy and smart. Plus, they're going *on top* of your head."

Maisy watched the proceedings as she leaned against the wall, waiting for Candace to make her grand entrance. Ten minutes after Candace said she would arrive, she could hear the sound of heels click-click-clicking down the hall. Candace appeared in the doorway wearing a shiny silver dress and a pair of high-heeled leopard-skin pumps. "I'm thinking an up-do, Christopher," she said, without saying hello.

"Brilliant! I'll get the hairpins," Christopher said, reaching into his bag.

Maisy looked at Candace carefully. She was glowing, as she usually did, but without the airy look of post-coital bliss she had exhibited the day before. "Is there anything I need to know about last night?" Maisy asked, looking intently into Candace's eyes.

"I went to bed early last night, Maisy," Candace said, matching her gaze. "I wanted to be rested for the show."

"Good," Maisy said. "That sounds wise. So. While I have your attention, let's go over some talking points."

"Oh, I know what to say," Candace said. "I'm proud of being a woman, blah, blah, blah, our bodies, ourselves, 'Chest in the Air.'"

"Well, yes, pretty much," Maisy said. "But I've printed out a cheat sheet for both of you, with complete sentences." She grabbed two pieces of paper from her desk, handed one to Candace, and placed the other beside Lauren, who was kneeling on the floor, fitting Rory into a baby-sized sundress covered in light blue flowers.

The paper had a list of words—PRIDE, WOMANHOOD, BEAUTY—followed by a list of helpful sentences. *If a mother has to hide, how will her child learn to be brave? I'll never be ashamed of feeding my child. I'm proud of what my body can do. I've got my chest in the air.*

"Remember," Maisy said, "our goal here is to make the MOMs look like self-haters. You're the real women at the table here. We want those MOMs to start to question their femininity."

That last idea had come from Jean Thompson, whom Maisy had met, the night before, in a decidedly non-baroque bar not far from Maisy's corporate apartment. The two had sat in a faraway corner, where Jean had told stories about her activism days and Maisy had regaled her with tales from the political trenches. When they finally got around to talking about the campaign, Jean had talked earnestly about how women should feel about themselves, about biology as destiny and the body meeting the mind.

Maisy had listened for a time, but soon began to focus instead on the nature of Jean's voice, the gentle sway of her body as she spoke. Jean wasn't feminine the way Candace was, flamboyantly aimed at men's fantasies, but she was sensual in her way, her low voice rolling across the table and down to the floor, unfolding like a warm, soft blanket. Her breasts were large and bountiful, maternal, a bosom. Maisy imagined they were warm to the touch.

"Maisy?" Candace was asking. "Hellooooo?"

"Sorry," Maisy said, looking up from her reverie.

"So what do you think?" Candace said. "About my line?"

"Oh—it's fine," Maisy said. "So long as it's not about getting pregnant, it's fine. And I mean it, Candace. No pregnancy talk." Just then her phone rang. It was the limo driver from the "Polly Park Show," ready to take them the roughly four blocks to the show.

POLLY PARK WAS TAPING her Boston show in Faneuil Hall, a grand, gilded auditorium that dated back to Revolutionary times. Once, colonists had protested the Sugar Act here, and Sam Adams had rallied against taxation without representation. Now, it was the centerpiece of an outdoor shopping mall, its lower floors converted to a warren of small shops that sold fudge and patriot bobblehead dolls and dishtowels festooned with lobsters.

The limo pulled up to the brick plaza in front of the hall. Maisy stepped out first. A "Polly Park Show" banner hung across the building. Several satellite trucks were parked nearby. Two massive TV screens had been set up outside to simulcast the show. A sizable crowd had already gathered, the BOOBs on one side of the building, the MOMs on the other, corralled into separate pens and fenced in by police barricades.

On the Calloway side, supporters were holding new campaign posters that said, "Women for Calloway: Chest in the Air." On the Winkle side, women stood with signs that said "MOMs," "Break These Chains," "Winkle = Respect," and "Calloway = Porn." There was a fair amount of New England Harshies among them, but also some women of childbearing age, likely followers of Claire Langoon.

A few local TV stations were filming the scene. Some tourists were milling around, taking photos on their cellphones and searching in vain for someone famous. Alice Andrews, the head of the MOMs, was standing with a megaphone, leading the group in halfhearted early-morning chants of "M-O-M."

When Candace stepped out of the limo, a huge cheer went up from the Calloway side. "Chest in the aiiiiiir!" Sheila Mc-Donough yelled into a bullhorn of her own. "Senator Calloway cares about women!"

"Oh, you only care about yourselves," Alice said. By the tone, it seemed she meant to be talking under her breath, but her lips were too close to her megaphone, so her comment came out loud and clear.

"Shame!" one of the BOOBs shouted. "You have no respect for women!"

"You have no respect for boys and men!" yelled one of the MOMs.

"You have no respect for babies!" the BOOB shot back.

A few Polly Park staffers wearing headphones and access tags ushered Candace and Lauren into the building. Maisy took an ID tag from one of the assistants, but lingered outside on the Fanueil Hall steps.

"Our babies are smarter than your babies!" one of the BOOBs shouted across the barricades.

"At least our babies sleep!" someone on the MOMs side yelled back.

"You probably let them cry!" shouted a BOOB.

"You probably spoil them!" shouted a MOM.

Maisy spotted Asher Griffin on the steps a few feet away, a small, amused smile on his face. She caught his eye, nodded, and walked over to his side.

"This is definitely weirder than alligators," she said.

"I've never seen anything like it," he agreed. "And I've seen a lot. I had no idea women could be so nasty to each other."

"That's because you're not a woman," Maisy said. "Nice find in Claire Langoon, by the way."

"Gift from heaven," Asher said. "She's nasty in the most productive way. And she's sensible. Sensible sells."

"I don't know," Maisy said. "Boston has an appetite for cream-filled doughnuts, too."

"See, now you're talking more like a man," Asher said. "So. Two weeks till the primary. How are your internals looking?"

"Same as yours, I'll bet," Maisy said. "Wish you luck."

She turned away, wondering if she'd sounded as confident as she intended—or if his internal polls were as inconclusive as hers. As she headed up the steps to Faneuil Hall, the BOOBs put forth a chant of "Chest in the air!" and the MOMs filled the spaces with their own refrain: "Cover it up! Cover it up!" The two sides shouted back and forth, a sort of call-and-response. Then someone arrived with a cowbell and clanged it along to a regular beat that Maisy still could hear after she'd entered the building.

She showed her ID tag to the security guards and production staff, then advanced to the main meeting room, where a small army of young men and women wearing headphones was scurrying about, finalizing the set. A hot-pink carpeted platform had been set up on the stage, equipped with four huge armchairs upholstered in turquoise velvet. The chairs flanked what appeared to be a golden throne—presumably, the place where Polly Park would sit. A thick purple curtain, decorated with two giant pink

"P's," was strung along a silver frame on the right-hand side, hiding a makeshift backstage.

Lauren, Candace, Stuart Winkle and Claire Langoon were all in their seats, sitting patiently as production assistants fished microphones up their shirts. Winkle and Claire were chatting amiably. Candace was tapping at her BlackBerry. Lauren was gazing at Jodi, who was carrying Rory around the outskirts of the set, pointing at fancy banisters and examples of Colonial crown molding.

"Studio audience arrives in 3...2...1!" one of the production assistants shouted. A pair of double doors opened wide, and a crowd of mostly women filed in, chattering loudly as they were ushered to their seats. Most seemed to be in the core Polly Park demographic, twentysomethings who were unlikely to be either BOOBs or MOMs, and who dressed, as so many college students did, only slightly more demurely than streetwalkers.

When most of them had settled into their seats, a young woman in black, her hair pulled into a severe ponytail, strode with purpose to the center of the set. She was holding a wireless microphone, which she tapped twice before she began to bellow into it.

"Your attention please!" she yelled, her face puckered into a tight frown. The crowd grew silent. "Thank you for coming to the 'Polly Park Show.' We're going on the air in five minutes. This might be your chance to be on TV—but only if you follow our rules. Turn off your cellphones. Sit quietly. And always keep an eye on Seth."

She pointed to a wafer-thin man in wire-rimmed glasses and a black T-shirt, who held a large cardboard sign that said "APPLAUSE."

"If Polly calls on you, stand up and wait for someone to pass you a microphone," the woman continued, unsmiling. "We're on a ten-second delay, but that doesn't mean you get to talk like Polly. The censors won't be happy, and we won't be happy, and we'll ask you to leave, and the rest of your day will suck. If you're asked to talk, get to the point. Don't say hi to your mother. Don't say hi to your boyfriend. Laugh when Polly laughs. Don't ask Polly a personal question. Have fun."

She retreated to the side of the stage. Maisy found her seat in a designated row for campaign staff on the far right-hand side of the room, beyond the cameras' view. The chair on her right side was reserved for Jodi, who had carried Rory outside the room. The chair on her other side was reserved for Christopher, who was still on the set, applying powder to Candace's nose.

Maisy made eye contact with Candace, who puckered her lips into a kissy mouth and winked. Maisy had never seen her look so relaxed at a campaign-related event.

"Thirty seconds!" one of the production assistants shouted. Christopher blew Candace an air kiss and walked toward his seat. Maisy glanced at Lauren, who was staring with interest at Claire Langoon, who was still chatting with Stuart Winkle. Claire wore a grey dress with a shiny black belt and a pair of high-heeled black boots. Her glasses were authentic, and rested on her nose.

"Ten seconds!" the production assistant yelled.

"I think Stuart Winkle went to a tanning salon," Christopher whispered to Maisy as he settled into his chair. Maisy studied Winkle's face and decided that Christopher was right, as usual. Winkle did look slightly orange.

"In five…four…three…two…one!" the production assistant yelled. A male announcer's voice, low and deep, reverberated over the public address system.

"Live from Boston, it's the 'Polly Park Show'!" said the voice. Seth held up his applause sign. The announcer paused for the cheers, then continued.

"Today, Polly talks about breasts! And the politicians who love them! And, of course, she talks to you! Now, it's time to welcome the meanest mouth on the Eastern Seaboard, Miss! Polly! PARK!"

The purple curtain was pulled aside slightly. A tall, black platform heel with a large silver buckle kicked its way through the opening, followed by a long, shapely leg in red fishnet tights.

Then came the rest of Polly Park, with a tall black Pilgrim hat atop her head and a black kimono wrapped around her body. She marched to the center of the room, stared directly at the audience with a serious look, and flung open her kimono to reveal a bright red bikini top and a matching miniskirt. Seth held up his applause sign. The crowd squealed with delight.

"Yes! Ve are in Boston!" Polly yelled, dropping the kimono to the floor. Inexplicably, she spoke with an accent that Maisy guessed might have been Swedish. "Zat's right, people! Motherfucking Boston!"

Seth held up his applause sign again and the crowd cheered. "I am wearing ze colors of a lobster!" Polly continued. "And ve are here to talk about one of my favorite subjects: Breasts!"

Seth held up his sign. Applause.

"Now, I know what you pervs are thinking," Polly said, dropping the accent. "But the breasts I'm talking about here are not for the boudoir. They aren't for your men, *no, no, no,* or for your ladies, if you swing that way. These breasts are reserved for your motherfucking babies."

Sign. Applause. Maisy was fully aware of Polly Park's penchant for saying words that had to be bleeped. What she hadn't known was that, in actuality, Polly almost always said some permutation of the word "motherfucker."

Polly marched over to her throne and settled herself in, crossing her legs coquettishly and gazing into a teleprompter attached to the camera across from her. A production assistant dashed onto the stage, grabbed her crumpled kimono, and dashed off again.

"We are sitting here in the birthplace of freedom," Polly said. "So we figured, what better place to talk about whether you should be free to take off your shirt?"

Seth held up his applause sign again.

"Our guests have very different ideas about how free those boobies should be," she said. "And I can say 'boobie' on TV, right? It's just some other things I can't say!"

Some people applauded, even without prompting from Seth.

"So let's get right to it," Polly continued. "We've got ourselves two people running for governor, and two hot mamas who know a little bit about how much the babies like the boobs. First, let's talk to Lauren Bruce, who has gotten pretty famous around here for breastfeeding in the open air!"

Seth held up his sign. The audience clapped politely.

"Welcome to the show, Lauren. That scarf is just gorgeous!" Polly said. "So. You dared to lift your shirt in front of other people, right? In a museum?"

"Well, thank you. And yes," Lauren said, looking nervous. "I was at an art museum, and I had my baby with me. She was six weeks old. And she was hungry, so I sat down in a gallery to feed her. Discreetly. I had a blanket, which covered everything, and…"

"But you shouldn't have to worry about being discreet. That's the point we're trying to make," Candace chimed in.

"Well!" Polly said. "I thought I was the only broad around here who liked to interrupt. I guess that means you must be a politician! Everybody, give a big welcome to Candace Calloway, who is running for governor of Massachusetts."

Seth held up his sign. Applause.

"So, Senator," Polly went on, "if you win, I guess the ladies will be lifting their shirts all day and night. It's gonna be like motherfucking Mardi Gras around here!"

Sign. Louder applause.

"I just want women to do what they need to do with their bodies, Polly," Candace said. "And I don't want them to be ashamed."

"Well, I am not ashamed of my body," Polly said, standing up and twirling around once before settling back down in her throne. The audience cheered. "Now, I want to go right to one of our other guests here, who has a different idea about what to do," she said. "Let's welcome Claire Langoon!"

Sign. Applause. Claire smiled and waved in the direction of the camera.

"You also have a baby," Polly told her. "But you say keep the boobies in or stay home, right? So tell me: Are you ashamed of yourself?"

"Not at all," Claire said. "I just know that there's a time and a place for everything. And I think if women didn't feel all of this pressure to breastfeed all the time, day and night, then more of them would be able to admit that there are certain things they'd rather do in private."

"Now, you have your own candidate, right? Professor Stuart Winkle," Polly said, looking back at the teleprompter. "He's here with us, too!"

Sign. Applause. "Professor Winkle, you also don't think women should be breastfeeding in public, right? No boobies for you! What are you, one of those butt-and-leg men?"

"Oh, on the contrary, Polly," Winkle said, flashing a leering grin. "I like breasts very much. Very much. And I like babies, too. It's just that I'm a philosophy professor, so I'm trying to think about this philosophically. Now, imagine that you're on a boat…"

"Oh, I have seen naked boobies on boats," Polly interrupted. "I've seen that lots of times. I think those 'Girls Gone Wild' videos all have scenes on boats. And men pay good money for them, right? What about my boobies? You think they look nice?"

Polly thrust her chest in the direction of Stuart Winkle's face.

"Well, yes, Polly, they're very nice," Winkle said. He sounded so nonchalant that Maisy wondered if his female students did this to him all the time.

"You're right," Polly said matter-of-factly. "They are motherfucking nice. So what's the big deal if you see a little flash of them in a museum?"

"Well, Polly, the point is that children are in that museum," Winkle said. "They're not asking for an anatomy lesson. And they might not be ready, developmentally ready, to appreciate just how nice your breasts are."

"So we are teaching them to be embarrassed, instead," Candace declared. "We're telling our sons that women's bodies are shameful.

And, oh, what kind of message are we sending to our daughters?"

"Ooh, this is getting hot!" Polly said. "They told me you people in Boston were stiffs, but they were wrong! Now I think we're gonna go to our audience and see what they have to say."

She leaned one hand against her forehead, as if she were trying to spot a boat far off in the distance, and pointed to a college-aged girl in a skin-tight Harvard T-shirt. The woman, who had been waving her hand ferociously, now stood. Her shirt rode up, revealing an outie belly button.

"Hi, Polly," she said.

"Hi, Doll!" Polly said. "What's on your mind?"

"Well, I haven't had kids or anything yet," the girl said. She was chewing gum. "But I'm kind of confused. I mean, why would you even want to take a little baby to a museum? It's not like they can, like, appreciate the art."

"Lauren, baby, I think this one's for you!" Polly said.

Lauren blinked for a moment and adjusted her scarf. "Well, here's the thing," she said. "Having a baby is great, but it's hard. You get so caught up in the baby's needs that you sort of stop feeling like a person sometimes. So you want to go to a museum, or shopping, or whatever, to remind yourself that you're you. So you can think about something other than babies for a little while."

"Something like boobs, maybe!" Polly said with a cackle. Then she pointed to a woman a few rows further back, who wore a low-cut sweater that showed off ample cleavage. "You!" she said. "What did you want to say?"

"Hey, Polly," she said. "I have to say that I just cannot imagine lifting up my shirt in front of anyone I don't know. I think the people who do that are excavationists or something."

About half of the audience started to hoot.

"Exhibitionists?" Lauren said.

"Yeah, you heard me," the woman said.

"Well," Lauren said, "there's a difference between…"

Candace broke in again. "Yes, of course, there's a difference,"

she said. "But with all due respect, we need to start changing at-
titudes like yours. We need to stop making women think they have
anything to hide. That's why I have a message for the women of
Massachusetts and beyond. If you have breasts, if you're near breasts,
look at them! Right now! And tell whoever's next to you to look at
them, too. Look at them good and hard. Look them in the eye. And
admit that they're the most beautiful, sexy things you've ever seen."

Here, Candace stood up, faced the audience, and cupped her
hands over her breasts. "Let's stamp out oppression, ladies!" she
shouted. "Tap into the maternal powers within us. Reveal…and heal!"

Maisy thought her heart might have briefly stopped. A murmur went through the crowd. And Polly Park's face peeled back
into a big, broad smile that stretched farther and farther until
finally, she spoke.

"Girrrrlfriend, that is mo-ther-fuck-ing *hot*," she declared. As
the crowd burst into peals of glee, Candace looked around the
audience, made eye contact with Maisy, and smiled.

Maisy thought back to that morning in her office, when she
had been so distracted by her daydream about Jean that she
hadn't listened to Candace's proposed new line. This was it, she
realized. Candace, as instructed, hadn't mentioned pregnancy.
Instead, she had taken it upon herself to advocate flashing.

"On that note, we are going for a commercial!" Polly said.
"We will be back to talk about bras! And we're gonna have some
models out, so you ladies out there might want to pull your men
into the living room to see. Provided you're not the jealous types."

Hip-hop music blared into the studio as Polly stood up and
danced in a circle, sashaying her hips.

"And we're out!" a production assistant yelled.

Polly stopped dancing and disappeared through the curtain.

Maisy got up from her seat and made a beeline for Candace.
"Did you just do what I think you did?" she asked.

"We're going to make women proud of themselves all over
again. It's like a second 'Feminine Mystique!'" Candace said.

"Maisy, I can't tell you how great it feels to be a leader. I feel like it's not just me who has a higher purpose now. This whole campaign has a higher purpose!"

"Candace," Maisy said. "People are going to think your purpose is to flash the public."

"Maybe it is," Candace said cryptically. "Maybe it is."

Maisy turned to Lauren. "See if you can steer the conversation away from nudity," she said.

"I'm not sure it's possible to steer anything around here," Lauren said.

"Point taken," Maisy said. "But if she asks you a question, see if you can squeeze in a few words about wearing clothes. I'm stepping outside to get a hold of Chip. He's about to get some phone calls from reporters."

Maisy pulled out her cellphone and headed out of the studio, glancing back to see what Candace was doing now. The senator was talking animatedly to Seth, standing in his personal space, hip cocked to one side. He held his applause sign limply by his side and stared into her face.

Maisy sighed, turned again and exited the studio, pushing through the heavy doors to the auditorium, running down the steps, and emerging into sunshine so bright that it felt like it was searing her eyes. Outside, the monitors were airing commercials and the women behind the barricades were chattering like crickets. They had clearly been watching the show.

"Maisy! Maisy!" somebody yelled. It was Sheila McDonough, wearing an extra-large Calloway T-shirt over her fleece jacket and holding a handmade sign that said "BOOBs in the Air."

"Hi, Sheila," Maisy said wearily.

"Can you send Senator Calloway a message?" Sheila said. "Can you tell her we are just so proud of her?"

"I think she already knows," Maisy said.

Behind Sheila, a few women started to chant: "Reveal and heal! Reveal and heal!"

"Oh, for crying out loud," said someone on the MOMs side.

"I'm gonna do it!" said someone on the BOOBs side. "For my baby! For me! For hope! For change!" She lifted her shirt and thrust her sports bra toward the MOMs.

"You can't do that!" one of the New England Harshies yelled, pronouncing it "*cahn't.*"

"Yes, we can!" said another woman on the Calloway side, and she lifted her shirt, too. "Reveal and heal!"

"Reveal and heal!" said the woman next her. The woman beside her did the same.

One by one, the women on the Calloway side of the barricades started lifting their sweaters and jackets to expose their bras. Then one woman reached inside her T-shirt with both hands, wiggled around, and fished out her bra, waving it in the air like a rally towel from a sports game.

"Show them, sister!" shouted another Calloway fan. She lifted her shirt, too, revealing her bare breasts. She had apparently not been wearing a bra at all.

"Reveal and heal!" another woman shouted, pulling up her sweater. Both flaps of her nursing bra and been unsnapped and were hanging down to her waist, exposing two more bare nipples to the bright sunlight.

"Police!" yelled one of the MOMs. "Police! Indecent exposure!"

"Police! HELP!" yelled another MOM.

Two police officers were standing nearby, assigned to watch over the crowd. They stood stock-still and stared, mouths slightly agape.

"*Offisahs! Offisahs!*" one of the MOMs shouted at them in a thick Boston accent. "Do your *jawwb!*"

"Do your *jawwb!* Do your *jawwb!*" several women behind them started to chant. A minute or so passed. One of the officers reluctantly lifted his walkie-talkie to contact headquarters.

It was 9:15. A handful of male tourists stood on the steps of Faneuil Hall, watching intently, filming the episode on video cameras and cellphones. A group of construction workers, wearing heavy work boots and carrying lunchboxes and Thermoses, stopped in their tracks when they saw the fracas. They looked at each other with grins, as if they couldn't believe their luck. Then they pounded their meaty palms in slow, steady applause.

CHAPTER 16

"COCK-A-DOODLE DOO! Are you ready to admit that this is getting out of hand?" Rob said. He was sitting at the kitchen table in his shirtsleeves, holding Rory in his arms, doing his barnyard animal impressions again. He was taking a rare late morning, having worked until midnight the night before. And he was tilting his head to indicate the front page of the Globe, which was spread out on the table. The lead headline read, "14 ARRESTED FOR INDECENT EXPOSURE OUTSIDE SHOW."

Yes, Lauren had to admit, things were getting a bit out of hand. The rest of the "Polly Park Show" had been fairly benign: Polly had introduced a fashion show of lacy nursing bras, which Candace Calloway had declared "a modern woman's dream" and Stuart Winkle had called "lovely for the boudoir." Lauren had held Rory up for the studio audience to see, garnering some modest applause prompted by Seth, and then had been allowed to leave the stage and feed Rory in the empty makeshift green room.

But by mid-day, the flashing episode outside had made it onto every local and national newscast and had become an instant viral sensation on YouTube, thanks to a grainy video uploaded from someone's cellphone. Late-night comics made jokes about "Flashachusetts." Lauren's pump, adjusted to increase the suction, had started saying, *"What a cult. What a cult."*

And yet there was no backing down, according to Maisy, who

had convened a quick huddle for messaging after the telecast had ended, with a nervous-looking Chip now at her side.

"Where's Candace?" she had said. Lauren hadn't mentioned that she had spied the candidate in the back hallway, talking intently to Seth the applause guy.

"Whatever. I'll catch up with her later," Maisy had said. "For now, we've got to ride this. Consider it earned media. Just press on the message of empowerment if anybody asks. Chip, go book Candace on some cable news shows. I'll see if the Pep Boys can come up with an ad about noble naked women."

"Lady Godiva," Lauren had said, automatically. She hadn't thought of the name in a decade or two, but there it was, rising to the surface of her memory. In her mind, she traced the outlines of a woman on horseback, with hair long and thick enough to cover her delicate parts.

"Hmm," Maisy had said, and Chip had started frantically fiddling with his iPhone.

"Wikipedia says she was an English noblewoman," he had announced, skimming through the text. "Born in 1040…rode her horse naked through the streets of Coventry to protest her husband's taxation policies."

"I like it," Maisy had said.

"I guess she's kind of a cult heroine," Chip had said hopefully.

"And she used her nakedness to look out for the little guy," Maisy had said. "That's key."

"So should we take a picture of Candace on a horse?" Chip had asked, with a dreamy tone in his voice. "She would look really great on a horse."

"Cool off, Chipper," Maisy had said, giving him a strange look. "I would advise you not to think about Candace on a horse, naked or otherwise. But we'll definitely add it to the talking points."

So far, Maisy hadn't asked Lauren to use any of those points, to represent Candace on any TV shows that night. Lauren felt relieved, but also a little bit hurt. She wasn't sure precisely what she would have said, but she felt an obligation—or maybe, if she was being fully honest with herself, an egotistical inner urge—to remain a symbol for the Calloway campaign. Just in case she got the call, she decided to try out a few lines on Rob.

"I think," she offered tentatively, "that maybe it's good that things have gone this far. This is how progress gets made, right? The radicals on the leading edge? Maybe we're, I don't know, teaching young girls a message about personal pride."

"Should we teach Rory to be an exotic dancer? Would that be a message of personal pride?" Rob shot back. "The only good I can think of is that nobody's talking about *your* boobs anymore." He lifted Rory high in the air and made a sound like a goat. The baby smiled.

"She just ate a few minutes ago," Lauren told him. "You're going to make her spit up."

"She'll be fine," Rob said, sounding defensive. "I leave all the feeding to you. You can leave some of the playing to me."

The doorbell rang, which Lauren thought was fortunate. It was Mia, toting Lyle, who was asleep in his car seat.

"I know I'm early," she said, not sounding especially apologetic as she brushed past Lauren and Rory and set the car seat on the floor beside the couch. She ignored Rob, who was bouncing Rory up and down and quacking like a duck.

"Early for what?" Lauren asked.

"We're visiting a toddler gym class today, remember?" Mia said. "Before we go, we need to talk about our message."

She marched into the kitchen and dropped her diaper bag on the floor, pulling out a brown paper bag from within it. "Campaign headquarters couriered these to my house," she said, placing the bag on the kitchen table. "They've bought some individually-wrapped Godiva chocolates for us to hand out."

"I figured they'd do something like that," Lauren said.

Rob galloped into the kitchen like a horse, neighing in Rory's ear. He grabbed one of the chocolates, opened it expertly with one hand, and popped it into his mouth. Mia stared at him for a moment, eyebrows raised, then turned to Lauren again.

"But Sheila McDonough and I have also been talking," Mia said. "And we have some issues with the way things have been going."

"It's pretty strange that we're talking about nakedness now," Lauren said. "Candace really surprised us with that whole 'Reveal and heal' thing."

"Oh, Candace is doing nothing wrong," Mia said. "Absolutely nothing. What Sheila and I were talking about was you."

"Me?" Lauren said.

"Ah, this sounds like fun," Rob said. "Too bad I have to go to work. Hey, Rory, want to learn how to tie a tie?" He carried the baby out of the room, honking like a goose.

Mia watched him disappear into the bedroom, then turned back to Lauren. "Look, we're fighting a war on two fronts here," she said. "We want to empower women. But we also want to make them the best mothers they can be. Which is why we're a little concerned about something you said."

"What did I say?" Lauren said, confused.

"You said you wanted to think about something other than babies!"

"But you're the one who told me to do that," Lauren said. "That's how this whole thing got started, remember? You told me to think about art."

"Lauren," Mia said, sounding frustrated. "That was *me* talking to *you*. When you go on national TV, it's different. Being a spokeswoman is a big responsibility. People are listening to you. They're thinking about you. I mean, you've read the comments."

"What comments?"

"The comments online, below the newspaper articles."

"Oh, God, I never read those," Lauren said. "Who has time to read those?"

"Ohhhhh," Mia said, as if she had just had a revelation. "Well, that's probably for the best."

"Why?" Lauren said. "What are they saying?"

"I shouldn't have brought it up," Mia said.

"What are they saying?" Lauren repeated.

Mia sighed, reached into her diaper bag and pulled out her iPhone. "I'll pull up today's Globe story," she said. "Read for yourself."

Lauren took Mia's phone and clicked on the comments. The first one said, "Candace Calloway is hot." The next few were about Lauren.

"It's so selfish to take a baby to a museum full of germs!"

"She thinks we all want to be around her miserable wailing kid."

"People like her shouldn't reproduce."

There were about 30 more, similar in tone. Exactly seven people called her a moron. A few more called her a "pioneer" or "heroine," and said Claire Langoon was a selfish baby-hater. One commenter called Candace Calloway a "socialist man-hating sex slut." Another said Stuart Winkle was a "fascist pinhead Neanderthal."

"Wow," Lauren said when she had finished. "These people don't even know us."

"They're watching," Mia said, in a scolding tone. "You're a public figure now."

DRIVING WESTWARD WITH MIA on the Massachusetts Turnpike, listening to gentle '60s protest songs on one of Mia's "Baby Baez" CDs, Lauren felt even more exposed. First, they passed a "Got Milk" billboard, Rory's face towering high above the city in the environs of Fenway Park. Then they zoomed beneath an underpass where someone had put up a handmade sign, painted onto what appeared to be an old bedsheet. "NO BARE NAKED LADIES," it said. "WINKLE FOR GOVERNOR."

When both Rory and Lyle seemed safely asleep, Mia turned off the CD and flipped on the radio, which was tuned to a public radio station.

"...and I lived in Paris for several years, Bob," a woman was saying. "They have a much healthier attitude than we do about the naked body."

"Yes. Yes. And why do you think that is?" said a man's voice, slightly effete.

"I think it's Europe," the woman said. "They have a sophistication that you just don't find in this country. Their cheese is better, too."

"Well, thank you for the call," said Bob. "Now, we're going to Olivia in Cambridge, Massachusetts. Olivia, you're on 'As it Were.'"

"Thanks, Bob," said another female voice, youthful and bright. "I just wanted to agree with your last caller. I live in a co-op at Harvard, and every other Sunday we have a nude brunch. It's, like, a totally liberating experience."

"Interesting," said Bob. "I'd like to ask our guest about that. Fritz, do you find that your nudist colonies are popular among college students?"

"It's certainly a market we're trying to grow," said the man, in a buttery voice. "I've considered doing a college tour to spread the word."

Mia reached for the dial. "NPR was always on our side," she declared. She turned the channel to a sports-talk station.

"So, you know, I'm starting to like that Candace Calloway," one of the hosts was saying. "I have no idea what women are thinking these days, but at least she knows what men want!"

He and his cohost chortled. "I was always happy just looking at her gams," the cohost said. "Now, I've got something else to look forward to. OK, let's go to the phones! Gus in Southie, you're on with Mike and Mac."

"Yeah, guys," said a gruff, gravelly voice with a thick Boston accent. "I want to issue Ms. Calloway a *fah-mal* invitation to join us in the L Street Brownies. She can skinny-dip in the *hahbah* this *New Yeahs* and really get to know her constituents. And her breasts can get the effects of the cold *ay-ah*."

The hosts broke into hyena-like guffaws.

MIA AND LAUREN LISTENED to 20 more minutes of naked-Calloway humor before they pulled up to a strip mall in Natick, a town west of Boston that had been overtaken by chain stores, big box merchandisers, and slow-moving traffic. They were going to a massive tot complex called the Brain and Body Zone, where stay-at-home mothers, part-time-working moms and high-salaried nannies brought their toddlers for mid-weekday stimulation.

Once again, Lauren and Mia grabbed the car seats and bags of campaign literature and hobbled inside. In the lobby, pop music from the '80s blasted over the loudspeakers. The walls were colored with painted swirls in primary colors, punctuated with metallic lightning bolts. Behind a rounded desk were doors marked "A," "B," and "C" in bright neon-pink letters, plus a spiral staircase leading to more rooms upstairs.

"Be Young at Heart! Hold Your Next Corporate Gathering Here!" read a banner above the stairs. Lauren glanced down at Rory, still strapped into her car seat. The baby was wide awake, her eyes shifting back and forth with wonder.

"I think we can just go anywhere and hand out pamphlets and candies," Mia said. "The owner is apparently a big Calloway supporter."

They headed through a door marked Studio A, and into a room with padded walls and floors. A dozen toddlers had been let loose, their parents trailing behind them helplessly, as "Groove is in the Heart" played loudly in the background. A few kids were attempting to scale a faux rock wall. One boy tried to lift a basketball toward a hoop, like an ant wrestling with an enormous crumb. Two well-dressed mothers chatted animatedly as their sons bonked each other over the head with foam baseball bats.

Across the room, a crowd of kids and mothers stood beside a trampoline, where a small girl was jumping vigorously. A sign beside the trampoline said, "One friend at a time! Sharing is fun!"

"Eight…nine…ten!" the girl's mother was saying. "OK, Annabel, time to get off."

Annabel kept jumping.

"All right, Annabel," the mother said calmly. "Let's just count one more time. One…two…"

One of the boys who were waiting began to whine. "Don't worry," his mother said loudly. "I'm sure Annabel's mother will do the right thing."

Lauren and Mia headed to another corner, where a young woman with a nametag that read "KIMMIE" was holding a toddler upside down, demonstrating a handstand.

"See, moms? This is great for their gross motor skills," she said. "While Loretta's standing on her head here, why don't we sing the ABCs together?" She looked up and spotted Lauren, a jolt of recognition flashing across her face. "Omigod! It's YOU!" she shouted, still holding Loretta upside down. "I saw you on Polly Park!"

The other mothers turned around and stared at Lauren, who tried to put on her most convincing smile.

"Hi!" she said. "I'm Lauren Bruce. I'm here from the Calloway—"

"We know who you are!" one of the mothers said. "We saw you on TV!"

"What is Polly Park like?" another one said.

"Did you hear her swear?" another one said.

"Did you touch her?" said another.

"Did she take off her shirt?"

"Did you take off *your* shirt?"

Suddenly, they were swarming, the mothers from across the room abandoning their children and collecting around Lauren, all asking questions at once. Lauren, her arm still hooked beneath Rory's car seat, started instinctively backing away from them. Out of the corner of her eye, she saw that six toddlers had crowded onto the trampoline and were jumping gleefully.

"Where does Candace Calloway get her clothes?"

"Do you really like to go naked?"

"Do you have any breastfeeding tips?"

Lauren decided to try out some of her spokeswoman lines.

"Can I tell you a little bit about Candace Calloway?" she yelled. "She really cares about mothers! She knows that breastfeeding makes us proud!"

"Is Candace Calloway going to outlaw formula?" one woman yelled. "I heard she was going to make formula illegal."

"Amen!" another woman shouted.

"I heard that if you get caught using a bottle in public, you'll get a call from social services."

"Could she do that?" someone said. "Take your baby away if it isn't breastfed?"

"She's the government," someone else said. "She could do anything."

"No! People!" Lauren said, edging backward toward the door. "Candace Calloway isn't taking anyone's babies away. She just wants women to feel good about breastfeeding. To feel empowered."

"Yeah, I feel really empowered when people are staring at my tits," a woman said.

Lauren found the doorknob with her right hand, opened it, and backed into the lobby. The crowd of women followed. Lauren turned, looking for a place to escape, and spotted an empty receptionist's desk. She set Rory's car seat down on the floor, climbed on top of the desk, and looked down on the crowd, which was still pelting her with questions and commentary.

"Candace Calloway should change the law!" one woman shouted. "If men can take their shirts off, why not women?"

"I wish men wouldn't take their shirts off!" said somebody else. "Can Candace Calloway stop men from taking their shirts off?"

Lauren clapped her hands as loudly as she could. "Stop! No!" she yelled "Candace Calloway can't make anyone do anything! She just wants everyone to make a healthy choice…"

"Healthy choice, my ass!" someone yelled.

"I had a premature baby! I couldn't breastfeed him!" another woman shouted. "Do you have any idea how bad you people made me feel?"

Lauren froze, filled again with self-doubt. Then she spotted Mia in the crowd, and got an idea. "Mia!" she shouted. "Come up here! And bring the bag!"

In a minute, Mia had pushed her way through the crowd and climbed up to the receptionist's desk, where she stood beside Lauren and surveyed the group. Lauren reached into Mia's tote bag and pulled out a handful of chocolates. "Ladies!" she yelled. "We've got Godiva!" She started tossing the chocolates into the crowd, the way she had once seen an aquarium worker toss live fish to a pack of seals.

The women stopped talking momentarily and focused on the chocolates. As they jostled and shoved, extending their arms high into the air, they started to argue among themselves.

"What do you mean, you don't breastfeed?"

"How could you do it for so long?"

"I did it in an elevator once."

"Maybe they *should* take your baby away."

"Wow," Lauren said quietly to Mia, watching the commotion.

"Low blood sugar," Mia replied. "The chocolate will take care of it."

"Think you can handle it from here?" Lauren said. "Give them your campaign pitch?"

"Of course," Mia said. She held her fingers up to her mouth and let forth a whistle so long and loud that most of the women fell silent.

"Ladies!" Mia said, when she had their attention. "Let's talk about solidarity!"

"Solidarity?" someone shouted.

"Oh, yes," Mia replied. "This is just what the patriarchy wants. They want us fighting with ourselves. They want to keep us down.

It's a good thing Candace Calloway can help us stand together."

As Mia vamped, Lauren quietly stepped down from the receptionist's desk and hooked her arm around Rory's car seat. Slowly, she made her way toward the front door, hoping none of the women would notice. As she approached the glass, she felt a tap on her shoulder. *Oh, no,* she thought. *They'll never let me go.* Then she turned around to find herself face to face with Claire Langoon.

Lauren's campaign nemesis was wearing sweatpants, a hoodie, and a wry smile on her face. "I thought there was a riot going on in here," she said. "I should have known it was just you and your breastfeeding talk."

"We were campaigning," Lauren said tentatively.

"So I see," said Claire, sounding friendlier than Lauren expected. "But you seem kind of done. Want to join me for a smoke? I promise I won't blow in the direction of your baby."

Lauren turned back to the crowd of women. Most of them were eating chocolate. Mia was yelling something about empowerment. None of them seemed to be looking for her. So Lauren quietly followed Claire through the heavy glass doors. There was a chill in the air that made her rub her arms together. They walked around the building and toward a loading dock, and ducked behind a delivery truck. Lauren put Rory's car seat on the ground and bent down to fasten the buttons on the baby's sweater. Then she stood up and faced Claire.

"So," she said. "What *are* you doing here?"

"My son takes a junior tae kwon do class," Claire said, leaning her back against the truck. "My mother lives in Framingham, so I take him here and then go over to her house for lunch, and it kills, like, five hours."

"And you left him in class?"

"Parents aren't allowed inside," Claire said. "It makes the kids less likely to cry. I could watch it on closed circuit TV, but it's like looking at a black and white postage stamp. So I usually go downstairs for a smoke. Today, I get down to the lobby and hear this commotion. For a second, I thought I'd stumbled on another MOM rally."

She reached into her messenger bag and pulled out a lighter and a packet of Marlboro Lights. "It's my weakness," she said. "So I grant myself two a day. Used to have them at bars, but I don't get out much these days. Now I pull them out when I'm around too many little kids."

She lit a cigarette, took a long drag, then turned and exhaled so that the smoke trailed into the breeze, a delicate wisp, in the opposite direction from where Lauren held Rory.

Lauren stared, in a little bit of awe. The mere fact that Claire was breaking such an enormous rule of motherhood was exciting to witness. Lauren hadn't had so much as a sip of alcohol in nearly a year. She still avoided tuna, since Mia had forwarded her an article about the way mercury spreads to breastfed children. Sometimes, in moments of deep hunger, she missed tuna sandwiches terribly. She imagined that Claire ate tuna with abandon, day and night. Tuna omelettes for breakfast, tuna melts for lunch, seared tuna for dinner on a bed of baby greens. She probably had tuna ice cream for dessert.

"So," Claire said, her cigarette already smoked down to half its original size. "How do you like being a media darling?"

"Media darling?" Lauren said. "Didn't you see those women? They were ready to rip my throat out."

"They were ready to rip *each other's* throats out," Claire corrected. "You, they worship. You're, like, the symbol of pure motherhood. I do PR, you know, when I'm not watching my kid. And I have to say, I'm impressed. They made a martyr out of you, fast."

"If I'm a martyr, it doesn't seem to be doing me any good," Lauren said. "I don't think anyone's listening to me."

"Maybe they would," Claire said, taking another drag, "if you had something to say."

"I have something to say," Lauren protested. "I'm saying that…breastfeeding is good. For babies' nutrition. And women's empowerment."

"That's the Calloway campaign's message," Claire said. "They're just using you to mouth it. Which is fine. That's how it works. But you've got power here, too. You could throw out a message of your own."

"What, a message like yours?" Lauren said. "That breastfeeding is awful? That it's a disgusting act?"

"That's what you think my message is?" Claire said, "Wow. You've been listening to too much BOOB propaganda."

"Isn't your blog called Hurtslikeabitch.com?"

"Yes. Because that's easy to remember and it gets good press," Claire said. "But if you listen to what I'm really saying, it's not anti-breastfeeding. It's pro-moderation. It's about being reasonable."

"You're telling people how good your life got when you quit."

"I never said I quit," Claire said. "I said I gave Tyler some formula. I broke the spell of the evil breastfeeding fairies. But that doesn't mean I stopped nursing."

"You didn't?" Lauren said.

"Nah," Claire said. "I still kept it up, at night before he went to bed, in the morning when he woke up. A lot longer than I thought I would."

"How long?" Lauren asked.

"Long," Claire said, dropping her cigarette butt onto the ground and smashing it with her sneaker. "Like, one of your crazy BOOB ladies long. And here's my dirty little secret: I loved it. I loved it so much that it kind of scared me."

"Scared you?"

"It was so intimate," Claire said. "Maybe it's a mother-son thing, I don't know. But it was like he was my little boyfriend. It was sensual. He would play with my hair. He would touch my cheek. He was more loving than any guy I'd ever known, my husband included. He was into me completely, obsessively. And I thought, 'This is like an addiction.'"

"I can see that," Lauren said. "Well, I guess I can. To me, right now, it feels more like an obligation. A nice obligation. But an obligation."

"When you don't feel obligated," Claire said, "that's when it gets really good." She lit another cigarette.

"So when did you finally quit?" Lauren asked.

"It tapered off," Claire said. "He lost interest in the morning. And then my husband would sometimes put him to bed at night, so he got out of the habit. But still, you know, every once in awhile...if he's sick, or he's having trouble going down for a nap, he'll give me a tug...and I can't really say no."

"How old is he now?" Lauren asked.

"Four."

"Four," Lauren said. "Wow. Wow."

"OK, I have no idea why I told you that," Claire said. "If you tell anyone else, I'll deny it. And if you tell that Sheila Mc-Donough woman, I will seriously slit your throat."

CHAPTER 17

THAT SAME MORNING, Maisy awoke at 4 a.m. after a fitful sleep. She stared at the ceiling and wall, trying to will herself to sleep again, until she saw light struggling through the thin metal blinds in her corporate apartment. She decided a long walk to the office might help her clear her head. So she hoisted herself out of bed, showered, dressed, and stepped outside, joining the quiet parade of joggers and early-bird dog walkers in the dewy autumn air.

She bypassed the T for the Longfellow Bridge and a long walk up Charles Street, stopping at a Starbucks to buy a large coffee and several newspapers. This, she thought wryly, was the path Mrs. Mallard and her brood had taken in "Make Way for Ducklings," a book she had been reading to her nieces and nephews for years. She had always considered it an allegory about real estate and how to cultivate relationships with public servants. But to all of these young mothers, she thought, it must seem like a tale of maternal duty: Mr. Mallard chooses a string of inappropriate places to live, then skips off on a self-indulgent personal "journey" at the moment when the ducklings need guidance, leaving his wife to teach them life skills and get them across the highway.

Maisy diverted from the ducklings' route at the edge of the Public Garden, heading across the Common toward Washington

Street. She reached campaign headquarters, unlocked the door, and stepped past the empty reception desk into the cavernous main room. Some volunteers had been phone banking the night before, and the room was strewn with plastic cups, paper plates, and nacho chip crumbs. Maisy figured she'd get one of the interns to vacuum. She turned away from the mess and headed toward her office. That's when she heard a stifled giggle.

"If those interns camped out here all night…" she muttered, half-aloud. Then, she saw a tall man with sandy hair, completely naked, scuttling down the hallway toward the bathroom. He clearly hadn't heard or noticed Maisy. He had the deliberate, half-limping gait of someone who badly needed to pee. Maisy only saw him from behind—his slender torso, his hairy legs and back, his small rear end—so she stood in her office doorway and waited for him to return.

In a few minutes, he ambled down the hall more comfortably, his face glistening with water from the bathroom sink. Maisy tried to keep her gaze above his waist. He had a close-cut moustache and beard, a shock of reddish hair, an arrogant expression that Maisy knew too well. Scott McFeeney. From the Herald.

Maisy retreated into her office, heart pounding, and counted to 100. Then she stormed over to Candace's office and flung open the door, her anger overriding her fear of what she'd see inside. To her relief, Candace was dressed for work and sitting demurely at her desk, tapping gently at her laptop. McFeeney was sitting on the couch in an undershirt and a pair of boxer briefs, pulling up a pair of wrinkled corduroy pants. He turned to see her, startled, his cheeks reddening.

"Well, if it isn't the Fourth Estate," Maisy said. Then she pointed at him and ordered, "Out. Get your hairy little ass out of this office and do not come back, ever. Unless you want me to call your editor and tell him he's got a firing offense on his hands."

"Hi, Maisy," Scott said, trying to sound casual. "How are you? I was just interviewing Senator Calloway for the profile—"

"Scott, do I look like a moron?" Maisy said. "Put your shirt on and make yourself scarce."

"Goodbye, Scott," Candace cooed quietly, putting a finger to her lips and turning an imaginary key. She winked. McFeeney gave her a slight, sheepish smile, then pulled on a T-shirt and ducked out of the office. Maisy listened to his footsteps hurrying down the hall and heard the heavy front door swing open and click shut.

"Candace," she finally said. "What the hell are you doing?"

"I told you I was ovulating," Candace said. "What do you expect?"

"I saw you talking to that kid from the 'Polly Park Show,'" Maisy said. "God knows what you did with him. And now a Herald reporter? Really? Can't you find some anonymous banker type who doesn't follow politics?"

"Scott's no Osterville, I know," Candace said. "But I like his height. And he has that cleft chin. I would love a child with a cleft chin."

"He's a tabloid reporter!" Maisy shouted. "You're going to wind up in the gossip pages!"

"Maisy, you never have faith in me," Candace said. "Scott is a climber. He thinks sleeping with me will help him get a cushy job at a state agency. But he knows that depends on his silence. Besides, he'll never breathe a word of this. It took him a few tries to accomplish the task at hand. I think the poor guy was a little intimidated."

"For God's sake, Candace," Maisy said. "If you're so intent on getting knocked up, can't you just go back to the sperm bank?"

"I want to know exactly what I'm getting," Candace said. "These are my child's genes we're talking about."

"Please, then. Stop ovulating," Maisy said weakly. "Or wait until the next cycle. We have less than two weeks to go. We have work to do. We have the Pep Boys coming in to show us a new ad."

"The Pep Boys," Candace said, contemplatively.

"Oh, Christ," Maisy said. "If you look at any one of them sideways, I'll cover you with a burka."

• • •

THREE HOURS LATER, Maisy and Candace sat beside each other in the conference room, watching Mike LaDuke insert a DVD into the player. Maisy shifted her gaze from Mike's face to Candace's, trying to read her thoughts. Then she was distracted by the music vamping through the TV speakers.

Bow, Chicka-wocka-chicka. Bow, Chicka-wocka-chicka.

An empty fireman's pole appeared on the screen, bathed in purple light.

Bow, Chicka-wocka-chicka. Bow, Chicka-wocka-chicka.

A woman in a blue metallic teddy slithered into the frame and wrapped her body suggestively around the pole.

"I was going to be a lawyer or a doctor," she purred, looking directly at the camera. "But Candace Calloway convinced me that I had a higher calling. She said that to really have self-esteem as a woman, I have to take it off. Take it *all* off."

She grabbed one of her shoulder straps and started to pull it down, her lips curling upward in a naughty smile. The screen cut to an image of Stuart Winkle, wearing an argyle sweater and sitting in an office surrounded by leather-bound books.

"Is this the message Massachusetts wants to send its girls?" he said. "I'm Stuart Winkle and I approve this message because I believe our children can do more. And I have a five-point education plan to prove it."

The camera cut to an elementary school classroom where Winkle sat at a table with four small girls, talking earnestly about a book. Minimalist music tinkled in the background.

"Stuart Winkle," a woman's voice said. "Because women can do more."

LaDuke clicked a button on the remote control. The screen turned blue.

"This is what they're airing on the 6 p.m. newscasts," he said, leaning back in his chair and stretching his arms behind him. "They're trying to scare the bejeezus out of the soccer moms."

"Doesn't he look creepy?" Maisy said, her hands locked around a warm, tall paper cup filled with her second Starbucks coffee of the day. "Am I the only one who thinks he looks creepy? If I had a six-year-old girl, I wouldn't let him within 50 yards of her."

"Nonetheless," Bob Brooks said. "They've also put out direct mail." He handed Maisy a glossy flier that blared, "THE NAKED TRUTH ABOUT CANDACE CALLOWAY."

"We need to take back the message," Brooks said. "The internals are, I have to say, a bit alarming. Our favorables with women spiked about a week and a half ago, but they've been declining ever since. The female voters are confused. They're responding to this stripper stuff. They're losing focus. And I never thought I'd say this, but I think we need to talk more about babies. So we put together this."

LaDuke had inserted another DVD in the machine, and now hit "Play." The screen filled with a picture of a park, the grass green and lush, the sky so blue and bright that it made the conference room, with its grey-tinged walls and industrial carpet, look especially bleak. A tune played through the speakers, choppy and sweet and vaguely familiar, as a parade of cute babies of varying ethnicities toddled across the screen happily. One walked clumsily, fell, laughed, and got up again. Another played with a flower. Another chased a ball.

"This is your future," a woman's voice said. "Feed it well." The Calloway campaign logo appeared on the screen as Candace's voice delivered a tagline in rapid speed: "I'm Candace Calloway and I approve this message."

LaDuke hit "Stop." The screen went blue again. He was smiling, as were Brooks and Albee.

Maisy glanced across the room at Candace, who was staring at the blue screen with a rapturous look.

"Brings a tear to your eye, doesn't it?" Brooks said.

"The kid with the ball is my nephew," Albee said.

"Was that a ukulele?" Maisy said.

"Yes," Brooks said. "You know that dead Hawaiian guy? Iz

Kamakamasomethingorother? The one who did a version of 'Somewhere Over the Rainbow'? We have a studio guy who knocked it off for cheap. If you change just enough notes, the copyright people won't come after you."

"Is that your way of telling me this ad wasn't expensive?" Maisy said. "Because it looks expensive."

"Thank you," Albee said. "And don't worry. Baby models are a bargain. You have no idea how many mothers are willing to put their kids out there for free."

"Well, that's good," Maisy said. "Because our fund-raising has slowed down in the last few days."

"Time to pick up the pace, then," Brooks said. "We have a direct mail piece, too."

"I think we should change the message even more," Candace declared. Everyone stopped and stared. This was the first time she had spoken since the meeting began.

"You've got another idea?" Maisy said. "Are there more parts of the anatomy you'd like to reveal?"

"That's not what I'm talking about," Candace told her, sounding irritated. Then she turned her attention to the Pep Boys.

"You know how much I love babies," she said. "But I think we should talk about more than just feeding them. What if we pitched a comprehensive campaign about women and families? Better medical care. The work-life balance. Child-care tax credits. Early education. This isn't only about breastfeeding and modesty, you know. It's about real issues that affect people's lives."

She looked at Steve Albee, who was sitting to her right. "Steve," she said, placing her hand over his. "You understand the importance of families, don't you?" Albee turned and looked at her, eyebrows raised, then let his gaze fall to her legs.

Bob Brooks didn't seem to notice. "So now you want to start taxing and spending like every other Democrat," he said dismissively.

"I want to make life better for women and children," Candace said.

"That's what every Democrat says," Brooks said. "And that's

why Democrats lose. Senator, with all due respect, it's too late for complexity. We've got two weeks to go, we're stuck in the polls, and our opponent is calling us a stripper. We've got to fight back with a single barrel, and that barrel is full of babies."

"I can't disagree," Maisy said, a little wistfully. "But I think we fight with two weapons. Babies and dirt."

"What dirt?" Brooks said.

"Damned if I know," Maisy said. "But as soon as y'all get out of here, I'm calling Dark Tim."

DARK TIM WAS AN opposition research guru Maisy had discovered a dozen or so years ago, when she ran a Congressional race in Ohio. That time, Dark Tim had worked wonders, unearthing the fact that the opponent, who was campaigning on fiscal austerity and moral superiority, had a time-share in a Jamaican condo complex known for pot busts and lavish swinging parties. Dark Tim worked for Democratic candidates across the country, but had never been known to set foot into a campaign office. Maisy didn't even know where he was, whether in a ranch house in some East Coast state or squirreled away in a shack in Costa Rica. She contacted him only through his cellphone. He didn't even use e-mail, preferring to send documents by fax. He either had a network of minions who frequented local courthouses, the ability to hack into databases everywhere, or both.

And he always answered the phone on the first ring. "Yo," he said when Maisy called him from her office, a few minutes after the Pep Boys had left for the airport. His voice was high-pitched, boyish, and a little bit scratchy, as if he were perpetually going through puberty. The first time Maisy had spoken to him, she had wondered if he were much older than thirteen.

"Tim," Maisy said. "Maisy Street. How's it going, hon?"

"State?" Dark Tim said in a clipped voice.

"Massachusetts. Governor's race. It's me, Tim. Maisy. We go way back."

There was silence for about five seconds. "Ah," Tim said finally. "Maisy. Right. Hi. Sorry, I'm juggling eight candidates this cycle."

"I understand," Maisy said. "But hope you've got something up your sleeve for this one. I could use a Hail Mary right about now."

"Let me get his file up," Tim said. Maisy could hear the sound of a keyboard, clacking in the background. "Stuart Winkle," he said presently. "He's the one who went to Bermuda with World Book, right? Exciting dude." He sighed. "Yeah, I've spent a fair amount of time digging on this guy. He's a tough nut. Real estate looks clean. Owns a place in Cambridge and an apartment in Fort Lauderdale that I think his mother is living in…"

The keys clacked some more. "Pays his taxes on time." More clacking. "Skipped a couple of votes for Cambridge City Council and a ballot question about dog parks, but I'm not sure how much you can make of that."

"Come on," Maisy said. "You've got to have something. He's been porking one of his female students. Or he's secretly gay. Or he has a thing for goats. I don't know. I just need you to make the guy look disgusting."

"Moral failing," Dark Tim said. "Hmm. Divorce records always have the best dirt, but this guy's never been married. But we'll see what we can find…" More clacking. "Twenty-five dollars in outstanding parking tickets in Cambridge. He was late three times getting his car inspection sticker. Went to a Communist Party meeting in the '70s. But I'm not sure that would matter in Massachusetts…." Dark Tim continued to clack away.

"No sexual harassment charges, far as I can tell. Let's see if he was disciplined for anything." More clacking. "Wait a minute. He was called in to a Harvard review board ten years ago…this could be good…Oh, no, wait, he was turning in one of his students. For plagiarism. Bastard."

"Goddamn ethics," Maisy said glumly.

"Hmm," Tim said. "I should have done this already, but while I've got you on the phone, let's Google Map his neighborhood." He typed some more.

"Nice house," he said. "Big lawn. What's that on the front there, next to the walkway? Are those gnomes? Dude, those are really old-school gnomes. Heh. That's kind of cool. And in the front here…under that tree…That's the Venus de Milo, isn't it? Hmph. She's naked."

"She's naked? Boobs and all?" Maisy said. "Well, that's hypocrisy."

"I suppose so," Dark Tim said unenthusiastically.

"Hypocrisy is good. For us, I mean," Maisy said.

"Everyone's a hypocrite," Dark Tim said.

"Don't I know it," Maisy said. "But at this point, I'll take what I can get. Oh—and Tim?"

"Yeah?"

"You haven't heard any new dirt about Candace, have you? Through your various grapevines? Any nasty rumors about… reporters? Press secretaries?"

"Huh?" Tim said.

"Never mind."

ONCE SHE HAD hung up with Dark Tim, Maisy got up to smoke a cigarette outside and contemplate how to use the news of Winkle's naked sculpture. In front of Candace's closed door, she hesitated, then knocked twice loudly and turned the knob. She was terrified that she'd find Steve Albee inside, without pants. But Candace was sitting at her desk, fully clothed, The New York Times spread out in front of her.

"You couldn't manage to bag Albee?" Maisy said.

"He had a flight to catch," Candace said wistfully. "Maybe next cycle."

"Be my guest," Maisy said. "That's after the election."

Candace returned to her newspaper.

"You know," Maisy said. "Those are good issues you were talking about in there. Kind of makes me wish you had this baby fever a few months earlier. We could have built a platform around them, gotten a head start on that women problem."

"God," Candace said disdainfully. "Do you know how tired I am of you telling me I have a woman problem? Do you know how ridiculous that sounds? Especially now that I'm, you know, a pre-mother. I'm more woman now than ever."

"A pre-mother *and* a stripper. How useful for our gender," Maisy said under her breath, turning back around to leave.

"Wait just a minute," Candace growled, in a tone of voice that made Maisy obey. "You and the goddamn Winkle campaign with the stripper talk. And you, at least, should know better. I'm the stripper? *You* should be the stripper! I was just following your instructions!"

"I don't remember instructing you to tell women to take their shirts off," Maisy said.

"You didn't say not to!" Candace said. "What you said was, 'Chest in the air, take pride in your body, here's a microphone, Candace, go hang yourself with the cord.' That's how you parasites work: You sit in a room and think up things for me to say, and when I say them a little more artfully, I'm a bimbo."

Maisy stepped inside the office and closed the door.

"First of all, you're not a bimbo," she said, working to keep her voice steady and calm. "Second of all, I'm not a parasite. I'm a professional. I know how to run a campaign. I've proved that over and over again in half the states in this country. That's why you hired me to sit in a room and tell you what to do."

"But you change your ideas every fifteen minutes!" Candace

said. "'It's about babies.' 'It's about women's empowerment.' 'Say this.' 'Say that.' 'Dress this way.' 'Don't wear that.' The only thing that's consistent is that you treat me like I don't know anything. Like I'm a bimbo. You think I'm a bimbo."

Maisy felt her cheeks flush. "You have racked up an impressive body count over the last few days, Candace," she said. "But, honestly, I don't think you're a bimbo. I just never thought of you as an advocate for families."

"Yes, you do think I'm a bimbo," Candace said. "You thought I was a bimbo even before I needed sperm. You never took me seriously, and don't think I don't know why. It's because I dress well. Because I have good hair. Because I'm not some butch 65-year-old in a pantsuit."

"Candace—" Maisy said.

"I act like myself and you say I have a woman problem. I take your professional advice and start talking about babies and women's empowerment, and you act like I'm the one who's crazy."

"Boobie milkshakes are a little crazy, Candace," Maisy said.

"You barely tasted it!" Candace shouted. "You just assumed!"

"You have to admit, you got a little emotional," Maisy said.

"I am not emotional," Candace said, her voice quivering. "I am an accomplished woman. I am a state senator. But I think you'd rather think of me as a stripper. I could have started off this campaign with a whole list of Nobel Prize-winning ideas, and you would have rolled your eyes and ignored me because I can pull off a six-inch heel."

She actually has a point, Maisy thought to herself. "Look, Candace. I feel for you," she said. "I know where you're coming from. Campaigns are tough. You have to change the message sometimes. You have to pander. But when you get in office, you can do all the things you want to do. Have twelve babies. Give people paid maternity leave. Drink milkshakes. Whatever. But first you have to win. And if you want to win, you have to listen to me."

"So am I going to win?"

Maisy paused. "I don't know," she said. "Usually around this time I can tell. But this campaign is weird. The numbers aren't making a lot of sense to me. Maybe I just don't understand women. I think I understand women less now than I did when we got started."

"Maybe you're thinking too much about one particular woman," Candace said. "Have you made a move on her yet?"

"What?" Maisy said, stunned.

"Have you made a move on her?"

"Who?" Maisy said.

"Maisy," Candace said, shooting her a look. "My window looks out on Washington Street. I've seen you going out for coffee. She's not my type, obviously, but hey. Whatever grows your tree. Only you're not going to grow anything unless you make a move. Have you made a move?"

Maisy felt herself flushing. "No," she said. "No. I have not made a move."

"Wow," Candace said. "And you think I have a woman problem."

Maisy lowered herself onto Candace's couch. "It's too late," she said. "In two weeks, this campaign ends and I leave town. God only knows where I'll be next year at this time. It just doesn't make sense to start anything now."

"Oh, for God's sake, Maisy, there are airplanes," Candace said. "That is such a bullshit excuse."

"It's really just a business relationship," Maisy said. "She's offering advice. Guidance. I don't want to presume…"

"Maisy," Candace said. "I'll admit I don't know everything about campaigns. But I do know a little bit about flirtation. And that woman is into you. She could offer you advice on the phone. But she's waiting downstairs every day to take a little stroll to Starbucks."

"I haven't had a relationship in a long time," Maisy said. "I don't even know how to start."

"I'd say kissing is a way to start," Candace said. "And then you see where it goes from there."

"I can't believe we're having this conversation," Maisy said. "Why are we having this conversation?"

"So I can help you," Candace said. "I guess it's my turn to help you."

"Why do you want to help me?" Maisy said. "I didn't even think you liked me."

"I don't know if I like you or not, honestly," Candace said. "But I do want you to be happy."

There was a knock on the door. The knob turned from the outside and Chip poked in his head. "Um, hi," he said, blushing ferociously at the sight of Candace. "Hi, Senator, h-how are you? I'm, um, really sorry to interrupt. But I, um, needed to talk to Maisy right away. Are you busy?"

"No," Maisy said.

"Yes," Candace said at the same time.

"No," Maisy said again, emphatically. "Come in, Chip."

Chip pushed the door open further. "I've got some news," Chip said, doing his best to avoid eye contact with Candace. "The BOOBs are going rogue."

"What?" Maisy said.

"Take a look," Chip said. He handed her his iPhone, which was cued up to a story from the Globe's website.

BREASTFEEDING FANS PLAN 'TEA PARTY'
By Marion Mitchell, Globe Staff

Saying they're angry about attacks on breast-feeding women, a group of mothers is planning a "Real Tea Party" on the Congress Street Bridge on Sunday, where they say they'll dump infant formula into the Fort Point Channel.

"We're taking back the Tea Party name, and we're doing actual dumping," said Sheila Mc-Donough, president of the Boston Organization for the Oversight of Breastfeeding. "I am a little concerned about the health of the fish, when they start ingesting this poison. But better the cod than our babies."

McDonough said her protest was not linked to the Candace Calloway campaign, which her organization supports. "We feel we need to make a strong statement on our own," McDonough said. "But we hope that Senator Calloway will join us on the bridge."

Republican gubernatorial candidate Stuart Winkle criticized the protest. "This is just another example of why Senator Calloway and her friends are out of touch," Winkle said, reached outside a shrimp processing plant where he had spent an hour working on the assembly line. "The real people in Massachusetts, like these shrimp plant workers, know that our economy will never survive with such wasteful actions or immodest thinking."

Calloway campaign spokesman Chip Osterville declined to comment.

Maisy handed the iPhone back to Chip. "Declined to comment?" she said.

"They just called two minutes ago," Chip said. "I wanted to talk to you first. We can always call them back and have them update."

"Yes. Call back. And tell them we're not going," Maisy said.

"But I could give a speech!" Candace said.

"As long as I'm campaign manager, you're not going," Maisy said. "Save it for your inaugural speech." Then she turned to Chip. "Tell them Candace has a previously scheduled speaking engagement in…I don't know, find some small town and we'll set up a meeting with the PTO."

She pulled a ballpoint pen out of her pocket and chomped on the end, wishing she'd already had that cigarette. "What is with these BOOBs?" she said. "We're blasting this state with pictures of cute babies. We're talking about breasts night and day. If we send them a copy of the ad with the ukulele, will they call this circus off?"

"I doubt it," Candace said glumly. "I've gotten to know that Sheila McDonough. She's got more passion in her left breast than everyone in the State House combined."

CHAPTER 18

"OF COURSE YOU have to go," Mia said. "You're the link."

"The link?" Lauren said.

"The link between the BOOBs and the public. The shining example of a regular person who needs the BOOBs' help."

"I'm not so sure I need the BOOBs' help."

"That's why you need the BOOBs' help."

They were standing in the infant-care aisle of the Super Stop 'n Shop, preparing to buy a stash of formula that Mia could toss into Boston Harbor. The formula section was wedged between the diapers and the pacifiers, four shelves' worth of liquid and powder in brightly colored jars and cans, each featuring a photo of some cherubic baby covered in rolls of fat. The product names seemed designed to evoke the dual ideas of science and milk: "Lactoline," "Mammafil," "Infabrest."

"I still can't believe they're allowed to sell this stuff in supermarkets," Mia said, patting Lyle's bald head. He gurgled happily from his Baby Bjorn and reached out for the formula as if he wanted to grab some for himself. "Oh, no, none of this for you," Mia said, waving her hand derisively at the merchandise. "Seriously. Would they sell arsenic? Rotted fruit?"

"I think I did once get a rotten avocado here," Lauren said.

"That was an accident," Mia said. "This is purposeful. It's like a terrible plot against babies."

Lauren picked up a can of Lactoline and looked at the small print on the label. "'Manufactured by Argozyme,'" she read. "That does sound kind of evil, I have to admit."

She turned the can around and read some of the promotional copy. "Breastfeeding is best for your baby. But if you can't breast-feed, Lactoline has created this special formula, with vitamins and enzymes that boost brain development."

"They've been studying milk and trying to replicate it!" Mia said. "It's like Frankenstein!"

"It doesn't sound like poison, exactly," Lauren said. "It sounds more like...I don't know, one of those protein powders they put in smoothies."

"That's what they want you to believe," Mia said. "Because they're trying to make money. I wonder which kind I should buy."

"How about the cheapest one?" Lauren said, scanning the shelves. "There's got to be a generic."

"No. No generics," Mia said. "It's important to send a message with the brand name. It should be visible in the photographs."

As she peered at the cans, another woman rolled her shopping cart beside them. A baby car seat was balanced in the child-seat portion of her cart. Two feet stuck out, motionless and clad in blue wool booties. Lauren glanced over at her own cart, where Rory's feet were wiggling in their tiny leather shoes.

Mia looked at the stranger with a smile. "Are you going to the rally, too?" she asked excitedly.

"What rally?" the woman said.

"The tea party!" Mia said. "That's why you're buying formula, right? To dump it?"

The woman looked confused. "I'm buying formula to feed my baby."

"How old is he?" Mia said.

"Four months."

"Oh, my God," Mia said. "Please tell me you're not giving him this."

"*Mia*," Lauren said.

"Excuse me?" the woman said.

"Don't you love him?" Mia said.

"*Mia!*" Lauren said.

"What else would you feed him?" Mia said. "Beer? Tequila?"

The woman grabbed a jumbo-sized can of Infabrest, shot Mia an insulted look, and scurried down the aisle toward the pet food.

"How could you do that?" Lauren said, watching her go.

"All that is necessary for evil to prevail is for good people to do nothing," Mia replied.

"That woman isn't evil," Lauren said. "Maybe she has a problem with her breasts, or—I don't know. What does it matter to you?"

"It matters because it's a slippery slope," Mia said. "You really need to talk to Sheila about this. One of the things we have to do is stigmatize formula, so that it becomes socially unacceptable. So people are ashamed. Smoking used to look cool, you know, but now it just makes you look like a skank."

"Smoking actually kills you," Lauren said.

"That just gave me an idea," Mia said, suddenly sounding less agitated. "They should put a warning label on this stuff. 'Surgeon General's Warning: This product makes you a bad mother.'"

"*Mia*," Lauren said.

"It could be one of Senator Calloway's first bills!" Mia said.

"You can't make that a law," Lauren said.

"But I could make it a T-shirt," Mia said. "OK, let's get out of here quickly so I can call the silkscreener. Lactoline or Mammafil? Eenie, meenie, minie, mo..." She wagged her fingers back and forth while mumbling the rest of the rhyme. "Mammafil. OK!" With one arm, she swept half a dozen cans of Mammafil into her cart and turned to go.

Lauren followed her, impulsively grabbing a box of brownies from a bakery table on the way to the cash registers. Breastfeeding made her voracious, and she figured she might as well indulge; Mia's Moo Coalition handbook said nursing depleted huge amounts of calories.

LATER THAT NIGHT, Lauren held one of those brownies partway in her mouth and tried to balance the rest of it on her arm, leaving her hands free to hold the pump funnels over her breasts. She was sitting on the living room armchair, the shades drawn, the lights dimmed. Rory was in bed; Rob was still at work; her dinner dishes were in the sink, awaiting attention. And the pump, adjusted for suction again, was saying something new: "*Give it up. Give it up. Give it up.*"

Lauren chewed off a chunk of brownie and tried to hold the rest of it steady on her arm, just above her elbow. The brownie wobbled for a minute, then dropped to the floor. On the way down, it knocked into a dial, making the pump slow down. The voice changed its message to "*Not now. Not now. Not now.*"

Lauren looked at the brownie wistfully and contemplated turning off the pump, but the bottles were quickly filling up with milk, and she was reluctant to rearrange all of the equipment again. Just then, a key turned in the knob and the door swung open. Rob appeared in his trench coat and suit, his briefcase in one hand, looking tired.

"You're doing that here? In the living room?" he said, looking slightly alarmed.

"I'm almost done," Lauren said. "I didn't want to wake up Rory. And I didn't think you'd be home yet. Can you grab that brownie off the floor for me?"

Rob put down his briefcase and walked over to Lauren. He bent down and picked up the brownie, took a bite, and swallowed. Then he stuck the rest of the brownie in Lauren's mouth and backed away, trying not to look at the pump.

"That thing makes me nervous," he said, loudly, so his voice could be heard over the mechanism.

"Sorry," Lauren said. "Goes with the territory." She turned off the pump and unhooked the bottles, placing them carefully on the coffee table so they wouldn't spill.

"How's Rory?" Rob said as Lauren re-hooked her bra and rolled down her T-shirt.

"Fine," Lauren said. "You know that bunny in her crib? She was really staring at it today. And her hand moved a little bit, like she was trying to reach for it, but she couldn't."

"That's good," Rob said.

"Also, the diaper rash she had the other day is almost gone. She just has a little redness on her right cheek."

"That's good," Rob said again.

"I realize this isn't very exciting to a big lawyer like you," Lauren said. "But this is what I do all day. I watch Rory. Every detail. And there aren't that many details. That's why the Calloway campaign has been a good thing for me."

"God, I'm going to be happy when this campaign is over," Rob said.

"What do you care?" Lauren said. "You're at work all day and half the night."

"You don't think I hear about what those people are doing?" Rob said. "You don't think I have to talk about it? Dick Melman, the managing partner, couldn't stop talking about the 'Polly Park Show.' He said he was worried his teenage daughter was going to turn into a trollop."

"He actually said 'trollop'?" Lauren said. "I didn't think people said that anymore."

"Melman is pretty old," Rob said. "It's his daughter from a second marriage. Or maybe his third."

"What does it matter what he thinks?" Lauren said. "Those guys are all Winkle voters anyway."

"They've all donated to Winkle," Rob said. "He had a big fundraising cocktail party in our office before…before you got involved in politics. But you never know how they're going to vote."

"Really?" Lauren said. "You think they'd vote for Candace Calloway?"

"Let's just say Candace Calloway has a fan base of male lawyers."

"Hmmph," Lauren said. "How about female lawyers?"

"They don't talk about politics in the office."

"Do they talk about babies?" Lauren said.

"Why would they?" Rob said.

"Don't they have babies?" Lauren said. "Do they use lactation rooms?"

"I have no idea," Rob said. "It's not like it ever came up for me."

"Do they get paid maternity leave?" Lauren said. "I don't think we even found out whether you get paternity leave."

"I took a week off when Rory was born," Rob said defensively. "You know I couldn't have taken any more. If I want to make partner…"

"I know, I know," Lauren said. "If you want to make partner, you have to turn over your life to Hunt, Fitzgerald, Melman and Tinker. I guess the female partners do, too. There are female partners, right?"

"Of course," Rob said. "There's Glenda Fleming. She does criminal defense law. You must have seen her on the news. She's one of the most powerful people in Boston."

"What did she do when she had kids?"

"She doesn't have any kids," Rob said.

"There's her secret," Lauren said. She carefully disassembled the pump, then took the bottles to the kitchen and poured the milk into a freezer bag. She scrawled the date on the label and put the bag into the freezer, beside the growing cache she'd been collecting. One of these days, she figured, she'd actually use the milk. She'd make Rob watch Rory for a couple of hours while she went to the Calloway offices. Or the gym. Maybe she'd even do something supremely illicit, like have coffee with Claire Langoon, who had scrawled her cellphone number on a business card at the Brain and Body Zone.

She returned to the living room, where Rob had turned on the TV and was watching the local evening news. Gil Zilman, the political reporter, was onscreen, standing in front of a grand Tudor house. He was walking toward the camera and pointing backward at the same time.

"Stuart Winkle says his Cambridge yard, with its landscaped flowers and classic gnomes, is a testament to how much he loves nature," Zilman said. "But hidden behind the bushes, there's something else he apparently loves: Naked women in the great outdoors."

The camera cut to a large bush, the corners of its leaves turning red. "We didn't have permission to enter his property," Zilman said. "But Google Maps shows that behind this bush is a sculpture. A sculpture with *bare breasts*."

The camera cut to Zilman in an office, typing at a computer. The camera zoomed in on a fuzzy computer screen. "From this view, it looks like a reproduction of the Venus de Milo—which, according to Wikipedia, is an ancient Greek sculpture known for its seductive beauty."

The camera cut to the bush again.

"We asked the Winkle campaign for a response," said Gilman's voice. "His spokeswoman, Ashley Weatherby, said the professor is merely a patron of the arts."

Now, Zilman was standing in front of Winkle campaign headquarters, holding his microphone up to a perky twenty-something in a business suit.

"The Venus de Milo is one of the most famous sculptures in the world," she said, the wind blowing her long brown hair into her face. "The original is on display at the Louvre."

"But what about the children in the neighborhood?" Zilman said, pulling the microphone back toward his face. "The ones Professor Winkle has said he wants to protect from indecent exposure?"

"The statue is behind a bush," Ashley said.

"And when the leaves fall in a few weeks, that bush will be exposed to the street," Zilman said. "Along with the bare breasts behind it."

Now the cameras cut to a graying man with a moustache, standing near a busy street and holding a small dog. Beneath him was the name "John Smith" and the description "Concerned About Sculpture."

"In Central Square today, we talked to some voters who said they are definitely concerned," said Zilman's voice.

"I don't think anyone should have pornography on his property," the man said tentatively.

The cameras cut to Zilman again, in front of the bush. "It looks like the champion of modesty might have some explaining to do," he said. "Gil Zilman, Action News 6."

Rob clicked off the television. "I can't take it," he said. "I'm going to bed."

Just then, Lauren's cellphone rang. She pulled it from her diaper bag, saw that it was Mia, and glanced at the clock before answering. Then she braced herself. When Mia called after 10 p.m., she was usually in crisis. But tonight, she sounded elated.

"I just found a good purpose for my breastmilk," she said. "Yours, too. It's not just for our babies anymore. Come with me tomorrow and I'll show you."

TWELVE HOURS LATER they were back in Mia's Volvo, driving into Westwood, an upscale suburban town filled with large houses and manicured lawns. Political signs dotted some of yards: "Chest in the Air," "Break These Chains," and some new purple signs that read, "Modesty. Respect. WINKLE."

Mia pulled up in front of a green colonial that looked to be built in the 1980s. She peered carefully up and down the street.

"We're actually going to the house next door," she said. "But we don't want to leave a trail."

"You said we were going to a milk bank," Lauren said. "I thought it would be in a medical building or something."

"The legal banks give all of their milk to premature babies in hospitals," Mia said. "This bank is off the grid."

Satisfied that no one was coming, she quickly got out of the car, grabbed her diaper bag and Lyle's car seat, and beckoned for Lauren to do the same. Lauren followed Mia to the next house, a large white cape. They scurried up a long driveway to the back-yard, then followed a brick path to the back door.

Mia knocked rhythmically: *tap-tap-a-tap-tap.*

There was a pause. "Who is it?" a woman's voice said.

"Mia Hastings Hoberman," Mia called out. "We spoke on the phone."

"What's the weather like out there?" the woman asked.

"Severe flood warning," Mia called cheerily. She turned to Lauren and winked. They could hear the sound of several locks unlatching, and the door slowly swung open.

A woman was standing before them in a low-cut top and skin-tight jeans, her jet-black hair swept into an up-do, her fingernails long and painted bright red. She was sucking on a hard candy.

"Come in, come in," she said. "Sorry about the password. But word spreads, you know, and you never know when the health inspectors are going to come by."

She beckoned Mia and Lauren into a simple room in a fin-ished basement, blue linoleum on the floor, walls painted white. Along the back wall were three large freezers, humming loudly.

"You can put the milk in the freezer on the far right there," the woman said, clacking the candy against her teeth. "Make sure it's labeled with your name and the date. Sign your initials on the clipboard attached. And then if you can fill out one of those forms over there..." She waved her hand in the direction of a table across the room, her fingernails sparkling under recessed ceiling lights.

"Of course," Mia said. She pulled a small cooler out of her diaper bag and lifted out a freezer bag filled with breastmilk. "I only have six ounces here," she said apologetically. "It's my first deposit. But I'll be back."

"Don't worry, honey. Every little bit counts," the woman said. She turned to Lauren as Mia attended to her paperwork. "You got a donation?" she asked.

At Mia's urging, Lauren had brought along a small cooler filled with several freezer bags of breastmilk. But she suddenly didn't feel ready to hand them over. "Um, no. Not today. I just came for the ride," she said. "Can I ask—why are you worried about health inspectors?"

"Officially, it's supposed to be pasteurized," the woman said. "That's what they do at the regulated milk banks. And I did try it once, when I first started. Oh my God, I felt like I was back in high school chemistry class. I had to use, like, a centrifuge, and the milk got all over the fricking floor. And then I realized that primitive women, you know, in the bush, they didn't fricking pasteurize when they passed their babies from boob to boob. They used trust. So now I just give everybody a look-see to make sure they look healthy and sanitary and all. I can tell by instinct. And my clients have never had a problem."

"So…you charge women for this milk?"

"Just a small service fee," the woman said, looking at Lauren keenly. "To cover the cost of the electricity and all. Really, I make my money off my wet-nurse business."

"Your what?"

"You'd be surprised how many rich families want the breastmilk without the bother," the woman said, glancing down at Rory, scanning Lauren's outfit, and settling her gaze on Lauren's breasts.

"You'd be eligible, you know, since you have a baby," she said. "Once the spigot starts flowing, you can make as much as you want. Supply and demand. So you can hire yourself out for extra money if you need it. It's like babysitting, but you get to sit still."

"Wow," Lauren said. "That's so...feudal."

"Money talks, honey, and this stuff is liquid gold," the woman said. "I've got ladies with implants, ladies who don't want to sag, ladies who want to play tennis all day. I'm serious, you know, if you're interested. In a few months, you could buy yourself a new car. Like, a Corolla or something, nothing fancy."

"I'll, um, think about it," Lauren said. "Thanks."

"Just let me know," the woman said, peering carefully at Lauren's face. "I swear, you look so familiar to me," she said. "Wait! I saw you on Polly Park! You're the Calloway campaign lady. The one from the museum!"

"I am," Lauren said.

"Honey, I have got to thank you!" the woman said, suddenly sounding excited. "You have done wonders for my business. Things had kind of hit a lull, you know, and then suddenly everyone got all excited about breastmilk again. Wet-nurse demand is way, way up, just in the past couple of weeks. And my clients come talking about those 'Got Milk' ads. You and your kid are, like, icons."

Suddenly a cellphone rang to the tune of "We are the Champions."

"Excuse me," the milk-bank woman said, pulling a small pink phone from her back pocket and flipping it open. "Hello? *What?* Oh, crap. Well, thanks for telling me. Let me go make some calls. Feel better, honey. Have some soup." She hung up the phone.

"That was one of my nurses now," she told Lauren. "Trouble is, they sometimes get sick. So I've got to go find a replacement before this hedge-fund manager's wife freaks out because her kid has to suck down formula."

She disappeared into a back room, leaving Lauren beside the cooler, staring down at Rory in her car seat. The baby was sleeping peacefully again, satiated after a long feeding at home. Lauren thought about how lucky she was to be able to breastfeed at all, compared to the women she'd met over the past couple of weeks, the ones who were moving mountains, breaking laws, and battling tears to avoid giving their children formula. The ones who had cited her as inspiration.

Now, Rory was officially an icon, an influencer, changing people's fates with her Fluff-covered face. She was colluding with the BOOBs. Justifying wet nurses. Insulting mothers of preemies. And she had no idea that any of this was going on. Suddenly, Lauren felt wracked with guilt. She couldn't allow Rory to be co-opted so early in life, forced to stand for principles she might not share. This seemed like Lauren's first real test of parenthood—a matter far more important than what or how her baby ate. She didn't want to look back on these crucial first months and think she'd handed Rory over to the Calloway campaign. She'd have to show her daughter how to take a stand. Claire Langoon was right: She needed a message of her own.

"Aren't you going to give your donation?" Mia had finished her paperwork and placed her form on top of the freezer. Now, she was looking at Lauren expectantly.

"Nope," Lauren said. "Sorry. I'm not giving here."

"Oh, come on, Lauren," Mia said. "Don't be touchy. This is how sisterhood works."

"Don't worry, I've figured out a good use for the milk," Lauren said. "A sisterhood kind of reason." What she didn't tell Mia was that she had decided to go to the rally after all.

CHAPTER 19

WHEN SHE EMERGED into the sunlight from South Station, Lauren could already hear the drums. They were banging in some sort of primitive rhythm, a statement of purpose or anger or solidarity. Every major public protest she had ever witnessed, as a sideline participant in college or a bystander passing through Boston Common, seemed to include a few drummers. Maybe some protestors found that drums gave voice to their pent-up anger. Maybe they were frustrated musicians and this was their only chance to play in public.

Today's drumming came from the direction of the Congress Street Bridge, a busy thoroughfare near the site of the original Boston Tea Party, which the BOOBs had chosen for their formula-dumping extravaganza. Sheila and her crew had lucked into a beautiful day, unseasonably warm, with a bright blue sky. The few fluffy, oblong clouds that drifted by looked a little like breasts, Lauren mused; they were full and milky white, floating slowly toward the harbor. Seagulls flew past them, silhouetted in the light, before they swooped down to the sidewalk in search of dropped potato chips or sandwich crumbs.

And there were plenty of crumbs, because there were toddlers around, along with smaller babies pushed in strollers or carried in slings and Baby Bjorns. Hundreds of women with kids in tow were heading toward the bridge, clustered in small groups like schools of fish, some wearing matching T-shirts or bandanas. Surveying the crowd, Lauren felt like one of the only people who had come here alone—though of course, Rory was with her, peeking out from her Bjorn, wearing a small pink windbreaker and a purple cotton hat. Lauren patted the baby on the head, adjusted her diaper bag over her shoulder, and headed down the station steps.

Just outside the doors, a dozen women sat cross-legged in a circle, humming "We Shall Overcome." In front of them was a sandwich board with the painted words "NURSE-IN." In every woman's lap was a baby or toddler suckling away, kicking gently in the air or brushing a little hand against its mother's chin. People with suitcases walked wide loops around them, their gazes fixed determinedly on the ground.

Lauren walked around them, too, nearly bumping into a camera crew as she headed toward Atlantic Avenue. As she waited for the light, she watched a cluster of counter-protestors, standing in front of an office building, wearing MOM T-shirts and holding Winkle signs.

"Mod-e-sty! Mod-e-sty!" they chanted in the direction of the nurse-in. The nursing women sang louder in response.

Lauren crossed the street and kept moving up Atlantic Avenue, walking to the rhythm of the drums, slipping into the stream of BOOB supporters headed toward the bridge. Another solo woman pushed a space-egg stroller with one hand and held a cellphone in the other. "Pretty huge," she said into the phone. "Like, maybe thousands. I think this is going to be our Woodstock." A pair of young women held ropes attached to monkey-shaped backpacks, worn by a pair of toddlers just ahead of them. The ropes looked like monkey's tails. The boys seemed to have no clue that they were leashed.

On the next corner, beside a woman holding a sign that said

"Jesus Was Breastfed," a twentysomething man in a beret had set up a stand selling energy bars and organic juice. An older man stood beside him with a rack of souvenir buttons and T-shirts, featuring slogans like "The Great Formula Dump" and "I Survived BOOB-a-geddon." Overhead, Lauren heard the rotor of a news helicopter. A small propeller plane flew by trailing a banner: "CANDACE CALLOWAY LOVES BOOBS." Another, just behind it, had the counterprogramming: "VOTE WINKLE FOR DECENCY."

Lauren paused for a moment and glanced down at Rory, who was looking up at the sky. Far across the street, by another office building, she thought she spotted Maisy Street half-hidden behind a pillar. Lauren turned away. When she looked back, the woman who might have been Maisy was gone.

At the corner of Atlantic Avenue and Congress Street, another group of MOMs stood in a cluster, handing out Winkle-for-governor fliers and chanting, "Real moms don't strip!" One MOM was standing to one side of the group, arguing feverishly with one of the passing BOOBs.

Lauren paused to eavesdrop. They were talking about Stuart Winkle's statue.

"It's different," the MOM was saying.

"How is it different?" said the BOOB, who was wearing a T-shirt that said "These BOOBs Vote" and patting a small baby on the back to force a burp. "She's naked. She's outdoors."

"It's a work of art," said the MOM. "It's beautiful. He's allowed to have beautiful things."

"Who decides what's beautiful?" the BOOB replied. "All breasts are beautiful. Yours are. So are mine."

"Don't even think about showing me," the MOM said, backing up in horror, as if someone were waving a cockroach in her face.

Lauren walked on, turning right onto Congress Street, passing several satellite trucks preparing for TV live shots, a recruitment booth set up by the Moo Coalition, and a cluster of college students dressed like babies, wearing giant diapers and filming themselves with a camcorder. As she approached the bridge, the crowd grew thicker and the drums banged more loudly. A woman with long braids and a flute stood on the sidewalk, playing the melody to "This Woman's Work." A few men milled through the crowd, apparently to gawk. Several male police officers patrolled the perimeter, some of them clearly having trouble hiding smiles.

As Lauren headed to the bridge, she passed a group of women who counted to three aloud and shouted "Reveal and Heal!" They lifted their shirts in unison, whooping and cheering. A group of videographers came rushing over. Lauren sidestepped them and suddenly spotted Mia a few yards away, pushing Lyle in his stroller and handing out Calloway for Governor brochures. Lauren wove through the crowd and tapped her on the shoulder.

"I thought you weren't coming," Mia said.

"I changed my mind," Lauren replied.

"I knew you would. You're a good mother," Mia said, in a cheerleader's tone. "I think it's about to start. How about we make some news?"

"Yes," Lauren replied. "How about it."

By this time, a large cluster of women had gathered at the foot of the bridge, which had been cut off from traffic and cordoned off with police tape. Two women with serious expressions stood atop a raised platform, playing acoustic guitars connected to a small amplifier. They were largely drowned out by the drums, but Lauren thought she could make out the strains of "Closer to Fine." A few people clapped when they finished. Sheila McDonough climbed up beside them, a large megaphone in her hand. She gazed out over the crowd and smiled.

"Let's hear it for Sisters in the Wildflowers," she said, reading from an index card. "They're playing Thursday night at the Mares Eat Oats Organic Café in Northampton."

"Go Northampton!" someone shouted out.

"Now, let's get started with the main event!" Sheila yelled. "Can I get my BOOBs up here with me?"

A group of a dozen women carrying "BOOB" and "Calloway" signs clambered onto the bridge and stood behind her.

"I hear we've got some of our milk sisters from Northampton here with us!" Sheila shouted into the megaphone when the women were in place. "We've got our milk sisters from Medfield and Wayland and Winchester! We've got our milk sisters from Cambridge and Norwell and Lenox! We've come to spread the message: Our babies need real milk, not poison!"

The crowd cheered.

"I want to read a message from Senator Candace Calloway," Sheila said, reaching into her flowered shirt and pulling a small square piece of paper from her bra. She unfolded the paper and cleared her throat.

"Dear BOOBs and BOOB supporters," she read. "I'm sorry I couldn't join you today. I had a prior engagement reading books to kindergarteners in Ware, and I care too much about children to disappoint them. But I applaud your efforts to feed your babies naturally and healthily. Please remember to vote on November 2. In the meantime, keep your chest in the air and be proud of what you do."

"Chest in the air, babeeeeeeeey!" shouted a male voice from the outskirts of the crowd. A few women booed at him.

"Thank you, Senator Calloway," Sheila said, ignoring the catcall. "And now, I'd like to read a passage from the Moo Coalition handbook." One of the BOOBs behind her held out a thick volume, which Sheila took and opened to a dog-eared page. She cleared her throat again.

"breastmilk is more than food. More than nutrition," she read. "It is a sacred compact, a promise to our children, a way of dedicating our lives to theirs. It is a message of world peace and understanding. It is a life force that must not be disobeyed."

She put the book down gently on the ground, then placed her

free hand underneath one of her breasts. "Look at this, formula companies! Look at this, MOMs! Look at this, Stuart Winkle!" she shouted into the megaphone. "This is a holy vessel! It gives life and health! It makes me a goddess! We are all goddesses!"

The crowd cheered.

"And you cannot replace a goddess with something you made in a chemical plant!"

The crowd cheered again.

"So today, we have a message to send to the formula companies!" Sheila yelled. "We're through with your brainwashing and your artificial promises! We are natural women, with natural babies! And we'll tell you where your formula belongs! Now, how many of you ladies brought your cans?"

A huge yell reverberated through the crowd, along with some whistles and catcalls. "Cans, baby!" a male voice shouted.

"OK, ladies, it's time to take them out," Sheila yelled into the megaphone. "Form a line here at the foot of the bridge. But don't pour anything yet! We need the TV cameras to get into their places."

Some photographers and videographers started moving into position beneath the bridge, jostling for camera angles. Within the crowd, women reached into purses and diaper bags to pull out cans and jars of infant formula. Many seemed to have purchased jumbo-sized cans, Lauren noticed; they'd make a bigger splash in the murky waters of Fort Point Channel, but they also required a bigger outlay of cash. This must have been a banner week for formula sales, she thought. If she had been smart, she would have bought stock.

"Are you ready?" Sheila said, addressing the TV crews. "Are your settings right? OK? OK." She held a giant yellow can of formula aloft. "Boooo!" she intoned.

"Booooo!" said the crowd.

"Goodbye, Lactoline Soy Blast with Extra Minerals," she announced, reading the can. "I banish you to the depths of Boston

Harbor!" Setting the megaphone down, she pulled off the lid, peeled open the aluminum top, and turned the can upside down. A pile of yellowish-white powder billowed down to the water. The crowd went wild.

"Wooooo! That felt good!" Sheila said into the megaphone. "OK! Who's next?"

A woman in khaki pants and a dark-blue sweater left the cluster of BOOBs and took the megaphone. "Goodbye, Mammafil Extra Concentrated Protein-Based Formula! I banish you to the depths of Boston Harbor!" she shouted, unleashing another stream of powder.

One of the drummers teamed up with the flute player and tried to recreate a Revolutionary War-era fife and drum tune. As they whistled and banged, a stream of women took the megaphone one by one, reading and overturning their cans.

"Goodbye, Infabrest A to Z Healthy Baby Concentrate!"

"Goodbye, Mammafil Sensitive Tummies Lactose-Free Formula with Colic Reducer!"

"Goodbye, Costmart Brand Vitamin-Enriched Baby Formula with Minerals!"

As women continued to shout and dump, Lauren pushed through the crowd until she could see the channel. The yellowish-white powder was congealing into a film that sat on top of the water, swirling in little eddies and following the current. Dozens more women were lined up at the foot of the bridge, awaiting their turns. Lauren thought about the plan she had formed in her head; it seemed like a fantasy, a daydream. She looked down at Rory and tried to feel emboldened. In the future, plenty of times, she'd have to set her daughter straight. She might as well practice on this group of angry women holding babies and cans of formula.

"Sheila!" she called. "Sheila!" Mia trailed behind her, shouting "Sheila!" too.

At first, Sheila didn't seem to notice; she was busy chatting with the women on the bridge. Lauren yelled louder, struggling to be heard over the flute and drums. "Sheila! It's Lauren Bruce!" she shouted. At last, Sheila turned around and made eye contact, her eyebrows rising with excitement. She gestured for Lauren to wait, then grabbed the megaphone unceremoniously from a woman who was about to read from her formula can.

"Ladies, I have news," Sheila said. "Lauren Bruce is with us! The woman who started it all! Her brave decision to feed her child at the Stonewall Museum will be remembered as a turning point in Massachusetts history!"

The crowd erupted into a lusty cheer. Some of the women whistled.

"Lauren, do you have something to dump?" Sheila asked. Lauren nodded yes. "Then come up and join us!" Sheila said.

The crowd parted quickly, allowing Lauren to climb onto the bridge. Sheila held out her arms to give her a hug. Then she turned Lauren back toward the crowd and grabbed her hand, raising it in a gesture of victory.

Lauren gently took the megaphone from Sheila and stared out at the sea of people. She could make out women's faces, expectant and giddy. Further out, she saw seagulls gliding and swooping low. An airplane crossed the sky high above, tiny and glistening, like a charm that could hang on a bracelet. Drums banged, a few babies cried, but to Lauren, the world suddenly felt silent. She took a deep breath, reached into her bag, and pulled out one of the pouches that had been sitting in her freezer for weeks. She held it up so the crowd could see. "I'm sorry, Sheila," she said under her breath.

Then she lifted the megaphone to her mouth and raised her voice. "This," she announced, "is breastmilk."

A murmur went through the crowd.

"And I'm willing to toss it," Lauren went on, "unless you people get some perspective."

Sheila looked at her in stunned silence. Someone deep in the crowd shouted, "Noooo!"

"I support breastfeeding, obviously. I like it," Lauren said. "But I can't take this anymore. Formula isn't poison! And you can't tell the women who use it that they're being bad mothers!"

The women around her started chattering more loudly. Lauren spotted Mia at the foot of the bridge, shaking her head in dismay.

"There's too much pressure!" Lauren said. "There's more to motherhood than how you feed your baby!"

This last statement seemed to shake Sheila out of her paralysis. Now, she lunged for the megaphone, grabbed the very end of it, and tried to pull it out of Lauren's hand. Lauren held on tighter.

"I don't understand why you people can't find some common ground," she went on, trying to brush Sheila away. "Why can't you give your babies breastmilk and formula, too?

By this point, most of the drummers had stopped banging and were talking to each other, gesticulating wildly. "Drums!" Sheila yelled at them. "Make the drums louder!"

"And honestly, what's wrong with using a blanket? Or going into a private place?" Lauren went on. "What if I didn't want to take my shirt off in front of a bunch of high school kids? What if *I* felt more comfortable in the bathroom?"

"Woman hater!" somebody yelled a few feet from the bridge. "Enabler!"

"OK, that's it," Lauren said. "This stuff is going down. And I've got more." She let go of her grip on the megaphone, causing Sheila to tumble backward. She lifted the bag of formula aloft again and set up for a throw. Before she could release, one of the BOOBs ran up from behind her and batted the bag out of her hand.

The milk had been out of the freezer for hours by now, so the bag was soft and squishy, slippery and wet with condensation. It sailed backward in a gentle arc toward the BOOBs on the bridge, many of whom tried to grab it, but couldn't get a grip. The bag bounced from person to person like a hacky sack ball, staying airborne for half a minute or so before it tumbled over the edge and into the water.

"Nooo!" yelled a woman on the bank, and to Lauren's shock, she ran toward the water's edge and jumped in. She stayed submerged for a moment, then popped up and started swimming, following the plastic baggie that was bobbing in the water. The women on the bridge cheered her on. Finally, she reached the bag, held it in the air, and started swimming back to the shore with one arm. She climbed back onto solid ground, raising two fingers in a victory sign, her white long-sleeved T-shirt clinging closely to her skin.

"Woo, baby!" some man shouted. "Wet T-shirt contest!"

Lauren reached into her diaper bag and pulled out another bag of breastmilk, tossing this one quickly into the water. It sailed high in the air, landed with a splash, then bobbed on the surface like a cork. She pulled out yet another bag and prepared to throw it, too.

"Stop!" Sheila shouted, now grabbing at Lauren's diaper bag and trying to pull it away. Lauren could see that she had tears in her eyes. Glancing down at the crowd, she saw Mia, who stood with her arms crossed, fuming.

But suddenly another woman appeared on the bridge with her own small freezer bag of milk. "I'm with you, Lauren Bruce!" she shouted. "I'm free!" She must have been a softball player, because she threw the bag so hard that it sailed far past the bridge and landed in the middle of the channel. The milk was still frozen, and quickly sank.

Another woman came up behind her, holding a baby bottle. "This is breastmilk, too! Just try to swim after it!" she yelled, unscrewing the cap and pouring the liquid directly into the channel. It was translucent and light, and seemed to disappear the instant it hit the surface.

Now, there was pandemonium on the bridge as the BOOBs and the breastmilk-dumpers started shouting at one another. Sheila had grabbed back the megaphone and was reading more passages aloud from the Moo Coalition handbook. The flutist was playing "Love is a Battlefield." A few more bags of breastmilk, thrown from various sources, were floating in the water, and several more women were in the channel swimming after them. Photographers and videographers were scampering across the bridge, trying to capture everything.

With all of the yelling, no one seemed to notice Lauren anymore, so she slowly walked away from the bridge. Suddenly, she felt something shaking at chest level. In the adrenaline rush of her rebellion, she had forgotten that she was carrying a baby. She felt a pang of guilt, thinking that the noise and jostling had made Rory cry. Then she peered down and saw that the baby was actually smiling. And doing something else she had never done before: laughing uncontrollably.

Lauren bent her neck and kissed Rory's head. "Let's go home," she whispered. "I've got a special treat for you to try. It looks like a milkshake, and it comes in a bottle, and I promise it won't kill you."

WHEN SHE OPENED the apartment door, she heard familiar noises in the background: rhythmic clicking, heavy wheezing, and a low-pitched, electronic voice that kept repeating "*Let it go. Let it go. Let it go.*" She walked tentatively into the bedroom, not sure what she'd find.

There was Rob, lying on the bed, tie off and collar loosened, playing with the breast pump. The plastic funnels and tubing were spread out across the bedspread. The cylinder was moving slowly back and forth as Rob fiddled with the dial.

"What are you doing?" Lauren said.

Rob looked up and smiled. "Channeling," he said. "I'm trying to figure out what it must feel like to be you."

"Let me know what you find out," Lauren said, staring at Rob skeptically. "Seriously. Why are you home?"

"I saw you on TV," Rob said. "I was having lunch in the corner deli, and the news came on, and there you were. Throwing breastmilk into the Fort Port Channel and telling people to screw themselves. I went back to the office and told them I was going to work from home this afternoon. I wanted to see you when you got back."

"Uh-oh," Lauren said. "What problem have I caused for you now?"

"No problem," Rob said. "None at all. The opposite of a problem. You looked good up there. Like yourself. Your old self."

Lauren pulled Rory out of her Baby Bjorn, where she had been sleeping off the afternoon's excitement, and placed her gently in her bassinet. Then she flopped down on the bed beside Rob, laid her head back on the pillow, and looked up at the ceiling.

"I don't think Mia is ever going to speak to me again," she said. "And I'll probably be persona non grata with the BOOBs. And the Calloway campaign will think I'm a betrayer."

"Maybe, maybe not," Rob said. "But those women are just trying to use you, anyway."

"I think they have good intentions," Lauren said. "Most of them do. They just get a little…excited."

"Well, they don't care about you like I do," Rob said.

"No," Lauren said, "they don't." They gazed at each other silently for a second or two.

"I still can't believe you pulled out the pump," Lauren finally said. "Usually you run from it like it's radioactive."

"And I can't believe you use this thing," Rob said. "It's even weirder when you look at it up close. And louder. Does it always talk like this?"

Lauren sat up, surprised. "You hear it, too?" she said. "I had wondered if I was going crazy."

"No, I hear it," Rob said. "It's saying 'Let it go.' But before I turned the dial, it sounded more like 'Get lost.' I thought it might be telling me that men weren't supposed to touch it."

"That's possible," Lauren said, patting the top of the pump as if it were a pet. "It does seem to hate men. Maybe it's jealous."

"No, I don't think it's jealous," Rob said. "I think it's wise. I think it's trying to say, 'Go take a break. Leave me alone. Let your husband give the kid a bottle of formula once in awhile.'"

"Ah," Lauren said. "Then this pump isn't as smart as it thinks it is. Because I was going to do that, anyway."

"You've come back from the dark side," Rob said, smiling.

"Yeah, but don't mess with me," Lauren said. "I'm not afraid to throw things."

She leaned over to Rob and gave him kiss, which went on for what felt like a long time. It was the sort of kiss they used to share when they were dating, when they had deep curiosity about each other, and all the time they needed to indulge it.

"Be careful," Rob finally said, lifting his head to glance at Rory in her bassinet. "This is how babies get made, you know."

"All in good time," Lauren mumbled, and kissed him again.

EPILOGUE

EVEN FOR A SEASONED event planner like Lauren, it was hard to pull off an inauguration party in an office filled with boxes. Beneath the thick crown molding and gold-framed portraits in the governor's suite, trays of hors d'oeuvres balanced precariously on stacks of files. Bottles of champagne and plastic flute glasses were set up on top of the copy machines. Interns and state police officers mingled with donors and volunteers, squeezing past each other on the way to the spinach dip. Lauren handed Rory off to Rob while she made the rounds, trying to make sure people were well-fed and properly greased with alcohol before the swearing-in.

She had taken this on as part of her job with Candace Callo-way's transition team, handling such delicate tasks as determining who got the offices with the best views of Boston Common. Maisy Street had recommended her, based on the events at the ill-fated tea party. "You're somebody who knows how to say 'no,'" Maisy had said. Lauren had liked the sound of that.

As she hovered over a receptionist's desk, sweeping up paper plates loaded with half-eaten shrimp cocktail, she heard a familiar voice say, "Hello, Lauren." She turned around to find Mia Hastings Hoberman, pushing a stroller back and forth to ensure that Lyle kept sleeping. For once, Lyle wasn't wearing one of his mother's onesies. Mia had dressed him in a tiny button-down shirt and a red bowtie.

"Mia," Lauren said politely. "It's great to see you. How have you been?"

She and Mia hadn't spoken since the tea party. More than once, Lauren had contemplated calling and inviting Mia over for a con-ciliatory cup of decaf. But between her transition team work, her mom-and-baby Pilates class, and her weekly coffees with her new friend Claire Langoon, her schedule had started to fill.

"Oh, I've been great," Mia said hurriedly. "So busy. Lyle has been getting a lot of modeling work. He did an ad for childproof oven knob handles last week. And I'm starting a new business."

"Something besides the T-shirts?" Lauren said.

"I'm now a certified elimination communication consultant," Mia said. "I'm going to train mothers' groups and do private coaching. Sheila McDonough and I are launching it together. We're calling it 'U Poo 2,' unless we run into copyright trouble."

"That sounds perfect for you," Lauren said. "The business, I mean. Congratulations." She looked down at Lyle, wondering if she'd ever see his private parts again. "And good luck to you, Lyle, on your modeling career. You look very handsome, as usual."

Actually, she thought, he still looked very much like a gnome.

MAISY WATCHED THE exchange between Lauren and Mia from across the room. She had made a quiet entrance, then leaned against a wall, visually checking in with the characters from the campaign. Leroy Mason was chatting up Tillie Lockerbie, who leaned on a cane topped with an alabaster sparrow. Christopher and Jodi stood in an office doorway, holding champagne flutes and giggling. Former interns milled about in too-high heels and designer-knockoff tops that showed off their cleavage.

After two months in Asheville, it was jarring to see these people again. Maisy didn't usually attend her candidates' inaugurations, but this race felt different—partly because she hadn't expected to win, partly because of what she had brought home.

The win had, indeed, been a stunner. The tea party debacle drew a flood of donations from out-of-state breastfeeding extremists, enough to fund a final blitz of the ukulele ad. Even so, Candace had lost the women's vote—by roughly the same margin the polls had predicted before the breastfeeding issue came up. But the naked images and strip club references had had an unintended effect. What had put Candace Calloway over the edge, it turned out, was overwhelming support from men.

"Hi Maisy," said a voice behind her. It was Chip Osterville, newly installed as the governor's deputy press secretary. In his slightly-oversized suit and tie, his hair weighed down with a bit too much gel, he looked like a boy playing dress-up. But his handshake was firmer than Maisy remembered.

"Deputy Secretary Osterville. As I live and breathe," she said.

"The Governor-elect would like to see you," Chip said, letting go of her hand. "She's happy that you're here. She talks about you a lot."

"Well, I'm glad you two are finding things to talk about," Maisy said, looking into his face to see if she could glean some sense of their current relationship. "Are they working you hard?"

"Just getting settled in," Chip said. "At least I know the press secretary pretty well. A guy named Scott McFeeney. He used to work for the Herald."

"I remember him well," Maisy said.

"And we have an assistant, Seth. He used to work for the 'Polly Park Show.'"

"You don't say," Maisy said, peering into Chip's eyes, concluding that he was oblivious. Someday, perhaps, when she was retired and Candace was out of politics, she'd tell him a long and interesting story. For now, it was best to leave him in the dark.

"And how are you?" Chip asked. "How's your...friend?"

"Jean," Maisy said. "She fine, Chipper. Thanks for asking." In fact, at that moment, Jean Thompson was at Maisy's house in Asheville, probably putting an extra coat of paint on the sun porch that had once been a repository for Maisy's dusty campaign files. Jean had arranged a purge, reupholstered some furniture she'd found at a yard sale, and converted the room into a plush nook for reading and drinking wine. In the warm weather months, she told Maisy, she would use it for Moo Coalition meetings. She had signed up to be a leader with the local group.

"So," said Chip, jolting Maisy back to the present. "Follow me." He led Maisy past desks and boxes until they reached the wide white door to the governor's suite. He knocked three times, then pushed open the door.

"I have Maisy for you," he said.

"Thank you, Chipper," Candace cooed, though te effect today was more maternal than flirtatious. She was wearing a pinstripe suit that was both businesslike and sexy. Her hair was piled above her head in a tight, prim bun. She looked anachronistic, a 21st-century power woman in an 18th-century room.

"Maisy," she said, a new note of formality in her voice. "It really is wonderful to see you again."

"Well, thanks for the private audience," Maisy said, looking around at the period details, the grand wooden desk and the Chippendale sofas. "Nice digs you've got here. A big step up from Downtown Crossing."

"Yes," Candace said, beginning to drop her guard. "With these couches, I don't have to worry that something with eighteen legs is going to crawl out."

Maisy thought about what else had happened on those campaign couches, and now looked at the Chippendale sofas in an entirely different light. "Speaking of crawling," she said, "I see you've done some careful hiring in the press office."

Candace smiled slyly. "My boys," she said. "One of them

is going to play a very important role in my life."

"You're keeping a stable of breeding horses," Maisy sighed.

"Well, I guess they could serve that purpose, for insurance," Candace said. "But one of them has already won the prize."

Maisy looked at Candace's svelte figure, amazed. "You're pregnant?" she said. "Already?"

"Who would have guessed I'd be so fertile?" Candace said happily. "Thank goodness for this campaign, or I might never have known."

Looking at the governor-elect carefully, Maisy did detect a different sort of aura. What she had assumed was Christopher's careful makeup application might actually have been a natural flush in Candace's cheeks, a brightness in her eyes. A glow.

"Well, congratulations," Maisy said. "Really. But…what are you going to do?"

"I'll announce it at the start of my second trimester," Candace said. "I'll explain about frozen sperm. That's one reason why I wanted to see you. To ask for your confidence. Woman to woman."

"Candace," Maisy said. "I wouldn't be where I am if I didn't know how to keep my mouth shut. But be careful; oppo research guys would have a field day with this."

"I know that," Candace said. "But even if this whole thing ends tomorrow, I'll still have gotten what I wanted."

A knock came on the door, and Lauren Bruce peeked in. "It's time," she said with smile. Then she rang a small silver bell to get the attention of the crowd. "Please make your way to the Doric Hall!" she called out. "The inauguration is about to begin."

Maisy allowed herself one more glance at Candace's belly, then left to join the crowd that filed into the hallway, down the marble steps, and into a grand room filled with columns and folding chairs. When everyone was seated, the pomp began. The outgoing governor exited the building to polite applause. A hymn was played on bagpipe, bouncing discordantly off the marble. Finally, a state police officer announced, "Ladies and Gentlemen, Governor-elect Candace Calloway."

Applause rang out as Candace descended the marble steps and strode to the podium, where the chief justice of the state Supreme Court was waiting to deliver the Oath of Office. Candace recited the oath and turned toward the crowd to deliver her inaugural address, brushing her hands almost imperceptibly against her belly, then laying them on either side of the podium.

Either she's going to set women back 30 years or move them forward like no one else has, Maisy thought. *Maybe both.* But Candace didn't seem concerned about anyone but herself. She smiled, teeth gleaming, and began the next phase of her life.

"Ladies and gentlemen, justices and mayors, members of the General Court," she said. "I think we can all agree that babies are our future."

ACKNOWLEDGMENTS

This book would not have been possible without the help and support of a number of people. My gratitude goes first to Ava and Jesse, my once-and-always babies, for inspiration and first-hand research. I'm also grateful to Wendy Strothman and Lauren Ma-cLeod for early support and encouragement; to Susan Kushner Resnick, Jenna Blum, and Margo Howard for reading drafts and offering insight and kind words; to Martha Kennedy and Heather Hopp-Bruce for invaluable advice on cover design; to Wendy Wahman for the world's most fabulous cover; to Joni Rodgers for a brilliant last read and a final push over the edge; to my parents, Gail and David Weiss, for ample advice and support. Most of all, thanks to Dan DeLeo, my first, best, and toughest editor, whom I'm lucky to have as a partner in all endeavors.

ABOUT THE AUTHOR

Joanna Weiss is an op-ed columnist for the *Boston Globe*. Her columns appear, via the *New York Times* newswire, in newspapers around the country. She lives near Boston with her husband, son and daughter. This is her first novel.

www.joannaweiss.net

Join the conversation at
www.facebook.com/MilkshakeMoms.

www.ingramcontent.com/pod-product-compliance
Lightning Source LLC
Chambersburg PA
CBHW050925120626
46552CB00001B/45